BE DARING, DUKE

A Very Fine Muddle
Book Two

Kate Archer

Dragonblade Publishing, Inc. is an imprint of Kathryn Le Veque Novels, Inc.
P.O. Box 23
Moreno Valley, CA 92556
ceo@dragonbladepublishing.com

Produced in the United States of America

First Edition June 2023
Trade Paperback Edition

ARE YOU SIGNED UP FOR DRAGONBLADE'S BLOG?

You'll get the latest news and information on exclusive giveaways, exclusive excerpts, coming releases, sales, free books, cover reveals and more.

Check out our complete list of authors, too!

No spam, no junk. That's a promise!

Sign Up Here

www.dragonbladepublishing.com

Dearest Reader;

Thank you for your support of a small press. At Dragonblade Publishing, we strive to bring you the highest quality Historical Romance from some of the best authors in the business. Without your support, there is no 'us', so we sincerely hope you adore these stories and find some new favorite authors along the way.

Happy Reading!

CEO, Dragonblade Publishing

Additional Dragonblade books by Author Kate Archer

A Very Fine Muddle
Romance Me, Viscount (Book 1)
Be Daring, Duke (Book 2)

A Series of Worthy Young Ladies
The Meddler (Book 1)
The Sprinter (Book 2)
The Undaunted (Book 3)
The Champion (Book 4)
The Jilter (Book 5)
The Regal (Book 6)

The Dukes' Pact Series
The Viscount's Sinful Bargain (Book 1)
The Marquess' Daring Wager (Book 2)
The Lord's Desperate Pledge (Book 3)
The Baron's Dangerous Contract (Book 4)
The Peer's Roguish Word (Book 5)
The Earl's Iron Warrant (Book 6)

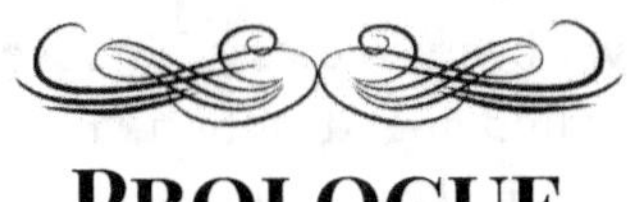

PROLOGUE

For any five sisters to lose their mother when young, it must be considered the tragedy of their lives. And then for their father to be faced with the situation, another question must present itself. Who would step in to guide his dear, darling girls?

Particularly, what lady would be stalwart enough in spirit when faced with so many of them? One is easy, two is a set…but five begins to approach a heap. A heap, as everybody knows, has far more ability to overwhelm than the sum of its parts.

The five daughters of the Earl of Westmont must count themselves among the unlucky, as the countess had died in childbirth. However, they must also count themselves among the *lucky*, as Miss Eloise Mayton had flown to their side upon becoming apprised of their situation.

Miss Mayton had been residing in Rome when she heard the call of five motherless girls by way of a letter from the earl. Being at loose ends, dwindling finances, and fading youth, and having a notion of being particularly suited to step in and lead five girls forward, she had decamped to Westmont House that same month.

The Earl of Westmont's daughters were prodigiously fond of their aunt, though to call her *Aunt* was to rename that which would usually be termed a very distant cousin of uncertain and winding connection.

Miss Mayton had cemented her place in these daughters'

hearts when they'd been fully apprised of her history. She had arrived to watch over them after having suffered through her own series of terrible tragedies.

Had any lady ever been so crossed in love! Had any lady lost so many suitors to undying devotion, morose dejection, and unfortunate and rather final rash actions?

Miss Mayton delighted in telling her charges about how she might have been a baroness or a countess, had not tragedy struck time and time again. Usually, it was a case of unrequited love that the gentleman could not recover from. In the case of Gregorio, it was a misunderstanding cleared up minutes too late to save the poor fellow. Fatal falls, deadly blows, impalements, poisonings, Miss Mayton had inspired it all when she had been young and beautiful.

The five daughters took these tales into their hearts and used them as their yardstick to measure their own ideas of romance. After all, it made sense that if a gentleman was in love and then realized that he would never have his one heart's desire, he was very likely to do a violence to himself.

The earl did not particularly believe any of it and had not the first idea of what Miss Mayton had been doing on the continent all those years. Nor did he know why she invented such tales. Though, he saw no real harm in her fanciful stories and was not the least concerned over their influence on his daughters. Did not all young ladies dream of improbable gentlemen and impossible love?

As far as the earl was concerned, Eloise Mayton was an indulgent and affectionate aunt willing to take on the raising of five motherless girls. Who could ask for more than that?

And so, under Miss Mayton's terrifically unsteady guidance, each of the five ladies would take their turn in London for their season.

The eldest had already married, though it had been an alarming path to get there. Now, Lady Rosalind was set to discover what the fates had in store for her.

CHAPTER ONE

The outskirts of London – 1803

ROSALIND BENNINGTON, SECOND of five daughters of the Earl of Westmont, had every reason to be delighted with her circumstances. It had been a jolly summer at Westmont House. Especially jolly after their eldest sister Beatrice returned to Somerset from her wedding trip to Venice and settled so nearby at Faversham Hall.

Naturally, all the sisters had found themselves mystified when Beatrice had married their scolding neighbor Van Doren. They had teased and defied that fellow all their lives—Rosalind's youngest sister, Juliet, had even named him Viscount Scoldy-Breeches and written dozens of insulting odes about him.

Yet, as the summer progressed, they began to see how it was between the couple. Oh, he lectured the rest of them as much as ever, but her sister Beatrice was suddenly never to do a wrong.

Beatrice must be made comfortable at all times. Should Beatrice even whisper that she might wish for something, she must have it. Beatrice was suddenly become a woman held superior to all other women. Were anybody to give a hint that they might trouble his lady, Van Doren would bite their head off.

The sisters had thoroughly discussed this new incarnation of Van Doren. He remained as tedious as ever to *them*, but they were quite satisfied with their sister's treatment.

The time had flown by with neighborhood parties and pic-nics, or family dinners and the comfortable scenes in the drawing room afterward—Juliet would read a recently composed ode and then Miss Mayton would read from a novel. It had all gone by so fast, until suddenly it was the day to venture forth to Rosalind's chance at love by way of a season in Town.

The Bennington caravan had set off for London six days ago. Van Doren did not accompany them on this particular journey as he and Beatrice would follow them in a week's time. The result of his absence was that there was nobody to drive them forward in a straight line with scoldings, warnings, and complaints. They zigged and zagged and circled back and dallied the entire way.

The earl had very sensibly declared that they should not even try to hurry. Their father was a comfortable gentleman who was never out of sorts but for a house fire. He also understood his daughters very well and saw no point in attempting to swim against the tide.

It was well that the earl was so easygoing. On the very first day and not five miles from home, Cordelia had shouted for the carriages to stop. She had spotted a dog in the distance who she was certain was in distress.

She, Rosalind, Viola, and Juliet had piled out of their carriage and set off across a field. There, they found the loveliest little brown dog with a twine leash that had been round her neck so long that it had begun to bind.

At least, they all assured each other she was lovely. Her fur was rather rough and patchy, and her eyes rather bulging, her proportions at once saggy and ribby, and her scent not exactly a flower bed. But other than those minor deficiencies, she was lovely.

With the help of the coachman, the twine was cut from the dog's neck and it was noted that the skin was very red under-neath, but no real damage had been done. They had remedied the situation just in time.

It was decided in a moment that whoever had once owned

this poor dog, they were either very cruel or had lost her somewhere. If they were cruel, they did not deserve her. If she'd been lost, then her owners must just now pray that someone had taken her in. She must be rescued from her dire circumstances.

Into the carriage she went, to the approbation of everybody. Except perhaps their butler. Tattleton was still recovering from the four kittens they'd found during last year's trip, those cats now residing happily at Westmont House in the country.

They had since named the dog Bess, scrubbed her with soap at the nearest inn yard, and showered her with bits of meat from every table they sat down to. All the food was seeming to have a very good effect, as Viola was certain little Bess had even managed to put on weight in the following days. Anybody could see that her ribs no longer showed as much as they had.

Of course, this sudden introduction of plentiful food had led to some rather noxious fumes, but other than that she was lovely.

What a delightful trip! They had stopped no end of times so that lovely little Bess might have a walk around or Juliet might write an ode to a charming vista.

Juliet, the youngest of them, was their resident poetess and these creations would be read to great approbation after dinner.

Her book of poems had confoundingly been left behind several times and, as they did not have Van Doren to send back to retrieve it like they did last year, the earl finally hired a fellow to do the job.

Young John Martin followed behind the caravan and would be alerted to the fact that Juliet had forgotten her book of poems again. She was certain it had been left in the last inn's breakfast room. John would tip his hat and set off for it.

Though Rosalind was continually surprised at how often Juliet lost track of her most precious possession, she was approving at how much more cheerfully John Martin went back for it than Van Doren ever had.

Viola, as had become her habit, had ordered plates of ham absolutely everywhere they stopped. Lovely little Bess was very approving of the idea as she always got her fair share. Further, everybody considered it a great success that Viola only had to get out of the carriage one time to walk about in the fresh air due to a stomachache from too much ham.

Bess had to get out rather more times, as they were alerted to by a sudden series of noises followed by noxious fumes in the carriage.

Cordelia, a natural actress, had performed her Desdemona speech to entertain them of an evening and while several candles were knocked over during her enthusiastic performances, no fires were started. This was very comforting to everybody, especially the earl who no doubt thought back to the two times the house had been on fire under similar circumstances.

Bess had, at first, been a bit startled by Cordelia's acting, as it was exceedingly energetic, but the little dog got used to it soon enough.

Miss Mayton had brought her latest favored romantic novel and read from it in the evening. Then, were they all not too tired, she might reminisce about one of her lost loves.

It was the merriest party going and Rosalind was exceedingly entertained by it all. In the quiet interludes between all these entertainments, she dreamed of her true love, whoever he might turn out to be.

It was the beginning of her adventure, and there had been surprises round every corner.

Just this afternoon, they'd descended upon The Angel in Basingstoke and encountered a charming French lady finding herself at sixes and sevens. Her name was Madame Marie Tussaud and she had been on her way to Town for a display of wax figures at the Lyceum.

Apparently, the lady had made it her business to construct these wax figures and they were to be shown for the first time in England. However, one of her carriage wheels had broken, necessitating an overnight stop.

The Benningtons had been determined to entertain the lady

and insisted she dine with them. The modest lady had hesitated and demurred, first claiming she was tired, then hinting she was ill. The Benningtons saw through it all—the poor madame feared she would be an imposition. They would not allow her to feel so, however, and pressed her from all sides. She had finally seen that they would not be put off over a false sense of delicacy and agreed to dine with them.

Now, they were having a jolly dinner with the lady. Unfortunately, Bess had made one little interruption of the noxious fume variety, prompting windows to be thrown open.

Madame Tussaud had appeared nearly overcome by it and held a perfumed handkerchief to her nose. She was mollified upon understanding that Bess was a lovely little dog who they'd rescued upon the road and the noxious fumes were her only fault.

"Madame Tussaud," Rosalind said, "our Miss Mayton has spent some time in Paris."

Miss Mayton nodded. "Oui, c'est vrai," she said.

"Ah, Miss Mayton," Madame Tussaud said, "you speak French."

"Just enough to exchange words with my dear Phillipe," Miss Mayton said. "All the words of love, you understand."

It did not appear to Rosalind that Madame Tussaud *did* understand, as she had just looked around as if wondering where Phillipe might be located just now. To clarify, she said, "Phillipe was one of Miss Mayton's desperately tragic loves."

"He was a poet," Juliet said, "as am I. He died very sadly, though."

Madame Tussaud nodded. "The terror has swept through all of Paris," she said. With a long sigh, she murmured, "The guillotine's word is sharp and cannot be unsaid."

"Oh, no," Miss Mayton said, "he did not leap to the great beyond *that* way. You see, he wrote me a poem declaring his undying passion. Unfortunately, the young fellow who was supposed to deliver it to me was distracted by a cockfight and forgot all about it in his pocket. Poor Phillipe had been watching out his garret window, hoping to see me come running down the street to accept his undying passion, which I can assure you I would have done. Alas, as the sun set over the rooftops of Paris, he finally surrendered to despair. He hung himself with a note pinned to his shirt—pour l'amour d'Eloïse je ne peux plus continuer."

"That means, for the love of Eloise I cannot longer go on," Juliet said.

"Yes, I understand French," Madame Tussaud said, appearing rather stunned to hear of Phillipe.

That did not surprise Rosalind. Nobody had experienced the terribly bad luck in love that Miss Mayton had.

"He could not wait a day to save his own life?" Madame Tussaud asked. "To discover whether you had even received his missive?"

Miss Mayton shook her head. "You see, Madame Tussaud, when the love is that passionate, rash action often follows."

"Does it?" Madame Tussaud said, seeming not to have known that fact. Rosalind thought it rather odd as the woman was a full-grown lady. Perhaps she had not had the good fortune to be loved as Miss Mayton had.

It was an idea that sent shivers down Rosalind's spine. Not every lady was blessed with finding true love. She had seen it in her own neighborhood. Mr. and Mrs. Wendall barely tolerated each other. It was said that they'd married because he'd wanted children and she'd wanted security. That was all that had ever been between them.

Surely, it would not be the case for her. No, it could not be. Her sister Beatrice had found love, as odd as it was that her particular love was for Van Doren. Surely Rosalind and her sisters would find it too.

Young waiters cleared the dinner plates and the innkeeper approached the earl. "The tea service and dessert cart will be in shortly, my lord. Will you wish for a bottle of port?"

The earl nodded, then he held his forefinger up as if he'd just had an idea. "I say, Madame Tussaud, I am not overfamiliar with how things are done in Paris. Do the ladies partake in port after dinner?"

Madame Tussaud, who seemed greatly affected by Miss Mayton's tragedy in love and was now rather pale, nodded and said, "They do now."

The innkeeper was as good as his word and the dinner was cleared and dessert served. The earl poured a glass of port for Madame Tussaud.

Juliet said, "Here we are, after dinner. I suppose everybody will wish to hear what I have written today?"

"Oh I am sure Madame Tussaud would be greatly appreciative to hear of some well-fashioned English poetry," Miss Mayton said.

Juliet rose. "I will read the one I consider most inspired. It is called *Ode to Hay*."

Reaching for the sun and sprung from the ground
As we trot on by, we see it all around
A farmer joyfully feeds his horses and cows
While the ground that sprung the hay graciously bows.

Everyone clapped, but for Madame Tussaud who missed the opportunity because she was draining her glass of port.

"So well done, Juliet, I really do not know how you manage to capture these bucolic scenes," Miss Mayton said.

"They inspire me, Aunt," Juliet said gravely. "They practically write themselves."

"Do you have such poets in France, Madame Tussaud?" Cordelia asked.

Madame Tussaud held her empty glass out toward the earl, who took the hint and filled it once more.

"We must make do with Voltaire," she said. "The French have created nothing approaching this."

Rosalind's sisters all nodded over the sentiment and Juliet

looked well-pleased.

"Now, Madame Tussaud, you are in for a real treat," Miss Mayton said.

"The poem was not it?" Madame Tussaud asked warily. "There are more treats?"

Rosalind began to fear that Madame Tussaud was becoming over-excited by all the entertainments. She began to sound almost nervous.

"Oh yes," Miss Mayton said, picking up a book from the table. "This is quite the treat. We have just begun reading a fascinating novel called *The Awful Happenstances of Grimwood Hall*. A young governess is raising the five children of the duke, his wife having just recently died under mysterious circumstances."

"She ended up in the bottom of a well," Viola said. "Nobody knows how she got there."

Miss Mayton nodded. "Now the interesting thing is, the governess has discovered that the duke has been in love with her for over a year. But, can she return his love when she does not know how his wife got in the well?"

"Mon dieu," Madame Tussaud muttered, draining her glass and holding it out for the earl.

Miss Mayton cleared her throat. "Chapter two," she said.

Rosalind sipped her tea and contentedly listened to this new story Miss Mayton had found for them. The duke had just insisted that the governess begin dining with him at table. During their dinners, he posited all sorts of ways his dead wife might have ended up in the well. Perhaps she was thirsty and had leaned over the side and then fell in. Perhaps she was running from a mad dog and accidently gone over the side. Perhaps a devilish ghost had led her there in her sleep.

The governess found herself torn—naturally, the duchess might have ended in the well for any of those reasons. And yet, the housekeeper kept telling her that the duke had strangled his lady and threw her in. Who to believe?

Miss Mayton closed the book with a satisfied sigh. "We are

left to wonder, are we not?"

By way of her approbation, lovely little Bess was gripped with a series of explosive and noxious fumes.

Cordelia and Viola ran to the windows to get them open, and then Juliet opened the door for good measure.

Madame Tussaud rose and said, "I am very tired, I must retire." She staggered from the dining room murmuring, "Jamais de ma vie—je suis sans voix."

They'd all turned to one another and nodded approvingly at the lady's parting words, as they were so perfectly apt. *Never in my life—I am speechless.*

Rosalind was not a bit surprised. Of course the lady *would* be struck speechless, what with all the entertainments they had offered for her benefit. When her carriage wheel broke, Madame Tussaud could not have had any idea that her evening would pass by so engagingly.

They all speedily agreed that they must visit Madame Tussaud and her wax figure display at the Lyceum. After all, she had become quite the friend and they all felt that nobody could need more propping up than a French royal sympathizer. It could not be comfortable to find oneself on that sort of a losing side. The English might have done away with a nobleman from time to time, but never so many at once!

THE FOLLOWING MORNING, Rosalind and her sisters were all looking forward to breakfasting with Madame Tussaud, but the innkeeper told them she'd set off in a hurry just before the dawn broke.

Now, their carriage trotted at a brisk pace, poised to enter the great city of London.

Rosalind had opened her window, on account of Bess' continuing stomach troubles, and watched the world go by.

Ever cognizant of what went on around her, she had taken in some lessons from Beatrice's adventure in Town. The primary thing she had decided upon was that Beatrice's list of requirements had been all well and good, but far too long.

Beatrice had been determined to find a gentleman with the courage of Beowulf, the strength of Hercules, the derring-do of Robin Hood, as gallant as Sir Gawain, having the depth of feelings of Shakespeare, and the stalwart heart of Henry the Fifth.

If one were to require so many attributes, then the fates might throw their hands up and deliver the likes of Van Doren, who had none of them.

Rosalind had decided that a lady must boil the thing down to its essence. What was the single thing that was most important to Lady Rosalind Bennington?

It had been the work of a moment to define it. Her gentleman must be daring and courageous, brave, and dripping in valor.

It really was the most sensible thing, as she was rather daring and courageous herself and a lady could not be happy with a man she could defeat before breakfast.

Had it not been she who had valiantly approached that hornet's nest to knock it down with a broom after one of the creatures had stung Juliet? Of course, she'd not got it knocked down and had ended up with far more stings than Juliet had ever got, but it had been the spirit of the thing.

Was it not herself who had pronounced the music tutor a sour-face for never smiling? Of course, she had missed several desserts after the fellow complained to the earl. Worse, that old sour-face had smiled at her ever after, as if he were forever thinking of her punishment. It had so discomposed her that she never did learn to read music. But again, it had been the spirit of the thing.

Had it not been Rosalind who had stolen down into the kitchens late one evening to secretly and silently prepare her sisters' favorite treat? Bread and butter, sprinkled with sugar? They called it faerie's tea and it was the remedy whenever they all caught colds. That she had somehow sprinkled the bread with salt rather than sugar had been unfortunate, but again it had been the spirit of the thing.

She was bold and would require an even bolder gentleman.

As she had such a short list of requirements, Rosalind was certain the fates would be pleased and her daring gentleman should present himself in all haste.

"How odd that we should be on our way to London and Beatrice is not in our carriage," Viola said.

"She could not be, though," Juliet said. "Van Doren must be making moon eyes at her at all times and will not be parted from her."

"They will follow us soon enough," Miss Mayton said, "and be directly across the street. Van Doren has bought the house he rented last season."

"Oh yes," Cordelia said, "Right across the street. Beatrice mentioned that she liked it and it was done."

"I hope he does not mean to make me any trouble," Rosalind said. "It's all well and good that Beatrice is delighted with him and I am so gratified that my sister is happy, but he does continue on with his lectures to *us*."

"Less so, though," Miss Mayton said, "as he is always so distracted by Beatrice."

"That is true," Juliet grudgingly admitted. "In any case, our dear brother Darden will be waiting for us and he shall understand your requirements perfectly, Rosalind."

"Courage," Viola said with a sigh. "If you found a brave man with red hair, I should go mad over it."

"Viola," Cordelia said, "you are the only one of us so tempted by red hair."

"I would not care if his hair were green," Rosalind said, "as long as he is brave and courageous." Rosalind paused. "Well, perhaps not green, I am hopeful he is attractive, but courage must be the primary thing."

They had entered the town proper and the carriage slowed as was always the way in London. One might race one's carriage all across England but there was no racing through Town in the middle of the day. Thousands of people of all sorts had places to go and were determined to go there.

Rosalind peered out the window at all of the bustle. Farmer's carts, hackneys, private carriages, pedestrians, and gentlemen on horseback all weaved and dodged and hurried to their destinations.

Very suddenly a particular gentleman on horseback caught her eye.

Rosalind's breath caught.

What was this magnificence before her?

He sat exceedingly tall in the saddle, his divine coat not showing the slightest crease. His hair was that of a gentle-baked loaf—a very light brown that was soft in its coloring and likely to darken in the cold months. His profile was so well-formed—a strong jaw, high cheekbones and straight nose.

As she was admiring this very wonderful-looking person, a young child escaped her mother's hand and ran out onto the street.

Rosalind watched in horror as carriage horses' hooves bore down on the little mite.

The magnificent gentleman saw the oncoming disaster, maneuvered round, and swept the girl up and out of the way of a carriage. He trotted to the pavement, depositing the girl in the arms of her hysterical mother.

The gentleman tipped his hat, turned a corner, and was gone.

CHAPTER TWO

ROSALIND SAT BACK. Her hands shook in her lap. That man, whoever he was, well, he was positively glorious in both person and action. She had never seen such a specimen of a gentleman. Surely, the fates had arranged that she see him at this moment—this fine moment of courageous action.

Yes, she felt in her heart that it was so.

"It is him," she said. "I have seen him. Gracious, he is marvelous."

"Seen who, my dear?" Miss Mayton inquired.

"Him. *My* gentleman."

Miss Mayton leaned over and peered out the window, as did Cordelia, Viola, and Juliet, all piling onto Rosalind's side and making the carriage rock on its springs.

"You will not see him," Rosalind said from underneath the muslin of Juliet's dress. "He has turned a corner and is gone. But Aunt, Sisters, he is here!"

"You felt the signs?" Miss Mayton asked, settling herself back in her seat and grasping Rosalind's hand from across the carriage.

Nobody had need of detailing the signs of true love, as Miss Mayton had explained them thoroughly. One felt as if one's hair had been struck by lightning, and one was drowning but taking in more air, and one's heart sped up though one felt well.

"Indeed," Rosalind said, "particularly my heart speeding up. As well, you can feel my hand in yours, it is shaking."

"Goodness," Cordelia said, putting Bess back on her lap, "he is here and now you must only encounter him at a ball or a party!"

"Then, he'll do something courageous to prove his love and before you know it, you are on your way to church," Juliet said.

"He just now saved a young girl from being trampled," Rosalind said. "The fates have arranged the display to point him out to me, I am certain of it."

"He has shown his courageousness," Viola said. "Surely he will show it on your behalf too."

"I will write an ode about it," Juliet said. "*Ode to the Heroic Gentleman.*"

"What did he look like?" Cordelia asked.

"Marvelous," Rosalind said with a sigh. "He is the most magnificent man I have ever seen—quite perfect."

"I wonder who he is," Miss Mayton said.

Rosalind wondered too, but she was certain that she should not wonder long. The fates were in her corner and would see to it that her magnificent gentleman was put in her view in all haste. The fates could not make her feel as she did just now if they meant anything other than he was to be her gentleman.

She must just be prepared for whatever courageous act he was determined to do for her.

"Until we meet, good sir," she murmured.

→》》》✦《《《←

BALTHAZAR REARDON, THE Duke of Conbatten, took a chilled glass of champagne from his valet. He had very particular habits and the champagne had been run up from the cellars at precisely twenty-six minutes into a bath that was heated to precisely ninety-eight degrees.

His valet, Henri, kept a close eye on the thermometer and poured in a judicious amount of hot water to keep the temperature up.

It was well he favored such habits. Henri had detailed them to a number of other valets and, as those persons had no ability to keep a thing to themselves, now all the *ton* knew of them. These, and other ideas about him, had turned him into some sort of mythical creature and he often found it amusing. He had recently been informed that the members of Lord Darden's *Young Bucks Club* continually debated inviting him in. The difficulty appeared to be the idea that he would refuse, or worse, accept.

All of this was an excellent mask for his real activities. Let them keep him at a distance, let them not know what to do with him.

His father had been one of the founders of the Queen's Knights—a select group of five heads of families who worked toward Queen Charlotte's primary aim. She wished England to be the envy of Europe, and London was to be the shining city, the lighthouse to all the world.

These aims had been continually stymied by how likely it was that one might be robbed on a lonely road, or robbed just by walking down the street in broad daylight.

Punishments, including hangings, had not had much effect. The queen was of the opinion that the worst offenders, the masterminds who directed their own armies of thieves, must be plucked out one by one like weeds from a garden.

So his father had sought to do, and so did he seek to do too. While the *ton* remained blissfully unaware of the Knights' activities, those with something to fear did not.

When five gentlemen masked and wearing black cloaks strode down a dirty street in the Rats' Castle, all who saw them knew that a powerful criminal was being hunted down. Shutters were closed and candles blown out.

Nobody dared fire at them, they had trained their eyes to spot the barrel of a gun poking out a window and the sot who tried it would find his one shot was countered by fifteen, as they all carried three pistols. Nobody dared approach them and stop their progress, as they would shortly find themselves sliced to ribbons.

Even the most depraved and daring rogue would prefer not to be the bull's eye when they came calling.

The Knights did not concern themselves with anybody other than the top of the ladder. They did not meddle with boys who stole out of necessity, nor did they tamper with a man only trying to feed his family or bother a woman picking pockets as an alternative to prostitution.

They were not unaware that people must eat and be housed and warm themselves in winter. Neither was the queen. She'd tried setting up schools, and bettering workhouse conditions, and paying for apprenticeships.

The efforts were worthwhile, but they were only a light finger on a scale with a very heavy weight on the other side of it.

The problem the Knights concerned themselves with were those who had satisfied their daily needs and would seek to build an empire. They sought out those who could increase the amount of crime exponentially through recruiting young men to work for them.

Every so often there was one of these men creating a deal of trouble for the queen's plans. There was one such now, who had grown so bold as to be training a legion of boys to be house-breakers.

Balthazar's information so far was that the efforts were highly organized and detailed.

Boys were not just trained on how to spot a vulnerable house and how to get in and out. They were also trained on the niceties—how to separate the paste from gem and the cheap metal from silver. How to bypass the jewelry box displayed and find the one that was hidden. Where to look for concealed compartments. How to understand which kinds of papers were valuable and which were not. Apparently, they were so bold as to take personal correspondence and he assumed they hoped to uncover a scandal they could use in a blackmail.

Their accents were worked on and references forged, as one

of the strategies was to get into a house through employment.

That was all the information the Knights had so far, but there would be more coming.

Now, the London season had commenced and Balthazar's door was to be battered with invitations. He would venture out and play his part in society until he received the summons.

One day, and he could not know when, he would receive a note from a certain marquess that read: *Our quarry is identified and within reach.*

Until then, champagne, warm baths, and lovely ladies at balls and dinners would do very well.

Of course, there was always the problem of some of those lovely ladies fluttering their eyelashes and delicately hinting that they might not mind becoming his duchess.

He'd got very experienced at dodging those subtle displays of feminine wiles. He would not be caught until he meant to be caught.

Exactly when he might mean to be caught, he could not say. He was well aware of his duty to produce an heir. There had been no end of ladies he might have taken on as duchess. But it was hard to tell them apart, so many of them were the same, as if they'd all had the same tutor and were taught the same conversations. Was he to chain himself to a lifetime of such uninteresting exchanges?

How many of those conversations he'd had—the weather, the traffic, how lovely the park was, or even more irritating, how edifying Fordyce's sermons were.

It was England, he hardly thought the fact that it was raining to be notable nor surprising. It was London, of course there was too much traffic on the streets. The park was a park, and generally crowded. As for Fordyce's sermons, it would be refreshing if some lady were to pronounce them what they really were—tedious.

And then there was another matter to consider when he thought of marriage. It would be nigh impossible to keep his activities for the queen hidden from a wife. Women sniffed out secrets like dogs sniffed out a fox. It would be inconvenient to have some lady handwringing at the door when he left for the Rats' Castle. It would be really inconvenient if she could not keep the secret to herself.

"Do you attend Almack's on Wednesday?" Henri asked, interrupting his thoughts and taking his empty champagne coupe from him.

Balthazar rose and Henri draped a towel round his shoulders and handed him another for his waist. "Of course I must attend. Conbatten must go to Almack's just as the sun must rise in the east. One does not like to disappoint the Patronesses."

Henri nodded. "Signor Ribaldi brings your new coats on the morrow. I have arranged he come disguised as a grocer and enter through the servants' door, as I believe there is at least one gentleman who has set a watch on the house in an effort to discover who your tailor is."

"Poor sots," Balthazar said. "If they were ever to discover it, they would also discover that I pay Ribaldi not to tailor for anybody else. The arrangement suits us both."

"This is why you are Conbatten and they are not," Henri said, thoroughly satisfied with the idea.

Balthazar smiled to himself. He knew his valet to be satisfied with the idea that there was only one Conbatten because that meant there could be only one Henri.

He was not particularly opposed to the opinion. He rather favored having a valet who was superior.

The fellow was remarkably good at tying a neckcloth and had traveled throughout the continent to finally locate the finest tailor. Ribaldi was found in Rome and Henri offered him such compensation that the fellow could not refuse. He'd done the same with his chef, practically smuggling him out of Paris. If one wished for the best, one only had to send Henri to find it.

Furthermore, if one had the great good luck to be born to a dukedom, one ought to have the sense to act like it.

⟫⟫⟫⟪⟪⟪

THE HOUSE ON Portland Place was just as Rosalind remembered from last season. Though, at the same time, everything looked different too. Last year, she had been the younger sister staying at home and listening to late night reports from Beatrice about this or that outing.

Now it would be she who would sally forth and bring home her own reports to her sisters. It was positively thrilling.

They had gathered in the drawing room before dinner, awaiting Darden's arrival. Their father had sent a note to The Young Bucks Club, a gentlemen's club that Darden had himself founded. Darden was to know that his family had arrived to Town and he was expected to dinner.

"I do hope our dear little Bess is comfortable in the kitchens," Cordelia said.

"I do not see why she wouldn't be," the earl said, "what more could a stray cur hope for—to be rescued by a gaggle of young ladies and deposited in the warmest room in the house, which also happens to be the place food is so helpfully located."

"Tattleton," Viola asked their butler, "how does our dear Bess get on?"

"When I left," he said gravely, "that canine was stretched in front of the hearth and gnawing a chair leg. Young Charlie has promised to keep her from devouring all of the furniture."

"Charlie has taken a shine to our Bess," Cordelia said.

"Very predictable," the earl said. "The poor boy was rescued from his own unfortunate circumstances and must find sympathy with a creature in a similar situation."

"Oh I am glad they have found each other as friends," Viola said.

Rosalind could not help but notice that Tattleton did not seem to be as joyful over it. She supposed the butler was suspicious of any new animal coming into the house on account of the four kittens that had come along with Charlie last year. While Charlie had proved himself to be ever so helpful in the kitchens, the kittens had been less so and had got up to much mischief.

Tattleton would see, though—lovely little Bess was an absolute angel. She had not filled their carriage with barking even one time on their journey. She *had* filled it with fumes, but then, everybody had their problems.

They all heard the front doors crash open and were on their feet in a moment.

"Darden!" Juliet cried.

Darden himself came into the room and braced himself for the inevitable onslaught of sisters.

They rushed him and nearly knocked him over with their enthusiasm.

"Darden!"

"Dear Darden!"

"Our dear brother!"

"Darden, we have brought a dog," Juliet said, having thrown herself at him and rumpling his coat.

"Of course, you have," Darden said, picking her up for a hug.

"We found her on the road," Juliet said by way of clarification.

"Where else?" Darden said, well used to his sisters' habits.

He untangled himself. "Father," he said, "and Miss Mayton. You are both looking well. Everybody is looking exceedingly well."

"Rosalind especially," Viola said, hanging on Darden's arm.

"Naturally Rosalind especially," Darden said. "It is to be her season after all."

"Now my girls, unhand your brother," the earl said jovially. "Tattleton has signaled we may go through. At table we can tell Darden all of our news and he can tell us all of his."

Viola had her brother's one arm and Rosalind took the other. Cordelia and Juliet followed close on their heels as they made their way to the dining room.

Rosalind was to take her place to the right of Darden this year, as Beatrice was gone from the house. It was rather thrilling to take the place of eldest sister in the house.

They arranged themselves with Miss Mayton to the earl's right, and Viola now on her own across the table from Cordelia and Juliet.

"Darden," Cordelia said, "you would have been so proud of us all while we traveled. We even entertained a French lady who was stranded and she was so overcome by our attentions she could not even find the words to thank us."

"She was speechless," Juliet said nodding.

"That would not surprise me," Darden said, laughing.

"And Darden," Viola said, "you are not to have nearly as much trouble this season as you did last. Rosalind has already seen her one true love."

"Already? How can it be so?" Darden asked, looking mystified.

"Indeed," the earl said, "I am interested to hear of that myself. We only arrived to the house three hours ago."

"We were in the carriage, just coming into Town," Rosalind said. "He is magnificent and he saved a young girl from being trampled on the road."

"Gracious," the earl said, "I missed that excitement. I suppose I was too deep into my book to notice what went on outside my window."

"A bit of derring-do and that was it, eh?" Darden said, obviously amused. "Who is this paragon?"

"We do not know him yet," Rosalind said. "But I cannot imagine the fates will keep him long from my side."

"None of us saw him but Rosalind," Cordelia said. "She says he is very wonderful."

"And," Miss Mayton said, "the signs of true love were there—Rosalind's heart beat faster and her hands shook."

"He is magnificent," Rosalind said once more.

"Then let us hope he is not magnificently married or some sort of bounder," Darden said.

"Rosalind would never be struck with true love for a married man or a bounder, Darden," Juliet said, looking very indignant.

"I am sure not," Darden said in a conciliatory tone. "Well, I will be most interested to see who this fellow turns out to be. I must suppose he was dressed to indicate he is a gentleman, so the *not a married bounder* is bound to turn up somewhere."

"The fates, Darden," Rosalind said. "The fates will make it so."

"Perhaps he will be at Almack's?" Cordelia said. "Darden, you will see that Rosalind gets a voucher from Lady Jersey? And then a ticket for Wednesday?"

"Done and done," Darden said. "As busy as I am with my club, you do not think I would let down our Rosalind? I had to smooth Lady Jersey's feathers a bit on account of Van Doren's various missteps last season, and it was no easy feat, but she is very fond of Father and so it is all smoothed."

The sisters all sighed contentedly over this, as Darden really was the best of brothers.

"Now, Son, tell us your news," the earl said. "I presume by what you said just now that your club goes along swimmingly?"

"Indeed it does, Father," Darden said. "We are up to twenty-two paying members. We have kept it very exclusive of course."

Darden paused, then said, "We still have not decided what to do about Conbatten though. If we extend the invitation to put him forward, he might decline it. Or accept it. Both outcomes feel a bit...fraught."

"Beatrice says you all ought not be so frightened of the duke," Juliet said. "She says he is just a regular person."

Darden seemed taken aback by that idea. "For one, it is not that we are frightened...exactly. We are more...concerned and undecided. But the idea that Conbatten is a regular person? There is nothing *regular* about Conbatten!"

"He does have a terrific name," Rosalind said. "I remember

when Beatrice told us of meeting him. I thought, well, the Duchess of Conbatten sounded rather good."

"Whoever Conbatten takes as a bride," Darden said, "she is certain to be a paragon among women. It cannot be any other way."

As Rosalind did not think herself entirely left out of the *paragon among women* category, she said, "Unfortunately, it cannot be me. My heart is already taken."

"What I like about this, Rosalind," Juliet said, "is how easily it is all happening. Beatrice's season was so much confusion and then she goes and marries Van Doren."

"Steady on, my girl," the earl said, "Van Doren is your brother-in-law. He is family now and will be forevermore."

Juliet appeared rather dejected to hear it.

"Do not despair, Juliet," Miss Mayton said. "Lord Van Doren is bound to give up his lectures entirely when he has his own children. He will be far too busy trying to fill *them* up with his ideas."

"That's very true," Juliet said, brightening. "Think what a time our little cousins will have, dodging and weaving from his stare. I shall help them hide whenever they wish and fill them with sweets they aren't meant to have and teach them all the little tricks on how to escape a governess."

"Well, now," the earl said, "that is something to look forward to, I suppose."

TATTLETON HAD GIRDED himself for another season in Town. Lady Beatrice's season had quite knocked it out of him, what with Lord Darden's plot to bring his sister and Lord Van Doren together. It had seemed impossible and heading toward disaster until somehow it had not. He was still rather lost on how the whole thing had come about. One minute they had disdained one another and the next they were mauling each other with kisses in the front hall.

He supposed he must be satisfied with the idea that all parties to it seemed happy.

Then, of course, there had been the matter of four unruly cats who could not catch a mouse between them being brought into the house. Those wily felines were in Westmont House in Somerset now, no doubt shredding all the curtains as an army of mice strolled confidently toward the kitchens.

Despite the cats now forever underfoot, he had somewhat recovered from the last season amongst the soothing sounds and regular habits of the countryside.

Now they were returned to Portland Place. The staff were abed but for Mrs. Huffson and they had settled at table with welcome glasses of brandy.

The trip to Town had seemed a journey across China by foot, so long did it take. They did more stopping than starting.

Even so, he should perhaps be grateful that the only thing the young ladies had collected on the way was one dog. That canine was currently splayed out by the hearth in front of him. At least the thing was quiet, so he supposed he must content himself with knowing it could have been far worse.

The far worse that had hung in the balance was a French lady named Madame Tussaud. Apparently, they had urged the lady to come to stay at Portland Place. The young ladies found themselves dejected that it could not be so. The madame was staying with friends who would be devastated to lose her company.

Tattleton was not the least dejected. What on earth would they have done with a French woman in the house? Miss Mayton's maid Fleur, whose real name was the very usual and English Flora, already threw round too many French phrases at the servants' table. It drove the footmen mad. And then, he'd been informed that this Frenchwoman made wax figures as her employment. Did that not smack of witchcraft somehow?

Whatever that woman and her wax were up to, he was glad it

was not to go on in this house.

As his thoughts meandered, he was suddenly hit by a wave of…well, he did not know what. Never had anything so deadly assaulted his senses. It was at once the odors of rotting fruit, old fish, foul water, and sulfur springs all mixed together. His eyes watered.

"What…is that…the *dog*?" he asked Mrs. Huffson.

Mrs. Huffson had raised her handkerchief to her nose. "Aye, I am afraid so. 'Tis not uncommon in animals that have been starved for a time and then find themselves in the midst of plentiful food."

"It cannot remain in the house in that condition!" he said, leaping up to open the door that led to the garden.

"Now, do not fret over it, Mr. Tattleton," Mrs. Huffson said through her handkerchief. "Her stomach will settle and right itself soon enough."

He flung the door open and breathed deep the fresh cool air. He turned and regarded the wretched creature as she stretched out on the carpet, completely oblivious to the suffering she had caused.

As the crisp breeze blew through the room, Mrs. Huffson lowered her handkerchief and said, "Aye, that's better. Now, Mr. Tattleton, there is all sorts of talk from the maids that Lady Rosalind already fancies herself in love."

Tattleton cautiously closed the door, though he would not be surprised if he were forced to race to get it open it again at any moment. "That is entirely true," he said, returning to the table and taking a gulp of brandy.

"Who is the fellow?" Mrs. Huffson said. "None of the maids seem to know who he is."

"That is because Lady Rosalind herself does not know who he is," Tattleton said. "She is counting on the fates to bring him forth."

"The fates?"

Tattleton nodded sadly. Lady Rosalind had a great confidence in the fates, whoever they were.

"Well now, that's a very fine muddle," Mrs. Huffson said.

Tattleton was afraid it was more than a muddle. Who was this fellow? Would it ever be discovered? What if the fates fell down on the job and did not bring him forth? Or what if they did and he was not up to snuff?

As Tattleton considered those questions, he suddenly peered closer at the dog. He did not know how much that mongrel had managed to eat in the past hours, but however much it had been, it seemed to be roiling in its stomach. Tattleton was certain its intestines were moving of their own accord and he was becoming fearful of another explosion.

"Is something wrong with that dog?" he asked, cautiously getting up and hurrying to the door before another eruption occurred.

Mrs. Huffson turned to look at the creature, who had now rolled on its back with its legs in the air.

"No, not a bit of it," Mrs. Huffson said. "Bess is just having a stretch. She's showing us her stomach, which signals she feels safe here."

Tattleton was not so sure Bess *ought* to feel safe here. Not if she were intent on carrying on like a veritable Mount Vesuvius.

"She'll be all right until morning and Charlie said he'd take her into the garden first thing," Mrs. Huffson said.

Tattleton could only hope Mrs. Huffson was correct. And hope that poor Charlie was not suddenly overcome with fumes when he did so. He did not wish to discover that fine young boy splayed on the floor, eyes wide, with a blank expression on his features, having been assaulted unawares.

Tattleton did not know how this season would unfold, exactly. But they already had a lady above stairs who did not know the identity of the gentleman she was in love with and a dog who could fell a full-grown man in a matter of seconds.

And he'd thought last season was a trial.

CHAPTER THREE

As Rosalind prepared to enter the vaunted halls of Almack's, her flutter of nerves made her think of how Beatrice must have felt, treading this same path last year.

Rosalind had been at home with her sisters, all of them lamenting that they must be left behind and wondering at the fun Beatrice must be having.

She'd not once in that moment thought of Beatrice being struck with nerves.

Beatrice must have been though. Rosalind was herself struck with nerves and everybody knew how bold and courageous she was.

Miss Mayton squeezed her hand after they'd handed in their tickets. The earl and Darden led the way to the ballroom.

Rosalind remembered Beatrice talking of how wonderfully elegant everybody was and how it was not at all like their own little neighborhood parties. Beatrice had taken comfort that even if she did not quite measure up, her dress certainly did.

She glanced down at her own dress. Mrs. Randower had spent months composing gowns that would complement Rosalind's dark brown hair and hazel eyes. Mrs. Randower had named the shade of her hair "chocolate" and said that complementary coloring and cut were everything. She would not involve herself with a lady who went in for bits and bobs stuck on everywhere, not for all the pounds and pence in the world. A rose was not more of a rose by dressing itself up in ribbons and bows.

Rosalind must think Mrs. Randower right about it. There was something about the simple dark blue silk with embroidered rosettes of the same color round the neckline that made her feel very elegant.

It was well she did feel elegant. They'd entered the ballroom and there was nothing but elegance in it.

"Earl, Darden," a fine-looking lady said.

"My dear Lady Jersey," the earl said with an elegant bow. "May I present my daughter, Lady Rosalind. And of course, you are already acquainted with Miss Mayton."

Rosalind curtsied very deeply, as Beatrice had told her the lady would expect it.

She rose and Lady Jersey tipped her chin. "She is positively lovely, Earl. It seems you are in possession of a whole line of comely daughters."

Rosalind blushed and was also very relieved. Van Doren had vexed the lady last season and she had not known what sort of reception they would get on account of it.

"Mrs. Mayton," Lady Jersey said, noticing she wore black bombazine, "you are still in mourning?"

"It is *Miss*, I am afraid to say," Miss Mayton said, whether she'd been afraid to or not. "I fear I shall be in mourning all my life after the tragedies I've suffered."

Lady Jersey narrowed her eyes just the littlest bit. "And yet you attend entertainments. How original."

Miss Mayton nodded sadly. "I must carry on for Rosalind's sake. And then Viola, Cordelia, and Juliet, too. After all my girls are settled comfortably, I will retire to my sad reflections."

"I see," Lady Jersey said. Though, Rosalind was fairly certain that she did not see.

It was hardly surprising. Her aunt's situation was unusual. There cannot have been many ladies who were in mourning for a husband though they'd never married, and who'd also declared they would bravely carry on attending entertainments for the sake of the charges they had raised.

Miss Mayton herself had not realized that she ought to be dressed in black until she'd donned the garb for a masque last season. Once she had on her widow's weeds, she said she knew it was right and must keep them on.

Lady Jersey nodded her understanding of the matter, though not very convincingly. "Darden, Earl, any who approach Lady Rosalind this evening have been sanctioned by me. You know how we do it for a first outing."

The earl and Darden bowed and Lady Jersey moved off.

"Lady Jersey is struck by my particular plight, as so many people are," Miss Mayton said.

Rosalind's father and Darden nodded and attempted to appear grave, though she could not help but note the smile playing at the edges of Darden's lips. Her brother was exceedingly fond of their aunt, though often amused by her too.

An elderly gentleman approached the earl. "Westmont! How long has it been? And this is your son?"

The gentleman appeared to be an old friend of the earl and there was much exclamation between them.

While her father became reacquainted with the fellow and Darden was acclaimed as a very fine-looking young man, Rosalind gazed round the ballroom, wondering who Lady Jersey would give leave to approach her.

Just now, she was certain she was being discussed. Lady Jersey spoke to a young gentleman who nodded and looked her way. It was not *her* gentleman, but she found him interesting. His hair was a deep copper color and Viola was very taken by shades of red hair. Nobody understood why it was so, not even Viola herself.

Rosalind suspected it had to do with an early crush. There had been a red-haired tinker's boy who had passed through their neighborhood when she was very young. He had winked at her and she'd talked about it for ages.

Well, at least there was one red-haired fellow in the *ton*. Rosalind had been worried that there would not be many.

The copper-haired gentleman looked her way.

Rosalind averted her eyes, not liking to be caught out in such a manner. She looked to her right, and then her breath caught in her throat.

He was here. It was him.

She'd been at once certain he would be and despairing that he would not be.

The fates had not failed her. He was here and he was as magnificent as he had been on horseback.

He was exceedingly tall, which was far more noticeable now that he was off his horse. Everything else, though, was as she remembered. His tailoring was perfection, his slim frame and broad shoulders were perfection, his strong jaw and those high, prominent cheekbones, his hooded eyes...he was simply magnificent.

Rosalind felt a little sick, and she remembered Beatrice saying she had felt just the same when she realized her love for Van Doren. It was not on the list of Miss Mayton's signs of true love, but it could very well be an inherited family trait.

She leaned toward Miss Mayton and whispered, "It is him. He is here."

Miss Mayton followed her eyes toward the magnificent gentleman.

"*Him?*" she asked, her tone all surprise.

The earl interrupted them. "Rosalind, Miss Mayton, do be introduced to my very old friend, Lord Cannerly. He and I have not crossed paths these twenty years."

Rosalind was forced to turn away from her magnificent gentleman, but not before she saw Lady Jersey approach him. She prayed her name was on Lady Jersey's lips just now. It must be so, the fates would not disappoint her in such a manner.

Lord Cannerly was a jolly fellow and after they were duly introduced, he and her father spoke of long-past days and their various battles over piquet.

"Now Earl," Miss Mayton said, "while it is usual that you and I defeat another couple at whist, I insist that you and Lord

Cannerly have the opportunity to pick up your piquet battles once more. Lord Darden and I can stay with Rosalind in the ballroom."

The earl was delighted with the idea, as was Lord Cannerly. Rosalind was so admiring of her aunt's forethought on the matter.

The two gentlemen set off very happily together.

Behind her, Rosalind heard a deep voice say, "Darden."

She slowly turned, certain of who she should find there. She was certain no other voice could make her shiver, as if a cold breeze had blown through the room. It was him.

"Hello!" Darden said, seeming almost nervous. "Your Grace, may I present my sister, Lady Rosalind."

The duke bowed. "Miss Mayton, Lady Rosalind."

"Rosalind, this is the Duke of Conbatten," Darden sputtered.

Conbatten! Of course it must be Conbatten. Hadn't she known it the first time Beatrice had ever mentioned his name? Or, if she had not *known* it, she did remember thinking it was a very fine name.

Rosalind curtsied. "Your Grace," she said.

"Lady Jersey has given me leave to put myself down on your card, if you are not opposed to it," Conbatten said.

"Opposed to it?" Rosalind said. "I would think not."

The duke had a rather bemused expression as he took her card.

"I suppose it will be for supper," Rosalind said.

"Do you suppose that?" the duke asked her quizzically.

"Do not you think so?" Rosalind asked.

"Rosalind," Darden said, sounding on the verge of becoming hysterical, "I hardly think—"

Conbatten held a hand up and Darden stopped talking. "If Lady Rosalind supposes it, then it must be true," he said, penciling in his name.

He bowed and walked off chuckling.

"Rosalind!" Darden whispered. "That was Conbatten, you understand, and that was rather…my God I do not know what it was."

"It was rather direct, I would say," Miss Mayton said.

"Well, I only say, he is Conbatten," Darden said, sounding near hysterical. "*Conbatten*, you understand."

"Look, Darden," Rosalind said, holding out her card, "he has done it. He has put himself down to take me into supper."

"Because you ordered him to!" Darden said. "What he must think of it…"

"Now Lord Darden, you have got yourself tied up in knots over nothing," Miss Mayton said.

"No I haven't!" Darden said. "Rosalind, you cannot go round ordering gentlemen on what dances they are to take. Especially not Conbatten!"

Miss Mayton tapped Darden's arm with her fan. "Oh look, Lady Mary has spotted you and she heads in your direction."

Darden suddenly had the look of a hunted stag upon him. "Excuse me, I must go and…go somewhere. Do not forget what I said." He hurried off in the opposite direction.

Rosalind did not think Darden's flight would do him much good. Lady Mary had reset her direction to follow Darden's own and bore down upon him, just as she'd heard the lady did with Van Doren last season.

But then, that was Darden's problem. Her gentleman was here, and her gentleman was Conbatten.

"I find myself all aflutter," Miss Mayton said. "When you told us of seeing your gentleman out of a carriage window, I had not imagined it was the duke."

"Nor I, Aunt," Rosalind said. "I could not have cared less if he were a grocer. Goodness, is he not marvelous? I feel as if my whole person is abuzz just to be near him. When I heard his voice behind me, I knew it was him. There is not a more perfect person on this earth, I am sure of it."

"Darden will be felled by the shock of the idea, I think," Miss Mayton said.

"Oh, he must not be told," Rosalind said. "Nobody must know but you and my sisters."

"It is to be a secret? Why?"

"We must allow Conbatten to prove his courage and bravery for me before I reveal my own feelings," Rosalind said. "I must be wooed, you see. He must do something daring for love of me. I cannot imagine what it will be, but the fates will see to it."

"Oh yes, I understand you," Miss Mayton said. "Goodness child, you are full of good sense in these matters."

BALTHAZAR HAD TAKEN his leave of Lady Rosalind Bennington after putting himself down for her supper.

Or rather, being directed to put his name down for her supper.

He'd really thought Lord Darden might expire over his sister's brashness. He'd been rather taken aback himself.

Of course, he should have known a Bennington lady would be an original. Lady Beatrice had been too, and he had even anticipated the entertainment of further Benningtons on the horizon.

He had no idea what she would have to say for herself at supper, though he doubted there would be endless conversation about the weather.

When had a lady ever directed him on which dance to take?

Never, that was when. Oh, he had been the subject of hints often enough. Lady Mary or Lady Clara might even go so far as to hold their thumb over another dance that was free and not so significant.

However, he had dined with both those ladies and was determined to avoid doing so again—he had acquired the habit of gently pulling their card from their hands to get a better view.

Lady Rosalind, though, just might be a different matter.

And my God, she was a tempting creature. She had that coloring he so preferred—her hair as deep brown as strong coffee.

Hazel eyes that changed color in the light. A delicate bone structure, as if she might have been a ballerina had she been born other than she had been. An entrancing little minx.

Still, her danger would never be in her looks, those he could withstand if necessary. Her danger would be in her…well, he did not know what to call it exactly. Her forthright and surprising nature, he supposed.

She was different, and different always pulled at him.

He was both wary and looking forward to speaking with her. It was so rare that any woman sparked any sort of interest in him.

He just must be careful not to let it get out of hand.

A certain marquess appeared beside him. One of the five Queen's Knights. "Hamill," he said.

"Conbatten. I have heard something that might interest you, as I believe you are acquainted with the fellow. It seems a certain Lord Van Doren's household has been targeted through unlikely means by the ring of thieves we seek."

"Van Doren?" Balthazar asked. They still did not know who was at the top of this organized group of housebreakers. Whoever it was, how on earth had they picked out Van Doren of all people? He was not as rich as some others. He was just a new-married viscount from the countryside—why him?

"Crosby nabbed one of the young ones we've been certain were a part of this gang and wrenched the information out of him. The wretch claims there is a boy named Shrimps having been taken into Van Doren's household last season and that boy is one of their own."

"Ah, so their scheme of getting employed to get into a house is already in play."

"Not exactly. Not in this case, anyway. It seems that some-time last year, six of the younger ones were all one night hanging about the street and Van Doren chased them away. This Shrimps character fell on the cobblestones and Van Doren picked him up and put him on his horse. There was a dog of some sort taken too. The rest of the boys followed in the darkness and apparently

Shrimps was taken into the house. After that, they saw him coming and going and saw him leave Town last season with the rest of the household. They had planned to make contact with him if he arrived back with the lord so they might make arrangements to clean the place out some night."

"So it is not clear whether the boy is even still a part of the household."

Hamill nodded. "Or part of the gang. I suspect this plan of theirs has been at least put on hold as they will know that one of their own has been taken by us. They will fear we will discover it, which we have, and that a trap would be set for them. So, I think Lord Van Doren is safe from a robbery. For now, at least. Though he might want to reconsider having a person named *Shrimps* in his household."

Balthazar nodded. "I suspect you are right, they won't risk a robbery that's been planned when one of the planners has been taken. Would this boy that Crosby got hold of reveal who is running the operation?"

"No, and Crosby thinks he's telling the truth when he says he does not know. It seems each level of the organization only has contact with one level below and one level directly above. He is at the bottom of the barrel, so to speak. He thinks things are set up in pods, meaning small groups of boys, scattered in the vicinity of the Seven Dials and not having contact with one another."

Conbatten sighed. It was a clever way to do things. Anybody who got nabbed could only tell so much.

"I'll move on now," Hamill said. "Lady Mary has turned her voracious eyes upon me and I must be quick about it before I am caught in her uncomfortable net."

Hamill strode off, and Balthazar did too. He was in no mood for Lady Mary's hard, glittering eyes this night.

As he strolled about the ballroom, he thought over what to do about Van Doren and his street urchin named Shrimps. Perhaps he would set a quiet watch. After all, according to his information, this Shrimps had not even been approached yet. If the young fellow had found a comfortable place to lay his head, he might not be at all inclined to rob the provider of it.

He glimpsed Lady Rosalind across the room. Lord Jeffries was making an attempt to entertain, he supposed. And there was Michaels lining up for his chance.

Well, good luck fellows. Lady Rosalind has already directed a gentleman to put himself down for her supper and it was not you.

Balthazar smiled to himself. Really, despite the news about Van Doren and his wayward urchin, this was turning out to be a very pleasant evening.

ROSALIND HAD DANCED with any number of genial gentlemen. As none of them were *her* gentleman, and as *her* gentleman was so well known, she spent most of her time attempting to hear of Conbatten.

As far as she was to understand it, gentlemen were at once admiring and abashed. Very similar to how Darden acted over the duke. She was told of his ninety-eight-degree bathwater several times. One of the gentlemen practically lamented over the idea that nobody could discover the duke's tailor.

Her sister Beatrice had counseled Darden that he ought not be so bowled over by the duke, that Conbatten was just a regular gentleman like all others.

Rosalind could not remember when last she had disagreed with one of Beatrice's opinions, but she must differ on that idea.

Conbatten was not a regular gentleman like everybody else. Not one bit of it. He was a glorious specimen and she was certain there had rarely been such a one walking the earth. Of course, he must have a bath at ninety-eight degrees. Of course, his tailor was sought after.

It was positively delicious to imagine the moment when he would kiss her, though of course she could not know when that would be.

Now, the Earl of Baderston had come to collect her. After that, she would be led round the floor by the wondrous Conbatten.

Though she had steered all other conversations toward Conbatten, she would not with the earl. He was the earl of copper-colored hair and she must assure herself that he would still be available for Viola to have a look at next season.

Really, there were so few redheads of any sort and Viola was so set on it that Rosalind would be loath to allow one to get away.

"Lord Baderston," she said as they took their places, "I am hopeful of discovering that you adore ham."

"Ham. Well, yes, I suppose I do like it. Does not everybody?"

"Oh, I should think so. But some people particularly adore it."

"Do they?"

"Lord Baderston," Rosalind said as they waited their turn in the line, "I suppose you will put off marriage until at least next year?"

Lord Baderston looked exceedingly surprised to hear it. "Ah, well, I hadn't thought…"

"You really ought to," Rosalind said.

The earl appeared exceedingly startled. "Do you say, then, Lady Rosalind, that there is something…needing improvement? Some aspect of my person that time might remedy?"

"Goodness no," Rosalind said. "It is just not your moment."

"Not my moment?"

"You must wait to encounter someone who will appreciate your looks," Rosalind said pointedly.

The earl appeared entirely affronted. "Lady Rosalind, while I realize that I might not be to everybody's taste—"

"But that is just it!"

"I did not ask to be born a redhead!" he whispered heatedly.

"Of course you did not ask for it, but it is your good luck," Rosalind said. "My sister adores red hair. Viola, you ought to wait for her."

"Adores it? Viola?"

"Indeed," Rosalind said. "She is quite set on red hair and as there cannot be many of you, I would say you have a distinct leg up. Further, you have a very nice shade going for you—it is rather like copper and I imagine she will highly approve of it. You will adore her, of course. She is very pretty and the most charming lady you shall ever meet."

"Viola?"

"Lady Viola Bennington. She shall be here next season. Though, I will tell you something confidentially," Lady Rosalind said.

The earl leaned close to hear it.

"She is in Town *now* and we plan to often go out in the carriage all together. Were you to spot us in the park, you would know her as being the lightest haired of us. She is a charming strawberry blond with marvelous blue eyes."

"Well, of course I do go to the park quite often," the earl said thoughtfully. "Lady Viola."

"Just so, my lord," Rosalind said. "She is prodigiously fond of ham too. Which is why I asked for your own views on it."

"I see," the earl said. "Now, of course I may have downplayed my fondness for ham. One does not like to express too much enthusiasm for any sort of meat on such short acquaintance."

"Just as I thought," Rosalind said. "As well, Viola is a very loyal sort of person."

"Is she?"

"Oh yes, if Viola decides that she is in your corner, then that is it forevermore. She says loyalty is the hallmark of a true heart."

"It certainly is a very good quality. One would always wish for those in one's sphere to be loyal."

"What doesn't our Viola have going for her?" Rosalind said. "Beauty, charm, loyalty, and a fondness for red hair and ham."

"Gad, that is a remarkable list," the earl said softly to himself.

Rosalind nodded, thoroughly satisfied with the earl. Now that she had conducted that bit of business for Viola, she turned her thoughts in the only direction they wished to go—Conbatten.

CHAPTER FOUR

BALTHAZAR HAD LED a series of ladies through the sets. Some were rather tedious—nervous young ladies who seemed just out of the schoolroom. They were the ones Lady Jersey had pressed him to engage with. Any lady just coming into society must be shown to good effect at Almack's.

Those particular ladies generally had mamas standing at the edges of the floor, watching like hawks wishing to spot a mouse on a field before swooping down. He was well aware that he was considered a high-value mouse and at least some of these poor young women had been lectured to make a good impression on him. One had even been told, apparently, to litter her speech with French phrases.

He assumed this was to showcase her fluency. Quelle belle soirée, indeed.

Some other dances were far more pleasant, being with ladies he would consider more well-met friends than anything else. Lady Worthington was particularly amusing, as she always had a sharp wit about her. Young widowhood had not seemed to dampen her spirit and it having been over a year since her lord had departed the world, she was now well out of mourning.

Lady Rosalind was his next partner, and he had hopes she would prove herself equally amusing. He supposed she must be considered among those just out of the schoolroom, but she did not seem so. And, rather than having a sharp-faced mama watching her every step, Lady Rosalind was chaperoned by the rather flighty Miss Mayton.

He smiled to himself as he compared Miss Mayton to the hawk-like mamas. The hawks were examining and measuring every action and expression—calculating chances and next moves. Miss Mayton, on the other hand, would only be cheerfully waving and rather oblivious. He was beyond amused that she had taken to wearing widow's weeds to entertainments—Lady Jersey must have been entirely befuddled.

He collected Lady Rosalind from Lord Baderston, who appeared very struck by the lady. He'd even heard the fellow say, "I hope I encounter your family's carriage in the park, Lady Rosalind."

Lady Rosalind had smiled and nodded knowingly at the idea.

They had placed themselves near the top of the line and Balthazar said, "You seemed to have made quite the impression on Lord Baderston."

He did not know why he said so. It was the sort of fishing expedition that he himself had often been subjected to and he never liked it. Still, he found he did wish to know her thoughts on Baderston.

"Well, I suppose I would have," Lady Rosalind said, "he is a redhead and while he perhaps does not adore ham as much as one would hope, I believe he is determined to start adoring it."

Balthazar was entirely nonplussed by her response. What did it mean?

"Am I to take it then, that you *do* adore red hair and ham?" he asked.

"Not particularly," Lady Rosalind said.

There was a pause, and a charming wrinkling of her forehead. Balthazar was hopeful that Lady Rosalind had perceived that he was entirely lost on her meaning. Or, perhaps she had heard herself and known anybody must be.

By way of clarification, she said, "You see, my sister, Viola, is quite set on a redhaired man and she happens to adore ham, but she is not out until next year. I just thought Lord Baderston should be apprised of it."

Balthazar found himself strangely satisfied with the answer. "So you attempt a matchmaking?"

Lady Rosalind nodded.

"I see," he said thoughtfully. "I had at first assumed you spoke of yourself."

Lady Rosalind looked at him quizzically. "Certainly not," she said. "Had I spoken of myself, I would have spoken of my *own* proclivities."

It was their turn at the steps and Balthazar led her down the line. She was as graceful on the floor as her sister had been. Whoever the Benningtons' dancing master was, he knew his business.

They returned to their places and Balthazar thought he'd better initiate some more usual conversation, beyond red hair and ham. "I have been told that all the young ladies these days are exceedingly fond of Fordyce," he said, wondering what she would say about it.

"Reverend James Fordyce? The sermons?"

"I have been told they are popular," Balthazar said. He would be very sorry if she praised them, or worse, if she quoted them.

Lady Rosalind laughed. "I think you might be shocked over what I think of them."

"Then you do not agree with his ideas of modesty and meekness?" he asked, hopeful that she did not.

"Certainly not, they are absurd. Those like Wollstonecraft are forever pointing out their unfairness to women, and point taken but point also terribly obvious. I wonder why I never do hear of the unfairness to men. Do not you see? Fordyce has played a great joke on the gentlemen. He has led them to believe that they will wed some creature they might boss about. Particularly if they do not have sisters, they will be entirely fooled by Fordyce's notions."

So it was *men* who were damaged by Fordyce's advice? That

was indeed an original take on it.

"And then, they find out they were very much mistaken and go racing back to the sermons to check they'd read them properly and, of course, they have. Now they are left to think they'd married the only lady on earth with her own opinions."

Well, well.

"Goodness, if we were all so meek and mild as the reverend would prefer, I do not see how any of us would have even got ourselves to Town. Would we not have perished from delicacy on the way?"

Balthazar suppressed his laughter. "I trust your own journey to Town went smoothly and there was no threat of perishing, Lady Rosalind?"

As the lady talked on, Balthazar began to think that nothing was ever usual with Lady Rosalind Bennington. Apparently, they had managed to come out of the trip with somebody's dog, and she spoke at great length of a certain Madame Tussaud who made wax figures who had been left speechless over their various entertainments. One of those entertainments had been something called *Ode to Hay*, though Lady Rosalind could not recall the exact words, only that the ground took a bow at the end of it.

Then, apparently, Miss Mayton had found another dreadful novel to read to her charges. He still laughed about the one Lady Beatrice had described to him last season.

"I seem to remember Lady Beatrice describing a novel last year about a one-eyed duke," he said.

"Oh yes, that was terrifically good. He had his eye all along and was only a madman."

Balthazar pressed his lips together to stop from laughing.

"She accepted him as he was, in the end," Lady Rosalind said. "They went on quite happily together."

Of course they did. "Dare I inquire what this new duke's problem is?" he asked, hoping for something equally absurd.

Lady Rosalind nodded. "He's been in love with his governess for over a year, but his wife died under mysterious circumstances.

She went down a well. So, as you can imagine, the governess is torn."

"Another lovelorn duke and his hesitating governess," Balthazar said drily. "Let me guess, she wonders if she can love a murderer."

"That is just it! She does not know if he is a murderer. *He* says there are all sorts of ways the late duchess might have ended up in the well, but the housekeeper says he strangled her and put her there. Who is she to believe?"

"My money would be on the housekeeper."

"Would it really?" Lady Rosalind said, appearing very sorry to hear it. "That would be such a shame. The duke and his governess are terribly in love, you know."

"And that is enough?" Balthazar said, barely controlling his laughter. "Love must conquer all, even under threat of murder?"

Lady Rosalind gazed up at him under dark lashes. "If the man be courageous enough to make it so."

Balthazar did not know what to make of that and so said nothing.

As THE DUKE led her into the dining room, Rosalind felt as if her future was racing toward her at a terrific pace. Conbatten was everything she imagined. More than she imagined, really. So handsome, so graceful on the floor, and then his arm felt so strong through his coat that it made her wonder what his chest felt like. And then his lips, those very perfect lips. All of that, and he was so easy to talk to!

Goodness, all those lessons she and her sisters had endured from their governess about having conversations in society. According to that lady, almost every subject was off the table. A lady was to comment on the weather, or the charms of the hostess and her rooms, or general comments about carriage traffic, noting whether it had been light or heavy. One might mention a book, were it on a suitably elevated subject. If one were really struggling in the search for a topic of conversation, one might say something pious, which always had a good effect.

It had seemed an awful amount of tedious work and now she realized it was not at all necessary! At least, it was not necessary with the duke. Of course it would not be necessary with *him*.

She had spoken quite freely with Conbatten. It was just as it should be. The fates had arranged it all.

And then, there was something so thrilling about being near his person. She had a great wish to throw herself in his arms. Of course, she would do no such thing. At least, not yet.

Still, it was clear enough that they were destined for one another.

He must realize it too by now. It was a shame she could not tiptoe into his thoughts and see what was there.

The duke led her to a place at the table and a footman came running. Dry cake and sour lemonade secured, Conbatten said, "If I recall rightly, last season Lady Beatrice arrived to Town with a list of requirements in hand for the successful suitor."

"Indeed she did," Rosalind said. "A very long list."

"Yes, I do remember it being quite extensive. I suppose Lord Van Doren was able to check every box?"

Rosalind laughed and set her glass down. "He does not check *any* box as far as I can tell. She is deliriously happy in spite of it. Most importantly, we all approve of his treatment of her, so we are resigned to him."

"I am surprised the gentleman does not check any box at all," the duke said.

"There were just too many boxes," Rosalind said. "That was the problem all along."

"I see. And is it a family tradition to compose a list of requirements?"

Rosalind was most satisfied with his questioning. He wished to know how to go about winning Lady Rosalind's heart.

"It *is* rather a habit," Rosalind said. "Though, I hope I have learned something from Beatrice's experience. You see, I boiled the thing down to bravery and courage. I am exceedingly brave and courageous myself."

"Are you?"

"Indeed yes, I am quite known for it. Naturally, I must require the same in any suitor."

"Ah, so the successful gentleman will be known as a fellow who is particularly courageous."

Rosalind shook her head. It was imperative that Conbatten understand her thoroughly on this point. He could not hope to do what was required if he did not understand it.

"The successful gentleman will not just be *known* as courageous. He must *show* himself courageous in defense of his lady," Rosalind said.

"Indeed? And how is this gentleman to go about doing such a thing?"

Now they were getting to it. Conbatten wished for specifics on how to win her.

"I suppose it should be simple enough," Rosalind said. "When the lady is troubled by somebody or even some *thing*, the gentleman will swoop in and drive off the troublemaker."

"Lady Rosalind," the duke said with a small smile, "I am not certain what you think of this town. Are you under the impression that a lady faces danger at every turn? I cannot recall a recent circumstance where a lady needed rescuing from anything."

This idea did give Rosalind a pause. She had not really thought through how likely it would be that a particular opportunity would present itself.

Then, like sunshine breaking through the clouds, it came to her.

"The fates, Your Grace. The fates will arrange it all."

"I see," Conbatten said. "Of course that is how it must be."

Henri took his coat from him. Balthazar had never had such an interesting evening at Almack's.

"I suppose the gentlemen were green with envy and the ladies were all fanning themselves over Conbatten," Henri said.

Balthazar well knew this prediction had nothing to do with any allure of his person. As far as Henri was concerned, his dress clothes might have gone to Almack's by themselves, as his valet's arrangements were the real star of any outing.

"I did not see anybody green or anybody fanning," he said.

"They hide it from you then," Henri said, all confidence that his work had caused untold misery and despair upon every gentleman and intense admiration from every lady who had viewed his handiwork.

"There is another Bennington lady on the scene," Balthazar said. "She seems to be even more of an original than Lady Beatrice."

"Mon Dieu," Henri said. "You had so much trouble with the last one."

"I believe this one may be waiting for some gentleman to do something heroic to save her."

"Save her from what?"

"She has not the first idea," Balthazar said, with a laugh.

"These Benningtons are trouble," Henri said.

"Yes, you are probably right. Though, I will be interested in watching what sort of trouble this one stirs up."

"She is pretty?" Henri asked.

"Very."

"Even more trouble."

Henri was definitely right about that. As entertaining and alluring as Lady Rosalind was, he was not quite ready to be caught by any woman. It was not the right time. This was a season for taking apart a housebreaking ring, not pursuing a lady.

Nevertheless, he was certain he should be endlessly entertained to watch Lady Rosalind put other gentlemen through their paces.

⋙✕⋘

FORTUNATELY FOR ROSALIND, her sisters and Miss Mayton were well-versed in her expressions and signals. Her sisters had all been abed when Rosalind had got home and so had been eager to hear of Almack's over the breakfast table.

Rosalind had described it in the vaguest terms possible and claimed her beloved gentleman had not made an appearance. Finally, her father had retreated to his library and Darden had gone off to his club.

Now, they told Tattleton that he and the footmen need not stay—they were quite content on their own and would linger over cups of tea.

The door closed behind their butler and Cordelia said, "We must know, Rosalind. What has happened that you have not said."

"We can tell you have held something back," Juliet said.

"We know your looks," Viola added.

Glancing toward the door to be certain it was closed, Rosalind said, "Ever so much has happened."

"Goodness, I did have a terrible time at pretending it had not," Miss Mayton said. "I just kept eating toast so I would not have to speak."

"My gentleman *was* there, and my gentleman is…Conbatten."

"The duke?" Viola asked.

"The very one," Rosalind said.

"I was as shocked as anybody that it should be Conbatten," Miss Mayton said.

"And did you feel just the same when you viewed him again?"

Cordelia asked. "Are you still in love with him?"

"Oh yes," Rosalind said, nodding. "He is divine. And what a conversation we had! He pressed me on my requirements."

"Because he wished to know how he could fulfill them," Juliet said.

"Just so."

"Now he knows that he is to act courageous on your behalf," Viola said.

"Yes, he knows it very well," Rosalind said. "He did bring up one thing, though. He said it was not at all usual for a lady to need rescuing. He wondered how it would happen."

"Oh, dear, I hadn't thought…" Miss Mayton said softly, buttering her sixth piece of toast.

"But I said that the fates were sure to arrange something," Rosalind said.

"Do you think they will?" Juliet asked. "What I say is, there have been no end of times I've wished for something to happen and then it doesn't. For instance, just yesterday I was hoping that somehow a publisher of books would have heard of my poems and come to the door insisting that I share them with the world. So far, nothing."

"Maybe the fates only choose to intervene at the right time?" Cordelia said hopefully.

"Maybe the fates are like God, himself. After all, they must work for him," Viola said. "And does not the vicar always say that the Lord helps those that help themselves?"

"Goodness, that vicar does not care for your idea of the fates," Miss Mayton said. "It is well you only mentioned it the one time."

Rosalind nodded. She'd been strongly lectured when she'd broached the idea to Mr. Clayborne. He'd warned her that she was not to go believing old Greek myths ahead of her bible. But then, Mr. Clayborne also thought Fordyce's sermons were the height of good sense, so what did he know?

"Viola, what you say is that the fates will assist me when I assist myself?" Rosalind asked. It was an intriguing idea, though she was not certain how to put such a thing into action.

"It could not hurt, I do not think," Miss Mayton said.

That was very true. She just must think of a way to help herself.

Rosalind suddenly set her teacup down with a clatter. "Goodness, I have not told you of everything that occurred last evening! Viola, I have met *your* gentleman."

Viola sat back. "Mine? How? Who is he? How did you know?"

"He is the Earl of Baderston, he is a genial fellow *and* he has lovely copper-colored hair and is determined to like ham as much as you do. He is exceedingly genial and seemed very struck by my description of you."

"That does sound promising," Viola said.

"I told him we planned to often go out in the carriage to the park and he is to know that you are the lightest-haired among us so he would know who you are."

"Goodness!" Viola said. "That means I might well get a look at him."

"Oh, I think you will. He said he often goes to the park too."

"We ought to go this afternoon," Miss Mayton said. "Who knows who we will encounter or what might happen. We might see the duke or Lord Baderston or both."

"And an opportunity to help myself help Conbatten do something courageous might present itself," Rosalind said. "We must be on alert at all times and not allow an opportunity to pass us by."

Rosalind sighed happily. Being a lady out in society was so thrilling. Her future was at hand, and it was a happy future indeed.

Her dear, darling Conbatten.

I await your bravery, Duke.

SHRIMPS HAD REALLY rather have stayed behind in the countryside. Faversham Hall was so peaceful! He and Oyster were so calm there—he had got well-used to what Cook expected from him and Oyster liked to go out in the garden and chase rabbits.

The only upset that had happened all summer was the morning Oyster had actually caught a rabbit. The dog had panicked, Shrimps had panicked, and the rabbit had panicked and then lain still.

Cook had come out to investigate the ruckus, declared the rabbit only in shock, and then said he would dispatch him and broil him up.

At that idea, Shrimps had really panicked, which had made Oyster really panic. The end result was they had nursed the rabbit back to health, with Shrimps feeding it bits of lettuce and carrots from the kitchen and Oyster licking its face as encouragement.

The rabbit had since been set free to live its life and hopefully forget all about that terrible morning in the garden.

Though Shrimps would very much like to stay behind, it could not be so. Most of Lord Van Doren's household was moving to Portland Place for the season and Cook said he could not do without him.

He understood why. Nobody could peel a potato faster, nobody could chop as many onions without crying. As for his kneading of dough, well, there could not be a person in the whole of England who put so much muscle into it, even though he didn't have much muscle to work with.

He liked making Cook happy. But he did not like London. He did not like the people he used to know there. He did not like that he might run into one of them. Or that they'd come looking for him.

The workhouse had been bad enough, but then his mother died and it got even more difficult. With no parent to shield him, he'd been knocked around a lot. He'd escaped, only to fall into even worse circumstances. Before he knew it, he was expected to go about stealing out of gentlemen's pockets. He'd been terrible at it and been warned by the boy who ran the room he slept in that he'd better figure it out or he would be thrown out to starve.

Then, very unexpectedly, he'd been rescued by Lord Van Doren.

Shrimps was well aware that some of those boys knew he'd been taken into Lord Van Doren's house. He'd seen them follow the lord to Portland Place that first night. When the butler had tried to take him to the stables to sleep, he'd had a panicked fit. It would be too easy for them to get him out of there and make him come back to the room in the Rats' Castle.

Oyster had panicked that night too. Dogs had a sense for when danger was around and the dog had spent a good few weeks barking at windows. They'd been out there, lurking around, he was sure. Barney especially. He was the lead boy and a terrifying person.

Barney would not like for anybody to get away. He'd worry that a person might tell tales, though Shrimps had told none. The man who ran the whole operation, the man in charge of Barney, spent money on food and clothes and did not like to find he'd poured money down a drain.

But then, maybe they all would have forgotten about him by now. Maybe they had their hands full with other things. He could just stay quiet and not go out unless he was forced to run an errand.

Portland Place had a small back garden for Oyster and that seemed secure enough. He patted the inside of his coat. A paper was sewn in there that his mother said nobody in the workhouse must ever see. He did not know what it was, himself, nor could he read it even if he dared to look at it, but he liked to think it was a lovely message from her. It was like he carried her in his pocket everywhere he went.

When he got nervous, he patted his pocket and it calmed

him.

Whatever was to happen, he and Oyster were going to London. He just must be careful. This life was too good to let slip away. He would not go back to that dark and cold room near the Seven Dials.

He looked at Oyster, sitting at his feet in the carriage. The dog looked back at him and his underbite chattered. He did not want to go either.

CHAPTER FIVE

WITH THE EARL'S permission, the barouche had been ordered to take them all to the park. Though its seating was meant for just four people, Rosalind and her sisters had no trouble squeezing in. They had even squeezed in six when Beatrice had been with them. Though, that had been a *real* squeeze, as Miss Mayton was very comfortably padded.

Now, Rosalind, Viola, and Cordelia were in the forward-facing seat and Miss Mayton and Juliet opposite them. They had entered the park proper and their coachman, Sandren, steered them expertly along the carriage road.

They all kept their eyes sharp for Conbatten or the Earl of Baderston, Miss Mayton and Juliet having to lean forward to see around the hood.

"We should not have any trouble spotting either of the gentlemen," Rosalind said. "Conbatten is wonderfully tall and Lord Baderston has copper hair."

"I imagine Lord Baderston's hair glints in the sunlight," Viola said.

"I expect so," Rosalind said. "It was wonderfully shiny under candlelight."

"Rosalind," Juliet said, "what do you call Conbatten? Do you call him Conbatten, or Duke, or Your Grace?"

Rosalind bit her lip. "I have only called him Your Grace so far, but I think of him as Conbatten. I suppose I ought to begin calling him Duke to be going in the right direction."

"Very sensible," Miss Mayton said, nodding.

"Do you suppose," Cordelia said, "that if we saw him today, there would be anything you could do to help him along to rescuing you from something?"

Rosalind considered it, then leaned forward and said to the coachman, "Sandren, would it be possible to make the horses bolt so a gentleman could catch them and save us all?"

Sandren, a portly and taciturn fellow of middle-age, turned on his box. "Absolutely not, Lady Rosalind."

Rosalind sat back. She'd been afraid he would not be game to try it. Sandren was very careful of them all and had even once put his foot down on taking them to Taunton when the skies began to darken. He'd said, "The earl believes I am not an idiot and I have no intention of proving him wrong."

Of course, Sandren had been right. It had stormed terribly and the mud on the roads had made them impassable for a full two days.

Miss Mayton suddenly grabbed Rosalind's hand. "It is Lord Baderston. He comes from behind."

Miss Mayton waved to him. Viola was facing the wrong way, but her eyes were wide.

She and Viola listened to the hoofbeats approach while Juliet whispered, "Look at that. Hair the color of new pennies."

"Miss Mayton," Lord Baderston said, reining his horse in. "Lady Rosalind."

Rosalind smiled and said, "Lord Baderston." She liked the look of him just now. His complexion was going rather in the direction of his hair, which she took to be a very good sign.

"These are my sisters, Lord Baderston. *Viola*, Cordelia, and Juliet."

She made it a point to allow her eyes to make clear who was who.

"Lady Viola. Lady Cordelia. Lady Juliet," he said. He then cleared his throat very loudly. "Lady Viola, I understand from

Lady Rosalind that you are fond of ham."

"Prodigiously fond, Lord Baderston," Viola said prettily.

"I am devilishly fond of it myself," the lord declared.

Now that was really a very good sign. He'd not been *devilishly* fond of it at Almack's.

"Well, I suppose I must be off," Lord Baderston said. Rather than turn his horse to be off as he had just promised, he paused as if he had just recalled something. "I say, Lady Viola, I understand you will be out next season."

"That is true, my lord," Viola said.

"Excellent. Very good. Well. Yes. Of course. Indeed."

With that rather wonderful string of words, Lord Baderston tipped his hat and was finally off.

"I like the look of him," Viola said as he trotted away.

Rosalind nodded knowingly. "And he is now *devilishly* fond of ham."

"Just think, Viola," Juliet said, "next season you shall go to Almack's and the earl will be there, already waiting for you."

"I suppose he will pine away until he can properly be introduced to you and request to be on your card or sit next to you at a dinner," Cordelia said.

"I would not wonder if we do not find him standing near the doors of Almack's next year, to be sure of the opportunity to take your supper," Miss Mayton said.

"It is all so glorious to think about," Viola said. "But you do not suppose that he might encounter some other lady before then? Some other lady who prefers his hair color and is partial to ham?"

"I cannot imagine that would happen, my dear," Miss Mayton said. "It would be too cruel."

Viola sighed. "Then, I must trust the fates, just as Rosalind does."

"Very sensible," Miss Mayton said. "Now, where is that duke, I wonder?"

Rosalind had been looking everywhere but Conbatten was

nowhere to be found. Where was he, indeed?

"Perhaps we will see him tonight at Lady Hightower's musical evening?" Miss Mayton said.

"Oh yes, that would be marvelous," Rosalind said. She paused, then said softly, "Though I am hard-pressed to think of what sort of danger I might encounter at a pianoforte."

"Do not lose hope, Rosalind," Miss Mayton said. "After all, anything could happen. What if Lady Hightower's guests are attacked and robbed by a horde of masked intruders? Certainly, Conbatten must do something then."

"Now that would be something," Rosalind said. "It is the sort of thing that would be a perfect opportunity to show his bravery. He'd have to fight them off to keep me safe. I might even faint in his arms."

"You have never fainted in your life," Juliet pointed out.

"But I might pretend to faint, as it seems a very direct way into a gentleman's arms."

"Very good thought, Rosalind," Miss Mayton said, nodding approvingly.

"Is it usual, Aunt," Cordelia said, "that hordes of masked men attack and rob a musical evening?"

"Not that I know of, but so few things that are really interesting *are* usual. And then, Conbatten himself is not particularly usual."

Miss Mayton told no tales. Conbatten was anything but usual and so was it not likely that unusual things might happen in his vicinity? Rosalind reminded herself that she could not predict the future and Miss Mayton was right—absolutely anything might happen. She must just be ready.

After all, if they *were* attacked and robbed at Lady Hightower's house, that would really be something, would it not?

BALTHAZAR HAD ACCEPTED Lady Hightower's invitation to a musical evening, just as he did every season. It was a tedious event meant to allow various young ladies to showcase all their years of slaving over a pianoforte or a harp.

Very occasionally, there was a lady who seemed to have a real ear for music and would bring a piece to life. Mostly, it was a plodding along and he could practically hear the lady's music master in the background crying, "Remember, back straight and shoulders relaxed!"

As tedious as it might be, he would go as there were two salient facts to consider.

One, Lady Hightower had been a friend to his father and had always doted on him. He had long called her Aunt, though she was no relation. She had been a firm friend when he'd stumbled through his inevitably callow youth and she'd kept up a regular correspondence with him. She, of all people, had been depended upon for sage advice. The lady was a marvelous and seasoned matron and these days liked to refer to herself as the oldest bat in the rafters. He would never let her down.

Two, it was the stupidest thing in the world for a duke to complain about such entertainments. Compared to nearly everybody else in the world, his chores must be seen as exceedingly light duty. An unhappy man was the man who forgot his luck, and he would never forget it. By accident of birth, he had landed on the softest of pillows.

That idea had been given him by Lady Hightower in the most pointed way possible. During his fourteenth summer, he'd stayed at her estate. She'd put him into the stables for those months to get a taste for how others lived. Lady Hightower explained that nobody could appreciate their luck unless they had felt how it might be otherwise.

These days, whenever he felt himself becoming bored, he directed his thoughts back to those long days and nights in the stable. Sleeping on a badly stuffed hay mattress in the heat of summer, physical work all day, being bossed about by the stablemaster, and feeling as if he never had quite enough to eat.

He suspected the stablemaster had been directed to make things particularly hard on him and, though he had not been glad of it then, he was glad of it now. It had greatly affected how he ran his own stables. At his estate, he had separate cottages built for the stable master and the senior hands. He over-hired by most men's measure, so the work was not so onerous, and he made sure the food was plentiful and days off were liberal.

Now, as Bellforce led him into the lady's house, he put a smile on his face and prepared to be charmed.

"Conbatten!" Lady Hightower said, striding to his side. "Goodness, you are looking very well these days."

Balthazar kissed her hand and said, "Aunt Agnes, you look just as you did when last we met. Time has taken kindly to you and paused its march forward."

Lady Hightower snorted and said, "Well now, the ladies must be very gratified by your elegant phrasings. Please do inform *time*, if you would be so good, to pause the arthritis in my bones if it is really that kindly disposed toward me."

"I will put in a word," Balthazar said smiling.

Lady Hightower took his arm and led him toward the music room. "My boy, you are very good to come to my little evening year after year when some other young buck might have taken himself off to a gambling den."

"I would never disappoint you, Aunt Agnes. You know that."

"I do know it," the lady said, "and you well know I feel that those of us matrons who are as old as Methuselah must provide little opportunities for the youngest ladies among us to shine. Or at least, make a valiant attempt to shine."

He nodded, well-used to his aunt's views on the subject.

"But you are not to think I have forgotten about your comfort. I have arranged something that will ease the duty. You will find a glorious Tokay on the sideboard this evening. Bellforce says it is a Szamorodni style called a Száraz—it is dry and nutty and very difficult to get as there is so little of it to be had."

Balthazar was rather cheered by that news. He liked a dry Tokay and did not know why so many of Hungary's winemakers were determined to make their wine sickly sweet. "How on earth did Bellforce get hold of it?" he asked.

"Goodness, I have not the faintest. You know my butler—all mysterious dealings and then he just hands me the bill."

They had entered the music room and looked about at the gathering guests.

Well, well. The evening got more interesting by the moment. A dry Tokay on hand and Lady Rosalind just across the room. Though her back was turned as she talked to Lady Mary and the ever-in-black Miss Mayton, he could not fail to recognize that marvelous hair, her slim and rather regal bearing, and the way she had of tilting her head when she listened to someone speak.

He supposed Lady Rosalind would be as graceful on her chosen musical instrument as she had been on the ballroom floor. That was not what was so alluring about her, though. He looked forward to what she might say. So far, all he knew was that she was prone to say what he had not imagined she would say.

Perhaps he might hear of another ode to a farmer's field, or another dreadful novel about a duke and his demurring governess, or even another dog stolen from the roadside.

Miss Mayton spotted him and wildly waved. In fact, she waved so wildly that she caught the attention of not only Lady Rosalind and Lady Mary, but a number of people nearby them.

Now he had a dozen people looking his way to see who Miss Mayton flagged down in such a fashion. She was a strange creature.

Lady Rosalind turned, looked over her delicate shoulder, and smiled at him. He would make his way there.

ROSALIND HAD NOT positively known that Conbatten would

attend the musical evening at Lady Hightower's house. At least, she had not known it in any factual way.

She had been sure the fates would not let her down and now she was buoyed by the idea that she must just trust in them and they would provide.

He was looking so marvelous in his well-cut coat that she had the urge to knock everybody out of the way who stood between them and throw herself into his arms.

Fortunately, there was no need to cause a scene, as he made his way directly to her. There would be time to throw herself into his arms after he'd done his courageous task. Whatever that turned out to be.

"Miss Mayton, Lady Rosalind, Lady Mary," he said.

"Your Grace," Lady Mary said.

"Duke," Rosalind said boldly. She had been determined to try it, to tiptoe her way from Your Grace to Duke to the day when she would call him Conbatten.

He raised a brow but did not comment upon it, which she must take as approval of the idea.

Lady Mary had raised a brow too, though her raised brow did not seem as approving.

Miss Mayton said, "Your Grace, you will be pleased to know that you are not nearly as frequent a topic of conversation that you were last year. In the servants' quarters, you understand. The maids were wild over you, if you will recall."

Conbatten regarded the lady. Of course Rosalind could see that he did recall that Miss Mayton had informed him that the lady's maids were admiring of his person.

"I suppose I ought to be downcast to hear it," he said, "though I find myself rather sanguine to discover that I have made a departure from their thoughts."

"It is Bess, you see," Miss Mayton said. "They are quite taken with her and all thought of you has flown from their heads."

"The dog I told you about, Duke," Lady Rosalind said. "The one we rescued during our travels. She is lovely."

"I am replaced by a stray cur found by the roadside," the duke said. "That is somehow fitting."

Lady Mary sported a rather wrinkled brow over the exchange.

Rosalind instantly perceived that the lady could not follow their conversation, as it referenced a prior conversation between herself and the duke.

"You see, Lady Mary," she said to clarify, "as we traveled from Somerset we encountered a lovely little dog in terrible straits and took her into our carriage straightaway."

"I see," Lady Mary said, not looking nearly as interested in hearing more about Bess as anybody might expect.

"That reminds me, Rosalind," Miss Mayton said, "of who else we encountered on our travels."

"Oh yes, we met a very pleasant French lady," Rosalind said. "Madame Tussaud. She makes wax figures."

"We are going to the Lyceum on Tuesday to see her exhibit," Miss Mayton said. "She will be delighted to see us, I expect. After all, a fellow Parisian was once desperately in love with me."

"Poor Phillipe," Rosalind said, shaking her head. "He thought his love was unrequited and hung himself in his garret. He did leave a lovely note, though."

"As only the French can," Miss Mayton said.

Lady Mary's brows had come together and met each other atop her nose. "In any case," she said, "Lady Hightower is always so kind to host a musical evening. There is nothing I like so well as playing the pianoforte."

"Are you rather good, then?" Rosalind asked.

"Well, I…" Lady Mary stuttered.

"Oh, I see," Rosalind said. "You do not like to ring your own bell. You must be very good indeed!"

"Do you suppose everybody who will play this evening is rather good?" Miss Mayton asked.

"Well, I am sure they must be," Lady Mary said.

"And you, Lady Rosalind?" Conbatten asked. "Do you dare to

ring your own bell?"

She smiled. Of course he would wish to know what he might expect when they spent a cozy night in. Did he picture her in his drawing room, elegantly playing for him?

"I only lay claim to originality," she said. "I think I might, as I have been told it often enough."

"You see, Your Grace," her aunt said, "Rosalind does not become tied down to notes on a sheet. Her feelings guide her music."

The duke seemed surprised to hear it. She supposed he would be—so many people took the notes on the sheet as a veritable bible, never to be trifled with. But then, the Bennington line had been gifted with a boldness of spirit that would not be so hemmed in. And also, she had never learned to read sheet music, on account of her various run-ins with their dour music master.

"That is quite the original approach," Lady Mary said.

Rosalind nodded. "You are to know, Lady Mary, that my family are all artistic souls at heart. Cordelia does a terrific Desdemona to entertain us, Viola just took up painting two days ago and is turning out to be rather talented, and then my youngest sister Juliet is a first-rate poetess."

"*Ode to Hay,*" Miss Mayton said softly. "I am still moved by it."

"Lady Rosalind did mention that particular ode at Almack's," the duke said, a smile playing at the edge of his lips. "Though she could not recall the precise phrasings."

"But *you* do, Aunt," Rosalind said, pleased with the duke's determined remembrance of something she had spoken of.

"Ah yes," Miss Mayton said. She cleared her throat and recited:

Reaching for the sun and sprung from the ground
As we trot on by, we see it all around
A farmer joyfully feeds his horses and cows
While the ground that sprung the hay graciously bows.

In the silence that followed, Lady Mary said, "Well that is…that is rather…something."

"Do not think badly of yourself for feeling overcome, Lady Mary," Miss Mayton said. "It is often the case when one first hears Lady Juliet's poignant stylings."

"Lady Mary does seem a bit overcome," the duke said. "As that ode is indeed *something*."

Rosalind nodded approvingly at the duke. "Now," she said, "I was going to tell Lady Hightower that I could not play because of a sore finger. But what do you think, Miss Mayton?"

"It sounds to me as if everybody will be a rather good player, and so perhaps you need not worry that you will outshine them."

"Just as I thought," Rosalind said, pleased as anything that she would have her chance to play.

"I believe I will get a glass of wine from the sideboard," Lady Mary said. She made a stumbling curtsy and hurried toward that stated destination.

"The wine will calm her nerves, which seem all a-jangle," Miss Mayton said. "I suppose she is one of those who are deeply affected by poetry."

"Certainly, something has affected her," Conbatten said drily. "Now, may I retrieve a glass of wine for both of you? Lady Hightower has told me she has got a very good Tokay."

"None for me, Duke," Rosalind said. "I would keep my mind sharp to better commune with the music. By the by, do you suppose it is likely that these sorts of affairs are ever attacked by bands of masked thieves?"

The duke looked perplexed over the question. "Do you fear such a thing, Lady Rosalind?"

"Not fear, exactly. I was just wondering about it."

"It is highly doubtful, as I have never heard of such a thing. It being so improbable, I have very sensibly left my pistols at the door. Miss Mayton, may I get you a glass of wine?"

"Oh yes, and then since you will be there, perhaps a little plate of whatever is sweet."

The duke bowed and made his way to the sideboard.

"He is so wonderful," Rosalind whispered to her aunt.

"I find I must agree," Miss Mayton said. "He hangs on your every word."

"But he says it is not at all likely that we will be attacked this evening," Rosalind said. "I do wish an opportunity for him to rescue me would arrive in all haste. How else am I to throw myself into his arms and declare that his love is requited?"

"Do not lose hope, my dear. For all we know, a fire might be starting in the kitchens as we speak and he would have to carry you through flames and smoke as you laid lifeless in his arms. Absolutely anything could happen."

Rosalind reached out and grasped her aunt's hand and gave it a good squeeze. "You always do know how to buoy my spirits, Aunt."

CHAPTER SIX

BALTHAZAR HAD A terrible time not heaving with laughter as he made his way to the sideboard. *Ode to Hay* was a delightful insult to poets everywhere. He did not often sympathize with Lady Mary, but he could not help feeling sorry that she had been assaulted by such drivel. The poor lady had practically staggered to the sideboard so that she might drink wine to revive herself from the experience.

He could only wonder what another sister's Desdemona consisted of—he imagined some drooping over a sofa and lamenting before a slow closing of eyes and dying dramatically. And there was the other one who had taken up painting a few days ago and was fast becoming a master.

Balthazar dared not even think of some poor Frenchman hanging himself for love of Miss Mayton. It was too absurd and he would not be able to control his laughter at all if he pondered it.

Then, the idea that Lady Hightower's house might be attacked by masked thieves. Lady Rosalind had sounded almost hopeful that such a thing was in the offing. He supposed she would wish to use such a circumstance to measure the bravery of the gentlemen in the room, as she had made it clear that particular quality was of vast consequence.

Miss Mayton obviously encouraged these various idiosyncrasies. Lord Westmont seemed such a sensible fellow, how had he turned over the raising of his daughters to that erratic woman? He would not personally have hired Miss Mayton to feed his chickens, much less guide any children he produced.

Perhaps Lord Westmont did not understand the extent of Miss Mayton's flightiness. Balthazar imagined a father would not be too terribly involved in the day-to-day education of his daughters. He likely only got reports and if those reports were delivered by Miss Mayton…well, he could see how it might happen that a father went along comfortably in the dark.

Lady Rosalind was at her best tonight, though. The daring little minx had taken to calling him Duke, just as her sister had done. He greatly looked forward to her playing, particularly since she had thought she might claim a strained finger to avoid outshining the other ladies and had pronounced herself gifted with originality.

Perhaps he might visit this Madame Tussaud's exhibit on Tuesday himself.

No, he really should not. It was one thing to encounter Lady Rosalind by happenstance and another to seek her out. He should not cross over that line.

Lady Hightower dinged a glass and said loudly, "If everyone would take a seat, we are ready to begin. The young ladies who will play for us will all be seated in the front row. The rest of you arrange yourselves as you will."

Balthazar took a plate with a slice of iced lemon cake and a glass of wine and scanned the room for Miss Mayton. The chairs were set up in rows and he would have wished to take for himself a seat in the last to be near the sideboard. It was well on nights such as this to be comfortably nearby sustenance that could revive flagging attention. However, it seemed others had the same idea and that row quickly filled.

Finding Miss Mayton seated in an aisle seat in one of the middle rows, he walked her plate and glass to her. She took it from him as Lord Huston came into the row from the other side, making his way to the seat next to her.

"Oh dear no, my lord," she said to him. "I am holding that empty seat open for his grace. You see, he's got my refreshment for me and now must just retrieve his own."

Lord Huston nodded though he looked surprised and moved down a seat.

Huston could not be more surprised than Balthazar was himself. What was she doing, presuming to hold a seat for him like they were old friends?

"Your Grace," she said, "you really ought to hurry. They will soon begin."

Balthazar silently groaned and he made his way back to the sideboard. He would take the bottle from the footman and pour for himself. There would be no half measures, he would pour a *very* full glass of wine.

"Do be seated, everyone," Lady Hightower said to her guests. "I know it is always a trial to find just the right spot, but keep in mind it is only for an evening, not all eternity."

The shuffling and *pardon mes* began to quiet. Balthazar had no choice but to return to Miss Mayton, as very predictably the only other open seats were in the middle of the rows and he'd have to climb over people to get to one of them.

"Excellent, yes, here we are," Lady Hightower said as he sat down. "It is my view that a lady who plays an instrument is able to offer much entertainment to her family. Just imagine that you are at home and the weather rages out of doors. There is nowhere to go but your own hearth. Is there to be no music there?"

There were various murmurings about the sadness of finding no music there.

"So you see the advantage of it. Fortunately for all of us, every father worth his salt ensures that his daughters will bring music into any house they enter. This evening, we have several of those young ladies who have kindly consented to play for us."

Lady Hightower made some version of the speech every year, no doubt as a hint to young men everywhere that they should pay attention to a lady's musical ability.

Balthazar tasted his wine. It was high in minerality from volcanic soil and carried notes of apple and pear. It had a crisp finish that did not linger. It was very good indeed and he wondered if there were a way to make Bellforce reveal where he'd got it.

"First," Lady Hightower said, "we will have Lady Marie on the harp."

Lady Marie did as so many young ladies were prone to do at such a moment. She rose and looked about as if she had not known she would be asked to play and might demur the request out of modesty. Then a blooming blush, deep breath, and a determined striding to her instrument and she was off to the races.

Balthazar dearly wished he was off to actual races, preferably in Newmarket. As Lady Marie's harp twanged on, Miss Mayton was managing to get more crumbs from her lemon cake on him than on herself. He did not even know how she was doing it.

"So sorry, Your Grace," she said, making an attempt to dust off his trousers, which he only narrowly avoided by moving his leg out of the way. "This cake is rather crumbly."

Balthazar said nothing, though he was thinking it was Miss Mayton's *mind* that was rather crumbly.

Lady Marie concluded her piece, and then very predictably looked about her as if she had not known she were being listened to. Polite clapping all round and on to the next.

So the evening wore on. Some of the ladies were mediocre at best, some more skilled. Lady Jemima had obviously spent all her waking hours at the pianoforte and blazed through a Haydn sonata in a seeming effort to frighten whoever would follow her.

The only things that kept Balthazar from dozing off were the very good wine, the anticipation of Lady Rosalind's turn, and Miss Mayton spraying crumbs on him. Her cake had a thin glaze of icing that was leaving white spots on his clothes. Henri would be apoplectic over it.

"And now," Lady Hightower said, "we are charmed to have Lady Rosalind Bennington play on the pianoforte. Lady Rosalind, what sheet music can I set up for you?"

Lady Rosalind had hopped up from her chair. She said, "Oh, it does not matter, really. I only use the sheet music as a starting point."

Lady Hightower appeared surprised to hear it and backed away from the pianoforte. Balthazar was rather surprised himself. Originality was one thing, but what could she mean by sheet music only being a starting point?

Lady Rosalind sat herself down with alacrity, glanced at whatever sheet music was before her. She had not blushed, she had not hesitated, she had not appeared taken aback to be asked.

Of course she had not. There was nothing of artifice about Lady Rosalind.

The lady smiled and her hands struck down upon the keys.

What Balthazar listened to in the next minutes was of a type and style that he was certain had never before been heard in any drawing room in London. Or the world.

It occurred to him that it was usual to get a feel for where a piece of music was going and then one's ear naturally predicted what was to come next.

Rather than being able to predict anything, he found his free hand gripping the arm of his chair.

One minute, it was a soft Irish air, the next a lively reel, the next a funeral march. The tempo zigged and then zagged, there were several crescendos, it would go melancholic before suddenly speeding up, then make an about face to something reminding him of a baroque fugue. There were times when the lady paused dramatically with her hands raised, as if she considered her next move.

At those suspenseful moments, Balthazar noted the people in the rows ahead of him leaned forward. Then suddenly, Lady Rosalind would have picked her direction and her hands would come down upon the instrument with gusto and she would be off in another direction entirely.

Near the end, at least Balthazar had hope it was near the end, Lady Rosalind's fingers began repeating the same notes, only faster and faster.

Miss Mayton leaned over and whispered, "Her signature arpeggio. She ends every performance with it."

And what a performance it was.

Lady Rosalind very suddenly stopped playing and rose. The conclusion was so abrupt that nobody saw it coming and it took most of her audience unawares. There was a silence before a gentle clapping ensued.

The lady graciously curtsied and retook her seat.

As for Lady Hightower, that lady appeared very much bowled over by the performance. "Goodness, yes, well, all right, now, well I suppose…oh yes, let us hear from Lady Mary Gremington on the pianoforte. Will you need music, my dear?"

Of course, Lady Mary did require music, and then very faithfully followed its written instructions.

Lady Rosalind was simply bizarre on the pianoforte and it was about the last thing anybody would wish to have as a regular feature of their drawing room. The notion that she'd worried about outshining the others made him want to roar with laughter. Though, she had certainly not exaggerated when she laid claim to originality.

Everything about her was original.

TATTLETON HAD GONE down to the servants' quarters as finally the ladies of the house had gone above stairs with a tea tray.

Lady Cordelia had enacted her Desdemona again and quite naturally there had been overturned candles, but then he supposed that was what sand buckets were for. The footmen had since cleaned up the sand and moved a chair over the new burn hole in the carpet.

Benny and Johnny had also mopped up the drips of paint on the floor, as Lady Viola had taken to dragging an easel everywhere in an effort to paint portraits. At least, Tattleton had been told they were portraits—the one she was working on at the moment looked to be something seen in a frightening fever dream. The sort of dream where a person was being chased by an otherworldly being sent from the devil.

Though the ladies had gone above stairs, they were determined to wait up for Lady Rosalind and there had been no turning them from the idea. At least the maids would have got them into their nightclothes so when they inevitably fell asleep and then awoke sometime in the middle of the night, they need not ring the bell.

He sat with the rest of the servants as they had their nightly ale. The windows were open because as usual that dog on the floor was contaminating the entire place with her eruptions.

Tattleton glared at the creature while he mulled over a matter weighing heavily upon him. He was very afraid the ladies of the house were plotting something. The first tip-off had been yesterday morning, when they'd sent him out of the breakfast room and made sure the door to it was shut.

Then, he noticed that they would suddenly stop speaking when he entered a room. He had heard the name Conbatten more than once. Why did they talk about that duke?

Their plots were always so ill-conceived and even worse executed. The last had been over the summer, when they'd sent anonymous unsigned notes to Lord Van Doren, claiming the entire neighborhood was fed up with his scolding.

It had taken the lord all of three seconds to deduce who'd sent them. As restitution, the earl had made them each write Lord Van Doren a letter listing his good qualities. The effort had nearly killed them all and Lady Juliet had been reduced to complimenting a blue coat the lord wore occasionally, noting it *was very blue.*

What were they up to now?

For that matter, what was that wretched dog up to? It had been constantly getting up and turning round for the past hour. It was becoming distracting.

Now it whimpered and turned itself once more.

Tattleton could not imagine what that canine had the nerve to complain about. As far as he could see it, the thing was eating them out of house and home. The creature's belly was getting bigger by the day.

"What is wrong with that dog?" he asked. "Charlie, does it need to go outside?"

"I don't think so, Mr. Tattleton," Charlie said, peering at the creature. "I just took our Bess out to the garden not a half hour ago."

Our Bess, indeed. Why cannot she be somebody else's Bess?

Something caught Tattleton's eye. He stood up and pointed at the dog. "Charlie, get that thing into the garden this instant. The crass cur is defecating right where it lays."

"Oh dear," Mrs. Huffson said, leaning down to look closer. "I was afraid of that."

"Afraid of what?" Tattleton said, feeling a chill run down his back.

"The poor lass is having pups," Mrs. Huffson said.

"What? No! You must be mistaken. Perhaps it is only dying."

"She's not dying," Mrs. Huffson said, letting him down entirely over his only hope.

"But, you knew of this, Mrs. Huffson?" Tattleton asked.

"Only suspected, Mr. Tattleton," Mrs. Huffson said. "She did seem to be growing in the midsection."

"But that was from all the food! Everybody is always feeding it. I have been fearing to see the incoming grocer's bills."

"I am afraid that is not it, Mr. Tattleton."

The lady seemed a deal more calm than she should be. Mrs. Huffson was certainly a deal more calm than he felt himself.

"No!" he cried. "No, it cannot do *that* in here! I forbid it!"

"Charlie, get some towels, string, and scissors, there's a good lad," Mrs. Huffson said.

Charlie raced off as the maids and the footmen all surrounded the wretched dog.

"There now, mon ami," Fleur said in her French accent, "tout ira bien."

"She don't speak French," Benny said. "She's an English dog."

"You don't know what she speaks," Fleur said haughtily.

"She don't speak anything," Johnny said, "just pat her head, she'll get the idea."

Charlie came hurrying back with the supplies he'd been sent for. "Don't you worry, Mrs. Huffson, I helped the cats' mum birth all her babies. I'll help our Bess through her time just fine."

"Excellent," Mrs. Huffson said. "Everyone, give Charlie and Bess some room."

Tattleton slumped in his seat. He did not know how to stop this calamity from happening. It was like an unhitched carriage rolling down a hill.

The first pup came fully into the world and Charlie deftly cleared the creature's nose and mouth and tied and cut the cord. The wretched Bess peered with interest at the squirming mass that had just shot out of her and then licked the awful little creature's face.

Tattleton looked on in horror. The thing resembled a small rat. How many more of them did she have lurking in there? It was to be the cats all over again. No, it could be even worse than the cats, there could be more than four of them!

Lynette rose and hurried toward the door.

"Where are you going?" Tattleton asked her.

"To tell the ladies!" she said, racing up the servants' stairs.

"No, do not, oh never mind," Tattleton said softly. As nuisance number two entered the world, Tattleton was beginning to believe that no stops should ever be made on the road to London. A stop was an opportunity for something to get into the ladies' carriage. If they'd never stopped in the first place, they would not have four cats already and now who even knew how many dogs they would be plagued with.

That road was cursed.

"All right now, there's a girl," Charlie said. "Here comes pup number three!"

Oh, hooray.

BALTHAZAR HAD COME through another of Lady Hightower's musical evenings relatively unscathed, though he could not say the same for his clothes.

He had stayed behind to have a drink with the lady, she insisting the bottles of Tokay that had been opened should not go to waste. He'd not been sorry to do it, as he did enjoy his private talks with Lady Hightower and the Tokay was indeed very good.

She'd dismissed Bellforce and poured him a glass in her cozy library.

"What on earth has happened to your clothes?" she asked. "You look as if you had a run in with a bag of flour."

"Miss Mayton somehow managed to get more icing on my person than into her mouth," he said drily.

"Odd woman. Well," she said, "duty done for this year. But my word, I never did hear the likes of Lady Rosalind's playing. It was very disconcerting. One minute I assured myself it was a gentle Irish air, then the next I thought no, it is a fugue, and then the next I thought, goodness I am sure that is a Scotch reel—my thoughts could not keep up with it all. Please do assure me that this is not some new style that has come on the scene."

Balthazar had laughed and said, "It is her own original style and unlikely to be taken up by the *ton*."

"That is a relief. The lady really should keep her playing under wraps—what gentleman would be willing to take her on after hearing it?"

He'd tented his fingers and said, "Well, I suppose one need not keep a pianoforte in the house. Or one could just hire someone to play."

Lady Hightower had leaned forward and peered at him. "It is intriguing that you have thought of two solutions to the problem. Do I detect some interest there?"

"I find Lady Rosalind exceedingly interesting, though not in the way you mean it."

"I do not see why not," Lady Hightower said. "Aside from her ghastly playing, which you have already arranged to solve, she seems a lovely girl."

"Ah yes, she is lovely. However, it is not the right time for me to marry. When I do decide to marry, I shall wish all of my attention to be put to it."

"Hmm," Lady Hightower said. "Of course, it is up to you when and how you take the fateful step. I will advise you on one thing, though. I know you always have ladies chasing you who have their eye on becoming a duchess. Very right of you to be cautious. However, be certain you do not outrun a lady you should slow down and stop for."

"Do you hint that Lady Rosalind might be a lady to slow down and stop for?"

"I haven't the faintest—only you know your own heart. However, I will say this—no lady who is coldly calculating over how to make herself a duchess would have ever allowed you to hear that racket she produced on the pianoforte."

Balthazar had laughed, because of course a title would be the last thing on Lady Rosalind's mind. She had too much of a romantic and fanciful outlook to consider such worldly aspirations.

Perhaps it was a shame he was not in a position to slow down and stop at this particular moment.

He had thanked Lady Hightower for her continuing interest in him. She had called that sentiment a lot of nonsense and asked what else one of the oldest bats in the rafters had to do. She'd made him bend down so she could kiss his forehead before he took his leave.

Now, he heard Henri's light and quick footsteps heading toward his bedchamber and braced himself.

"Your Grace," Henri said, after a quick knock. "I assume you had a fine—"

Henri stopped mid-sentence, the look of horror on his features telling the tale. His valet had perceived the lemon cake's handiwork.

"What has happened to you?" Henri cried.

"A certain Miss Mayton, her clumsy hands, crumbs, and icing," he answered.

Then came a string of French oaths that would not bear repeating but had much to do with various ways Miss Mayton must die.

Henri took Balthazar's coat and held it in front of him as if it were a wild animal. "We will see if this can be rescued, but I am not hopeful. It is the finest of Italian wool and the finest Italian fabrics do not care to be disrespected in such a manner! The people of Florence would be up in arms if they knew of this insult! Tell that Miss Mayton she is not to show her face in Florence, lest the people throw her into the Arno River!"

"Yes, yes," Balthazar said. He had no idea why Henri thought the people of Florence were always to be revolting in the streets and throwing people into the Arno over a stain on his clothes. As it was a thing his valet mentioned often, he supposed they were a rather tautly strung sort of people.

"Ça ne fait rien, I will carry on despite this setback," Henri said in a certain tone.

Balthazar recognized it as the tone that indicated his valet expected to be commended for his bravery and valor in dispatching his duties.

"I have every faith in your abilities," he said to smooth ruffled feathers.

"Je suis courageux," Henri said.

"Nobody braver," Balthazar said.

"And so, now that Henri has calmed himself," Henri said, "I imagine Lady Hightower's musical evening was as riveting as it is every year?"

"Just so. Though, there were a few surprises. Lady Hightower provided a magnificent Tokay, very dry. You ought to talk to Bellforce about where he got it."

"Bellforce," Henri said, looking down his rather long and straight nose, "all mystery and 'I cannot reveal this,' and 'I cannot tell you of that,' and 'that is only for me to know.'"

Balthazar rather thought that would be the case. Bellforce had never shown any appreciation for Henri's particular brand of highhandedness.

Henri threw his shoulders back. "*If* that Bellforce person has found a superior dry Tokay, I will find one better! I will find the driest. It will be so dry you will not perceive you've had anything to drink."

Balthazar nodded, though it did not sound very appealing. "Lady Rosalind entertained with her very unique stylings on the pianoforte."

"What does this mean? Was she very good or very bad?" Henri asked.

"The adorable creature was positively ghastly. I believe she cannot read sheet music and so just strings together a bunch of notes she remembers, then when she runs out of memory for that piece, she reaches for another string of notes that come to mind. There are long pauses when she stares down at the keys and one holds one's breath to hear what she will do next."

"This sounds very English," Henri said.

Balthazar was well aware that was no compliment. Henri thought the English were, in general, unsophisticated brutes. Balthazar himself was given an exception, but only because he'd had the good sense to employ a remarkable French valet.

"She concludes every performance with an arpeggio of her own design that ends very abruptly."

Henri shook his head sadly. "For all this, though, you like to talk to her."

"I admit that I do," Balthazar said. "I never know what she'll say next. I find listening to her very entertaining."

"Just do not kiss her, then! Do not make that mistake! You do not want such an offense to music in your house."

Balthazar did not answer. For one, he had no intention of kissing Lady Rosalind, as interesting as the prospect might be. For another, he was certain his valet took far too many liberties.

He would not scold him over it though. Just now, his valet was in too fragile a state of mind after viewing Miss Mayton's assault on his clothes and considering that Bellforce would never tell him where he got the dry Tokay.

CHAPTER SEVEN

WHEN ROSALIND AND Miss Mayton had come home, Rosalind did not hear a peep from her sisters. Presuming them all abed, she'd waited for Lynette to come to help her into her nightclothes.

Once Lynette *had* come, she'd heard the exciting news from below stairs. Bess had been pregnant, was now the proud mother of eight darling puppies, and her sisters had dragged pillows and blankets down to the servants' hall so they might spend this first critical night by Bess' side.

Rosalind and Miss Mayton had quickly changed into their own nightclothes, donned robes and slippers, and gone down to see for themselves.

Rosalind found the table and chairs in the servants' dining hall had been pushed to one side of the room. Her sisters were all splayed out on blankets with a sleeping Bess and her snoring pups in the middle.

She and Miss Mayton had squeezed in among them and they had been happily exchanging news ever since.

"So you did play the pianoforte, then?" Cordelia asked.

"Oh yes, Papa and Darden were worried over nothing," Rosalind said.

Her dear Papa. He always was so considerate of other people's feelings. Upon hearing that Miss Mayton had taken the liberty of accepting Lady Hightower's invitation, he had said perhaps they should not go. He'd said that her original way of playing might intimidate those that were less original.

But then Miss Mayton had pointed out that they'd already accepted the invitation and it was a musical evening, not a rout. Those bowing out of such a small gathering would cause some disturbance to the hostess.

They had finally settled on the idea that Rosalind would claim a sprained finger. In that way, they would fill two of Lady Hightower's chairs, but would not fell the other ladies with Rosalind's playing.

"You see," Miss Mayton said as Fleur put her hair up in curl papers, "we were able to ascertain from Lady Mary that all the ladies who would play would be quite good. There was no danger in Rosalind frightening anybody with her talent."

"I suppose Conbatten was bowled over by Rosalind's playing," Juliet said. "It's so original, anybody must be struck by it. You never know, from minute to minute, where it's going."

"He seemed exceedingly struck," Miss Mayton said.

Rosalind sighed. "But when will his moment come? That delicious moment when he can rescue me from something?"

"No masked thieves turned up, then?" Juliet asked.

Rosalind shook her head. "Aunt even speculated that there might be a house fire and he would have to carry my lifeless body to safety, but that didn't happen either."

"I am convinced the fates want you to get the ball rolling down the hill somehow," Viola said. "Recall, Rosalind, that when you spoke of my red-haired gentleman perhaps haunting the park to get a look at me, what did we do? We went to the park. We took action and then the fates helped us along."

"I believe you may be right," Rosalind said. "We could arrange something. For instance, what if I were to encounter Conbatten on the street and then as we were having one of our lovely conversations, I was to be accosted by a pickpocket?"

"You could pay a pickpocket!" Juliet said. "You could pay him a fee and then he could return whatever was taken later."

"We do not know any pickpockets though," Cordelia said.

That was very true. Despite their ever-growing list of acquaintances in London, not a one of them was a pickpocket.

Rosalind sighed. "I believe we are going in the right direction in all of this, we will just need to think over how it is best accomplished."

"Very sensible," Miss Mayton said.

One of the pups yawned and stretched and then curled up.

"They are so charming," Rosalind said, gazing down at the little darlings.

"And guess what, Rosalind," Juliet said, "our dear little Bess seems cured of her only problem. We have not needed to open the windows even once."

"We think the noxious fumes must have been caused by her pregnancy," Viola added.

"Tattleton will be very pleased to know it," Rosalind said. "He's mentioned the situation to Papa several times."

"You would think he'd be delighted that she managed eight little babies all on her own," Cordelia said, "but when he retired for the night, he looked rather distraught."

"Poor Tattleton," Juliet said softly. "He always does take things to heart. I suppose another burn hole in the rug and eight new dogs was too much for him."

They all nodded, commiserating with their butler's nerves.

Viola suddenly sprang up. "Goodness, there has been so much that has happened tonight, we forgot about the note!"

"Oh yes!" Cordelia said. "Beatrice has written. She and Van Doren will arrive in Town on the morrow."

"That is good news," Rosalind said. "Perhaps Beatrice will know where we can find a pickpocket for my duke to chase."

"Careful there, though," Viola said. "Beatrice tells Van Doren everything and you know what he'll think about it."

"Van Doren," Juliet said. "Scoldy-Breeches would have an apoplectic fit."

"It is precisely the sort of thing that would set him off and there we go with an hour-long lecture," Cordelia said.

"That's true, of course," Rosalind admitted.

"I wonder if our footmen are acquainted with any pickpockets?" Cordelia asked. "Whoever knows where they go and what they do on their days off?"

"I'm not sure we can ask the servants that sort of question," Rosalind said. "They might be insulted by it."

They were all silent for some moments, each considering if the footmen would be aggrieved if they were to be asked whether they knew any criminals.

Juliet's eyes suddenly went wide. "Shrimps!" she cried. "We can ask Shrimps because we already know he was with a gang of boys when Van Doren found him. He must know pickpockets and there is no reason why he would be insulted over it."

"Shrimps," Rosalind said softly. "Yes, that might just be the ticket."

"I know what to do," Cordelia said, "we will give Bess a day to settle in with her babies and then when she's ready to receive visitors, we will send a note to Shrimps that he may come and see them."

"Because he's so fond of dogs!" Viola said.

"He and his dog, Oyster, are inseparable," Juliet said.

"Of course they are," Rosalind said, "how often has Beatrice said so? If you are looking for Shrimps, find Oyster, and if you are looking for Oyster, find Shrimps."

"I knew we should think of something," Juliet said.

"You girls are all so clever," Miss Mayton said.

"Do you suppose we might arrange a pickpocket for Lady Crinkleton's picnic in the park for orphans?" Viola asked. "Papa says we are all to go as it is a family outing sort of thing and all that's required is forking over a good amount of money, which he is happy to do."

"But will Conbatten be there?" Cordelia asked. "We must be sure that whatever we arrange, it is in his view so he can leap into action."

"I am sure he must go," Rosalind said. "Darden's whole club is going and he says Lady Crinkleton is in the habit of talking about people who do not turn up. As well, the Prince of Wales is to be there and make a speech. Certainly, a duke of the realm must go."

"Goodness, the picnic is in a week's time," Viola said. "We must have everything in place by then."

Rosalind's heart picked up speed and thump-thumped in her chest. If all went well, in just a week's time she would find herself in Conbatten's arms.

⤙⤙⤙✦⤚⤚⤚

BALTHAZAR HAD TAKEN one of the private dining rooms at White's. He and Hamill found it a convenient place to meet to discuss the Queen's Knights' business. They were both members of the club and so anybody watching their individual comings and goings would not see anything unusual in it.

The waiter had brought in a coffee service and closed the door behind him.

"I presume you have news or we would not be meeting at this ungodly hour," Balthazar said.

"There is nothing ungodly about ten o'clock," Hamill said, "I have been up with the chickens, ridden my horse, and done a few rounds of boxing before I came here."

Balthazar stretched out his long legs. "I have very sensibly been in a bath."

"Have some coffee," Hamill said. "You'd be better served if Henri was bringing you coffee instead of champagne in that bath of yours."

Balthazar poured himself a cup of coffee, which now always reminded him of the shade of Lady Rosalind's hair. "Better served, but not quite as comfortable. Now, what have you heard?" he asked.

Something very strange," the marquess said. "Crosby has been having some long conversations with the boy I told you about. He's taken him to his estate and made certain he is secure, but he's also been plying him with plentiful food and hinting that the boy might be able to continue on there as a stable hand if he spills everything he knows."

"Slay him with kindness," Balthazar said. "It is a good strategy, especially for a boy like that, as he's likely known little of it."

Hamill nodded. "Crosby means to keep his promise as long as he's convinced the boy, Jimmy is his name, has really said all he knows. The information seems to be coming out in dribs and drabs."

"What is the latest?"

Hamill leaned forward and said quietly, "This Jimmy says that months ago he was sent to a tavern with a note. The note was not even sealed as nobody imagines he can read, but he was raised for a few years by a vicar and he can."

"He read the note."

Hamill nodded and said, "It was addressed to Mondrian."

"Mondrian?" Balthazar said. "You do not think it is Harold Mondrian?"

"I think it just might be. The boy was given a description of who he looked for—he was told to seek out black hair, black eyes, pale skin. He would ask for the password before handing over the note, which was M."

Balthazar sat back. Harold Mondrian was presumed dead. He'd presented himself as the heir to the Dedmont barony and its estates, claiming he was a cousin.

He'd been unmasked when the dowager grew suspicious and began testing him on the family tree.

It was then revealed that it had been Mondrian who had supplied the estate's lawyers with the forged passenger list for the *Louisa*—a ship that sank on its way to America. That was how everyone had been led to believe that the real heir, James Conroy, and the bride he'd run off to Gretna Green with, Lady Edna

Edenborough, had perished.

Now, nobody was certain what had happened to them. Though, it had been eight or nine years with no word and Balthazar presumed them to be dead. The two families would not believe it of course, and were ever hopeful that the couple would turn up some day.

The whole fiasco could have been avoided in the first place, had those two families had a lick of sense between them. They were longstanding neighbors and a feud had raged for fifty years over a property line. When the couple announced their wish to marry, both sides dug in their heels and refused to sanction it. Now both sides had been left bereft on account of their own stubbornness.

"So, you think perhaps Mondrian was never on that sailboat?" Balthazar asked.

When Mondrian had been unmasked, he'd fled the neighborhood. The next anybody knew of him was when his overturned sailboat had been found in the channel.

"The boy, Jimmy, said the note he delivered to this man was long and about combing through birth records. There were several parishes listed and a set of years to be examined."

"Aside from the physical description, that is why you think it might be Mondrian," Balthazar said. "He has a habit of impersonation and birth records come in handy. In the meantime, he runs his housebreaking operation to finance whatever new project he has in mind."

Hamill nodded. "It is possible. Though, without getting hold of the villain, I cannot see how we discover who his new victims are to be."

Balthazar tented his fingers. "Perhaps we take it step by step. We take down the housebreaking operation, then worry about what else he has going on."

ONE BY ONE, Rosalind and her sisters had fallen asleep on the floor, all of them curled around Bess and her lovely new family. They were roused very early in the morning by Meg, the kitchen maid, who'd hurried in to light the kitchen fires ahead of Mr. James. Charlie had come in not long after and they discovered that he regularly rose early to help Meg get the kitchen set up.

They'd all had a merry cup of tea together and Juliet and Cordelia attempted to help Meg in her duties until Charlie very kindly pointed out that they were mostly just creating more work. It seemed there was a system to the whole thing and pouring flour into a bowl would not magically make bread.

The sisters had finally given Bess a kiss on the head, admired her babies taking full advantage of the milk supply they'd found so nearby, and taken their blankets above stairs.

As they found themselves quite exhausted from little sleep on a hard floor, they all went to bed and did not rise until noon. Since then, they'd taken a walk up and down Portland Place and lounged round the drawing room. Juliet had composed an ode to Bess, and Viola had begun painting a portrait of that canine matriarch and her brood. All the while, they'd kept an eye out for Beatrice arriving.

So far, they had not seen her and now they'd gone up to change for dinner. Rosalind knew her papa had sent a note over the road to invite Beatrice and Van Doren to dine, but it was getting so late that nobody could say what would happen. She was beginning to think they must be delayed and would not arrive until the morrow.

Lynette arranged her hair into order and once more, Rosalind heard carriage wheels rumbling down Portland Place.

She'd already driven Lynette mad with leaping up a half dozen times before to see if it were Beatrice, but she could not help it.

Rosalind ran to the window.

Three carriages had stopped in front of Van Doren's house.

"Finally, Lynette!" she cried. "They have come."

She struggled with the window to get it open and stuck her head out just as Van Doren helped Beatrice from the carriage.

"Beatrice!" she shouted.

Her sister turned at the sound. "Oh hello, Rosalind! Goodness we are arriving so late—you know how these trips are. And there is Juliet at her window too. And Cordelia. Oh, and there is Viola. Hello!"

"Beatrice," Juliet called, "Papa has sent a note that you must dine with us. You will come?"

"Of course we will come," Beatrice said laughing.

Van Doren said something, but Rosalind could not hear what it was. From his expression, though, he did not look quite as enthusiastic over the prospect.

Typical Van Doren. No matter though, Beatrice was coming and she could leave Van Doren where he was if he did not like it.

"We will just change our clothes and then be over," Beatrice called, as Van Doren led her into the house.

Rosalind had hurried Lynette to finish her hair and then flew down to the drawing room, as did all her sisters.

In under an hour, dear Beatrice was among them once more and Papa and Darden had looked ever so pleased to see Van Doren. Though really, their recently acquired brother-in-law seemed a bit grumpy from his journey.

It turned out that a carriage wheel had cracked and needed replacing and then a horse had thrown a shoe and Van Doren was convinced that all these delays could not be comfortable for his wife. His wife, however, seemed none the worse for wear.

They had already told Beatrice about lovely little Bess and her pups, and Beatrice had already declared she must have a pup once they were old enough to leave their mother.

Van Doren, who always had the ability to surprise them these days, said that if Beatrice required a dog, then she must have one. Rosalind had been certain he'd be against it. Especially when Juliet described Bess' intestinal problems and hinted that those problems might run in her family.

They then told Beatrice of their charming encounter with Madame Tussaud.

"We entertained her until she was speechless," Juliet said.

"I bet she was," Van Doren said.

Ignoring Van Doren's swipe, Miss Mayton said, "She was very touched to hear of my poor Phillipe, as he was a fellow Parisian."

"Oh yes," Cordelia said. "She was particularly struck to discover he'd hung himself in his garret. She really had not anticipated the story would end so."

"Nobody ever does," Van Doren said.

"Pour l'amour d'Eloïse je ne peux plus continuer," Miss Mayton said softly.

"That was the note pinned to his coat," Juliet said, brow raised in Van Doren's direction. "For the love of Eloise, I can no longer go on."

"They all leave such poignant goodbyes, don't they?" Van Doren asked.

"Beatrice," Viola said, "has Van Doren recently threatened to do a violence to himself over his love for you?"

"Not recently," Beatrice said, a giggle escaping her.

"Do not rule it out," Van Doren said. "I'm beginning to feel a violence coming on."

"Will you be pinning a note to your coat, then?" Juliet asked.

"Indeed," Van Doren said, staring at Juliet. "It will read, *'Done in by lunacy—could no longer go on.'*"

"Well, Beatrice," Viola said, "not exactly a note you could hold to your heart and treasure forevermore."

"I think I'd prefer to keep Van Doren *alive* and hold him to my heart and treasure him forevermore," Beatrice said.

This sentiment was received very well by Van Doren, but prompted a very distinct eye roll from Juliet, as she knew it drove him mad.

"That's enough teasing of Van Doren, I think," the earl said.

"Very well, Papa," Juliet said. "To make you happy, I will

even extend an olive branch. When we go to the Lyceum to see Madame Tussaud's wax figures, he may come. We plan it for Tuesday."

"Very magnanimous," Van Doren said.

"She never did say what the wax figures were," Cordelia said, "but we think it's likely to be faeries and woodland sprites."

"Yes, I think it must be some sort of magical forest scene," Viola said, "what else could it be?"

"That would be ever so charming," Viola said.

And so it was determined that they would allow Van Doren to come along, though he did not seem to feel the honor of it. Or wish to go.

Now they had gone into dinner.

"Rosalind, you must tell me of where you have been so far," Beatrice said. "Have you gone to Almack's yet?"

"Indeed, it was most pleasant once I got over the hurdle of being introduced to Lady Jersey," Rosalind said.

"Conbatten approached Rosalind, to be put on her card," Darden said. "*Conbatten*, you understand."

"The duke took me into supper."

"She ordered him to," Darden said. "Father, you must tell Rosalind she is not to order a duke about. Not that duke, in particular."

The earl laughed and said, "I presume His Grace is well able to fend for himself."

"I thought he was very handsome, Beatrice," Rosalind said.

"I suppose what Rosalind means to say," Juliet said, "is that she cannot imagine why Beatrice did not pick him instead of...you know."

Amidst Beatrice's peals of laughter, Van Doren said, "I sometimes wonder at it myself."

"You certainly do not," Beatrice said, looking at him with rather lovestruck eyes.

"Perhaps not," Van Doren admitted.

Rosalind noted Juliet's crestfallen expression. So often these days, they would try to get a rise out of Van Doren and he would confound them by being pleasant.

"Why couldn't you be in love with Conbatten, instead of this mysterious gent you saw out of a carriage window?" Darden asked Rosalind. "After all, somebody has got to tie him down one of these days. It would be very pleasant to be related by marriage."

Rosalind ignored the sentiment. Poor dear Darden's vision was clouded to what was right before him. He was too taken up with his own feelings about Conbatten to ever register her own.

CHAPTER EIGHT

"Rosalind, what is this about a gentleman out of a carriage window?" Beatrice asked.

"Indeed," Rosalind said, "I saw a magnificent gentleman out of my carriage window and am looking forward to when he might present himself to me."

There was a long silence over the table, then Cordelia said, "Beatrice, Rosalind went to a musical evening last night."

Beatrice nodded and Rosalind knew she understood the game—the gentleman out the carriage window was a secret just now.

"She stunned everybody with her playing," Juliet said.

"Playing?" Darden's glass slipped out of his hand and hit the table, wine running in all directions over the cloth. As the footmen rushed to mop it up, her father's fork clattered onto his plate. The earl hurriedly picked it up again.

"Rosalind, my dear," the earl said, "I had thought you were to claim a sprained finger to Lady Hightower."

"We *had* all agreed on it," Miss Mayton said. "You see, Beatrice, the earl was worried that the other ladies should feel entirely outshone. But then Lady Mary was able to put aside that concern, as she told us everybody would be very good."

"So…you played?" Darden said.

Rosalind nodded. "I played one of my travels through the world of music and ended with my signature arpeggio."

"Travels through the world…is that the one that goes…from one thing to the next?" the earl asked.

"*That* one?" Darden asked.

"Indeed," Rosalind said. "Of course, I never do know where it will take me. It comes out different every time."

Darden had gone very pale. "Where did it take you in Lady Hightower's drawing room last evening?"

"Let's see," Rosalind said, "if I remember correctly, it was an Irish air, a fugue, a Scotch reel, oh, I do not remember what else."

"The funeral march, my dear," Miss Mayton said.

"That's right, the funeral march," Rosalind said.

She could not imagine why her brother and her father were staring at each other in such a fashion. They really need not have worried that she would outshine the other ladies as Lady Mary had been correct—they *had* all turned out to be quite good.

As for Van Doren, he just snorted. He'd always been so disdainful of her playing and said if she could not read notes or remember an entire piece, she should not play at all.

"Did anybody…" Darden began. "What I mean is…were there any comments?"

"I sat right next to the duke," Miss Mayton said. "He talked very low, as if he were talking to himself and did not even realize he was doing it. He said: *Well, well, that was something else entirely.*"

"The duke appreciates originality," Rosalind said.

"Yes, I believe you are right about that," Beatrice said.

"Beatrice," Cordelia said, "Viola has taken up painting."

"Has she?" Beatrice asked.

Viola nodded. "I believe I may have a talent for it."

"Goodness, and there was our poor drawing master, Mr. Robbins, who could never get anywhere with us," Beatrice said.

"That was because he always insisted on pencils and charcoals," Viola said. "What I have needed all along was paint and a brush. A brush feels quite natural in my hand."

"We will show you the one she did this afternoon of Bess and her pups when we go into the drawing room," Rosalind said. "It is still in development, but you will see for yourself where it's going. It will be exceedingly fine when it's done."

"And Miss Mayton is reading us a story," Viola said. *"The Awful Happenstances of Grimwood Hall."*

"Let me guess," Van Doren said, "another gentle governess and her deranged duke."

"For your information, Van Doren," Cordelia said, "yes, the governess is gentle, *but* the duke is not deranged." She paused, then said, "He only might be a murderer."

Van Doren sighed. The earl said, "I know it sounds outlandish, but it is jolly good fun, a real page turner."

Beatrice sighed happily. "Viola's painting, our aunt's book, and Cordelia, I have not seen your Desdemona in over a fortnight," Beatrice said. "Now, Juliet, I will not believe it if you claim you have not written a new ode. And then, Rosalind might even try to recreate her travels through the world of music she played to such acclaim last evening. Goodness, we will have such fun tonight."

"A delight," Van Doren muttered.

"A *delight*," Juliet said back to him, seeming ever so pleased to see him looking grim.

"Well," the earl said, "I do not see that it matters what we do, as long as we are all together. That is what cheers me the most."

"Then I will be cheered by it too," Darden said, raising his refilled glass. "To the Benningtons."

"To the Benningtons," they all replied. Except of course, Van Doren, who was too busy being grim.

NEITHER SHRIMPS NOR Oyster liked chaos. They both preferred things to advance in a quiet and orderly fashion. Shrimps supposed a journey was one of those things that could very easily descend into chaos, and it had.

First a carriage wheel had broken, and then the very next day a horse had thrown a shoe. At each delay, Lord Van Doren had been very like a madman. Lady Van Doren was thought to be too hot or too cold. Or perhaps she was becoming overtired. Or had not eaten enough or must be thirsty. The world, according to Lord Van Doren, conspired to inconvenience his wife, and he railed against it.

As far as Shrimps could see, the lady was perfectly fine, but there was no accounting for lords and ladies. Having a noble title made a person go a bit off in the head. At least, that was what Cook said.

They'd finally got to Portland Place two hours ago and it had been a chaotic arrival, with Lady Van Doren's sisters calling out from their windows across the street. Then, everything had to be rushed into the house so the lord and lady could change clothes and stroll over to see their relatives.

"Well, Oyster," Shrimps said, opening the back door to the garden, "it seems everything has settled for now. We'll have a walk around and then we'll go to bed and recover."

Oyster seemed thoroughly agreed with this idea and his underbite chattered less than it had done all day.

There was only a sliver of a moon and clouds raced over it. Shrimps led the way in the darkness, having tread the paths dozens of times last season.

Very suddenly, a hand came out of the darkness and gripped his arm.

"Hullo, old mate," the person said.

Shrimps' breath caught. He knew that voice. Why wouldn't he? It had haunted his dreams.

Barney. The oldest of the boys he had once lived with in that dingy room in Rats' Castle. Barney was the oldest and the biggest and by far the prickliest of them all. Shrimps had once asked him how he got the big brown spot on his cheek and had been beaten for it. One of the other boys had told him later that it was a mark at birth and Barney would pound anybody who even seemed to notice it.

Oyster growled, but he backed away at the same time. A thing Shrimps would very much like to do himself.

"Ya didn't think we forgot about you, did ya?" Barney said.

"I had hoped so, actually," Shrimps said. In a fit of daring, he said, "I won't go back with you. I'll shout and scream and Cook will come out for me."

"We don't want you back," Barney said with a chuckle. "Why would we, you were practically useless. But here you are now, in this fine house, with riches at your fingertips."

"It's not *my* riches," Shrimps said.

Barney ignored that very salient point. "Now listen up. We had a plan for when ya came back. You was to let us into the house some night when all were abed and we could relieve the lord of some of his belongings. But that won't do no more. Jimmy got taken and there's too much risk he'll squeal. So, you're gonna think of a new way to enrich us."

"Think up a new way? I don't have any new ways!"

"Figure it out. I'll be back in two days' time to hear it and you better turn up right here. If ya don't, or if you decide to tell them anything, I'll knock right on the front door and inform them people of all the things you used to get up to and they'll kick you out before I'm done talkin'. A house like this don't employ a diver. Not even a bad one who couldn't get a handkerchief off a blind man."

Barney let go of his arm and disappeared into the night.

Shrimps stood there and wept. There was nothing he could do. Barney would make sure he was kicked out of the only house he'd ever wanted to be in.

"Don't worry Oyster," he said through his sobs. "Whatever I'm forced to do, I'll make them see you weren't in on it. I'll make them keep you here."

Oyster's underbite chattered and he weakly wagged his tail.

Shrimps nodded at him sympathetically. He knew they should not have come to London. He hated London.

He patted the inside pocket of his coat and the folded-up letter from his mother. It was the only thing that was entirely his and the only thing that brought him any comfort when his situation seemed particularly dire.

Cook had been threatening to get him a new coat. He said Shrimps was outgrowing the one he was in. So far, he'd been able to put him off by explaining that the coat he wore had sentimental value. He'd been thinking of taking up sewing so that when the time came, he could carefully remove the paper and resew it into a new coat.

Of course, once they all found out he'd used to be a very bad pickpocket, there would be no new coat. Or food. Or bed.

"We best go inside, Oyster. I want to enjoy my bed for as long as I have it."

BALTHAZAR HAD DIRECTED Henri to dress him all in black, along with his black cape. Naturally, his valet assumed he and the rest of the Queen's Knights were off to enter the Rats' Castle to take down a particularly harmful criminal. That had not been where he was going, but Henri did not need to be informed of where he *was* going.

"Your Grace," he'd said, "do not get shot or stabbed. What am I to do if you are dead? Am I to train another nobleman on the correct temperature of a bath? Am I to explain to him the necessity of cooled champagne at the end of it? Am I to order a whole new set of clothes to replace the ill-fitting coats that gentleman is just now walking around in? I'd rather throw myself into the Arno! Or worse, the Thames!"

It was the same speech every time—Balthazar's death would simply be too inconvenient for his valet. With dire warnings of death by Arno or Thames ringing in his ears, Balthazar slipped out of his house.

He did not take his carriage, nor even his horse. He walked along the side streets, avoiding the main avenues where it was too likely to be spotted by someone he knew, passing by in a carriage.

He was well aware that he might have simply hired someone to keep watch on Van Doren's house. In fact, he had. But when he got word that the lord had arrived to open the house, he'd felt the need to go himself.

Would anybody make an approach to the house? Or was it as Hamill had predicted—had the criminals who'd targeted the residence, on account of a young boy named Shrimps currently inside it, given up the scheme? Had they deemed it too risky now that one of their own, one who knew of the plan, had been taken?

If they had *not* given it up, it was possible that whoever turned up could lead him to Harold Mondrian. Some criminals were cautious and some were not. He did not yet know who he dealt with.

He'd arrived in Portland Place after sunset and concealed himself behind a stand of trees across the street from Van Doren's residence.

Balthazar had stayed still, unseen, as Lord Van Doren and his new bride had walked across the street and into Lord Westmont's address.

They seemed well-pleased with one another. Balthazar smiled as he thought back to last season and what trouble it had been to get them both to see that they would be.

After that, the street was quiet with only an occasional carriage pulling up and taking away a house's occupants. Nobody on Portland Place was entertaining this night and once the usual time for departures had passed, it got quieter still.

He'd almost determined he ought to give up his watch and return home when he saw him. A boy emerging from the trees at the end of the road, so badly dressed that he could not possibly be anybody's servant. Even a stable hand would be given new trousers if the ones he wore had two large holes in them.

The boy walked, cap pulled low to shield his face, hands in pockets. He paused in front of Van Doren's house. He looked up at the windows and then proceeded on his way.

Balthazar did not know where he'd come from. It was a little too coincidental, however, that he'd paused to have a look at Van Doren's house. He was determined to see where the boy went.

He allowed the boy to get some distance and watched him intently.

The lad was no fool, he was careful. He occasionally paused to look over his shoulder. When he did so, he covered his face with his hand in case anybody was interested in getting a look at him.

That was a boy who'd been long on the streets and made such moves without even thinking about it.

Balthazar allowed him to turn a corner and then set off. If he, himself, looked toward any house as he exited Portland Place, it was perhaps toward Lady Rosalind's.

He did not have the first idea of what she and her sisters would do to amuse themselves on such a night, but he had high hopes for Miss Mayton's alarming duke and governess, and then of course, Lady Rosalind's absolutely startling pianoforte playing.

The boy was exceedingly cautious as he made his way through London, as he was too.

After a time, Balthazar had no doubt of their destination. First south, then east, they made their way inexorably toward the Seven Dials.

Once he had confirmed the boy's destination, he turned round and left him to his evening. He would not be entering the Rats' Castle this night alone. In any case, he had discovered what he wished to know. The question had been: was there any reason to suppose that Van Doren's house was still a target?

The answer was: yes. He was sure of it.

It was time to return home and alert his valet that there was no cause to throw himself into the Arno on this night at least.

THE BENNINGTON LADIES had retired to the drawing room, leaving the earl, Darden, and Van Doren to their port.

Juliet scribbled a new ode, Viola added various touches to her painting of Bess and her pups, Miss Mayton went above stairs to retrieve her book, and Cordelia arranged candles for her portrayal of Desdemona.

Rosalind and Beatrice sat in front of the tea tray.

"Tell me everything you would not say in front of Papa, Darden, and my dear husband," Beatrice said, clasping Rosalind's hand. "Tell me of this gentleman you saw out of a carriage window. I know you held something back."

Rosalind was not at all surprised to be questioned so. After all, who knew one better than a sister?

"The gentleman was Conbatten. I am in love, Bea," she said.

"Conbatten!"

"It has not been as it was for you and Van Doren—a sort of growing realization. No, I knew the moment I saw him out that carriage window," Rosalind said, her voice all contentment. "It is Conbatten."

"The duke? Goodness, and what does he say about it?"

"He has not dared say anything yet," Rosalind said. "He knows of my requirement for courage and bravery and is biding his time until he can rescue me from danger."

Beatrice's forehead wrinkled just a bit over that idea. "But how is that to occur? That you would suddenly need rescuing and he would happen to be there?"

Rosalind had wrestled with that same question. She and her sisters had concluded that they must help the fates along and arrange something, but they had also decided that Beatrice could not know of it. Not yet. There was too much of a chance that she would tell Van Doren, who would go straight to their father.

"I am trusting the fates to make it so," Rosalind said. "By the by, do you suppose Shrimps would enjoy a visit with the pups? He is so fond of Oyster that I must think he would like it."

"I am sure he would," Beatrice said. "How considerate of you to think of him."

Rosalind nodded, though she wished she could tell Beatrice the real reason Shrimps had been thought of—they needed to hire a pickpocket in time for the charity picnic. She must be accosted and robbed within sight of Conbatten.

Miss Mayton returned with book in hand and not another moment passed before the gentlemen followed.

"Van Doren hurried us along," Darden said, smiling.

"I do not see why I should be separated from my wife over-long," Van Doren said. "She has had a very tiring journey."

"At home, as it is just the two of us, I stay at table," Beatrice said. "Sometimes I even have a glass of port."

"No harm in it, I do not think. What shall we do first?" the earl asked. "Now, I *ask* it, though I think you will all know what I would wish."

"*The Awful Happenstances of Grimwood Hall*, Papa," Cordelia said.

"You know me well, child," the earl said. "I just cannot get it out of my head—is he or is he not a murderer?"

Miss Mayton nodded graciously. She opened the book and said, "Chapter three."

As her aunt related the happenings at Grimwood Hall, Rosalind watched Beatrice and Van Doren. It was always so interesting to observe them these days.

Beatrice patted his arm when Miss Mayton read of the moon-lit walk between the gentle governess and the duke as he listed all the reasons he was not a murderer.

Van Doren pressed his lips together in a grim line and gripped Beatrice's hand while Miss Mayton read of the gentle governess listing all the reasons he *might* be a murderer.

"Finally," Miss Mayton said, "they came to the well. The very well where the late duchess had made her final adieu."

The duke seized his gentle governess and picked her up. "You see? I could throw you right over the side, and yet I do not. That must be ultimate proof that I am not a murderer!"

The gentle governess was confused. What he said was true—he could murder her this very minute, and yet he did not.

But then, why would the housekeeper tell her that she'd seen the duke murder his duchess? The housekeeper said she must never reveal what had been told to her and she must leave the estate quickly, to save her own life.

What to do? On the one hand, she did like the idea of becoming a duchess. But on the other hand, there was no happiness in being a dead duchess.

"How about this," the duke said, setting her down, "how about I seal up the well?"

"But how can you?" the gentle governess asked. "The magistrate said he was bringing men on the morrow to retrieve the poor duchess."

"Once they get her out then. Consider it sealed."

"How long has she been down there, exactly?" Van Doren said to Beatrice in a low voice.

Beatrice patted his hand to quiet him.

"If you will seal up the well," the gentle governess said, "then I will be convinced."

The duke and his gentle governess walked happily back to the house.

They could not know, of course, that when the magistrate exhumed the well, all of their plans would be thrown into disarray. If the duchess was not down there, where was she?

Miss Mayton closed her book. "One wonders what chapter four will bring us," she said.

"Wonders?" the earl said jovially. "I am on tenterhooks over it!"

Van Doren quietly groaned. Beatrice bit her lip.

The next hours were filled with amusements. Cordelia's Desdemona was a rousing success, and she did not start one fire from knocked-over candles. Tattleton had eyed the sand buckets while she performed, but he never had a need to race to them to put out a smoldering carpet.

Juliet read her newly composed *Ode to Pups.*

New arrived and what a surprise
Hear me, good dogs, and gently rise.
The time for slumber has come to be over
And soon you will be frolicking in clover.

Van Doren had muttered, "Might *we* frolic home now? I will even frolic in clover if you take me out of here." Beatrice was entirely amused by it.

Viola unveiled her portrait of Bess and her little family.

While it was true that the portrait might need a bit of refining, as just now it was eight small brown ovals and one larger brown oval, for a first effort it was going in a rather inspired direction.

Fortunately, Viola was confident in her abilities and did not so much as flinch when Van Doren said, "Wait. Those are supposed to be dogs?"

Everybody was so lively and entertained. Except Van Doren, of course.

Beatrice finally leaned close to him and whispered, "You are a very good sport, you know."

"I do know," he answered. "Perhaps I'll write an ode about it—*Ode to Suffering at my In-Laws' Hands.*"

Beatrice practically fell over with laughter.

While Rosalind could see very well that they were delighted with one another, it was in their very peculiar way. Her own marriage to Conbatten would be nothing like it.

Theirs would be all passionate romance and courageous demonstrations of love.

Rosalind felt she was inching ever closer to her future happiness. She must only secure a pickpocket to rob her.

CHAPTER NINE

WHEN SHRIMPS HAD been called to the library to see Lady Van Doren, he of course knew he was dismissed.

He'd been very surprised to find out he was not dismissed and that he was told he might go across the street to see eight pups just recently born.

Lady Van Doren had given him a note to give to Mr. Tattleton and then he would be shown into the servants' quarters where those dogs currently resided.

Shrimps had not told Oyster anything about the visit, as he could not guess if Oyster would be jealous over the idea.

Peering out the servants' entrance to assure himself that his old associate Barney was not lurking around somewhere, he'd made a run for it across the wide avenue.

Shrimps had handed over the note he was sent with and was let into the house by Jimmy, a wonderfully cheerful footman.

Below stairs, he was taken to the dog and her pups.

They were very small indeed and Shrimps had no idea how anybody could tell one from the other. Every single one of them had a brown coat and a white patch on the chest.

Their eyes were still closed and they clumsily crawled on top of each other, heading in the direction of their mother.

That made him think of his own mother and he thought he might cry where he sat. Between Barney's visit and being certain he was dismissed and not knowing when he really would be dismissed, as he knew he would be eventually, it was all too much.

Where would he go? He'd be out on the streets, but Barney and his gang would never take him back. He was no good at pickpocketing! He got too frightened in the attempt.

The poor pups! They could not even see the world they'd come into and probably thought it was wonderful. They did not yet know how the world really was. Oyster knew, he'd been out there, but these poor little things did not know yet.

They would be crushed when they figured it out.

A sudden loud clattering on the steps took his attention.

The ladies Rosalind, Viola, Cordelia, and Juliet all came barreling into the servants' dining hall, one after another.

Shrimps leapt to his feet. He bowed deeply and worried that they would be angry to find him there. He didn't have the note from Lady Van Doren to prove he'd been sent! He'd given it over to Jimmy when he came in.

"Shrimps," Lady Rosalind said, "we wished you to especially come and see Bess' lovely new babies."

"You did, my lady?" he asked. Lady Van Doren had not said whose idea it was. He'd assumed it had been *hers*.

"Now Shrimps," Lady Juliet said, "we wished to have a confidential conversation with you about pickpockets."

"Why? What have you heard?" he cried. Had he been lured out of the house to be dismissed here? He'd never had a job a person could be dismissed from. He didn't know how it was done! They might all be riffling through his little room across the street to make sure he had not stolen anything before he was given the boot.

"They'll not find anything!" Shrimps said. "I would not take even an extra biscuit!"

"Goodness," Lady Rosalind said, "Beatrice did mention you were a bit...nervous."

"Wouldn't you be?" he asked plaintively.

"Hmm, I couldn't say. Well, never mind, nobody thinks you

took an extra biscuit," Lady Rosalind said.

"Though I do not know why anybody should mind if you had," Lady Juliet said. "That's what napkins are for, in my view."

"Now that we've got that out of the way," Lady Rosalind said, "we need to hire a pickpocket for Lady Crinkleton's charity picnic for orphans. It is next Thursday, you see."

"Hire a pickpocket?" Shrimps asked. He'd no idea pickpockets ever got hired. Nobody had ever said anything to him about that.

"You see, Shrimps," Lady Viola said, "Rosalind is in love with the Duke of Conbatten, but she requires him to have an opportunity to save her from something."

"So we thought," Lady Cordelia said, "why not have Rosalind accosted by a pickpocket right in front of him. You see? It would be his chance to be heroic."

"Now of course, we understand you were hanging round the streets with some unsavory sorts when Van Doren found you and Oyster last season," Lady Rosalind said.

Unsavory sorts. Yes, he supposed the likes of Barney *were* unsavory sorts. He'd been an unsavory sort himself, though he never really took to it.

But surely these ladies did not think a person could stroll into a rookery and casually request a pickpocket for a certain day and time?

"We would like one of those unsavory sorts to steal a handkerchief from Rosalind," Lady Cordelia said.

"We understand that whoever you are able to contact about this will expect to be paid," Lady Viola said.

"We've pooled all our pin money together and can pay ten pounds," Lady Rosalind said.

"Ten pounds!" Shrimps said, in more of a squeak than a voice. A diver might steal sixty or seventy handkerchiefs to come out with ten pounds.

Maybe Barney would be satisfied with ten pounds and agree to go away. Barney had told him he better think of a new idea and so far he had none. Maybe this was the idea?

Then another thought occurred to him. What use was ten pounds when a duke had collared a person and turned him over to the magistrate?

"You can find someone, Shrimps?" Lady Rosalind asked.

Shrimps shook his head sadly. "Nobody will agree to it. It's fine money but nobody will allow themselves to be caught like that."

"Oh, he will not be caught!" Lady Rosalind said.

"Goodness, we have no intention of the fellow being caught," Viola said.

"You see, all of my sisters will be there with me," Lady Rosalind said. "They, and Miss Mayton too, will create a terrible confusion, giving the person ample time to get away."

"Rosalind doesn't require that Conbatten catch anybody," Lady Viola said, "just that he makes the attempt."

"And then catches *me* when I swoon in his arms," Lady Rosalind said nodding.

Shrimps mulled it over. It was the strangest plan he'd ever heard. On the other hand, it was the only plan anywhere near him just now.

And wasn't it better than Lord Van Doren's house getting robbed? He must think so.

"Well, I do know a fellow who has been looking for some employment," Shrimps said slowly.

"And you think he'd be good at it?" Lady Rosalind asked.

Shrimps nodded. Barney was *very* good at stealing handker-chiefs.

"Excellent," Lady Rosalind said. "I will wear a light blue spencer with small pockets and I will have my handkerchief hanging out of one of them. Your fellow will know me by my straw bonnet. The hat will display three red silk roses on the brim."

"Be certain that your pickpocket ascertains that the duke is nearby," Viola said. "He is very tall."

"Though, Rosalind, I think you need a signal," Lady Cordelia said. "After all, what if a second very tall man was to turn up?"

"Excellent thought, Cordelia," Lady Rosalind said. "I know, I will tug on the brim of my bonnet. That shall be the signal."

Shrimps took it all in—light blue spencer, handkerchief hanging from pocket, bonnet with three red roses. A pull on the brim was the signal.

"Oh, and the charity picnic is to take place at two o'clock in the north-west enclosure, nearby the keeper's lodge," Lady Rosalind said.

"And since we will be dealing with someone in the criminal way," Lady Juliet said, "he shan't be paid until the job is done."

"Quite right, sister," Lady Rosalind said. She handed Shrimps a small purse. "All the money is there, keep it safe until your fellow has stolen my handkerchief."

Shrimps' hands shook as he took the purse. He had never held such a fortune. He just prayed he did not get robbed while crossing the street. Once he got it safely into the house, he would hide it under his mattress.

Then, all he had to do was convince Barney to take a job as a hired pickpocket.

Cook was right—there was no accounting for lords and ladies. Who would believe they went about courting in such a manner?

⊰⊱

BALTHAZAR RARELY FOUND himself in the position of not being quite able to account for his actions. He found himself in that situation now, though.

He had just tapped the roof of his carriage and it had come to a stop, a few buildings down from the Lyceum.

Lady Rosalind had mentioned that she and her sisters would attend a Frenchwoman's exhibition of waxed figures at that theater. Not a thing that would usually interest him.

He had certainly not planned on going—he was meant to be

on his way to White's.

However, he could not resist being entertained by Lady Rosalind. Or Miss Mayton for that matter, as long as that lady was not attempting to eat a slice of lemon cake in his vicinity. And then, he would be further amused to have a look at those sisters—one had just taken up painting and was a regular Holbein, one fancied herself treading the boards as Desdemona, and another wrote odes to hay.

The doors were to open at two o'clock and it must be past time by now.

He exited the carriage and followed a stream of people heading toward the doors.

Handing over a shilling and six, he made his way into the large foyer.

"Your Grace!"

He turned toward the sound, knowing perfectly well who it was—Miss Mayton. He suppressed the urge to laugh. The lady could attract the attention of a crowd at a fish market.

Miss Mayton, Lady Rosalind, Lady Beatrice, and three younger ladies all looked at him smiling. He made his way over.

"I thought you should hear me, Your Grace," Miss Mayton said.

"I believe nobody has missed it, Miss Mayton," Balthazar said. "Lady Beatrice, welcome back to Town. Lady Rosalind, how do you do?"

Done with the niceties, Balthazar waited to be introduced to the allegedly talented younger sisters.

"Duke," Lady Rosalind said, "these are my younger sisters—Lady Viola, Lady Cordelia, and Lady Juliet."

"Charmed," Balthazar said, executing a very formal bow for this collection of young ladies.

"Your Grace," Lady Juliet said, "we understand you attended Lady Hightower's musical evening. I imagine you were bowled over by Rosalind's performance. She calls it a travel through the world of music."

Balthazar attempted to keep his expression neutral lest he allow a smile to escape. A travel through the world of music, indeed. It was certainly a trip through something. "I had not known the style had a name."

"Rosalind's playing is ever so thrilling," Lady Cordelia said. "We never know where it's going."

"I certainly did not," Balthazar said.

"All the girls are so creative and talented," Miss Mayton said.

"Ah, yes," Balthazar said. "Lady Cordelia, I believe you have a penchant for Othello?"

"Indeed, Your Grace. But only the very end where Desdemona very elegantly dies."

"And Lady Juliet is the poet?"

"Poetess," Lady Juliet corrected, "I write odes to what I see, to capture their essence."

Balthazar nodded gravely. *Ode to Hay*," he said. "And Lady Viola, I understand you are a gifted painter."

Lady Viola nodded in the affirmative and said, "Mind you, I am very new to it. But the brush does feel very natural in my hand."

Balthazar bit his lip to stop from laughing. All over England, ladies were taught to be modest. They were never to own any particular accomplishment. If one were a great proficient at the pianoforte, one must claim only a glancing acquaintance with it. If one were particularly skilled at drawing, one might only dismiss one's work as dabblings, and only a pleasant way to pass the time.

Somebody had clearly forgot to stop at the Earl of Westmont's estate and inform his daughters of this British proclivity. As far as they were concerned, anything they put their hand to was bound to come off brilliantly.

What made for further hilarity was the idea that if Lady Rosalind's playing and *Ode to Hay* were their measuring stick to brilliancy, he could assure himself that Desdemona and any paintings produced were equally dreadful. He hardly dared think about it lest he roar with laughter.

"Shall we proceed in and see what Madame Tussaud has in store for us?" Balthazar asked.

The ladies all nodded with real enthusiasm.

And there was their charm.

Whatever their lack of modesty might be, there was nothing of artifice about them. They were comely enough and happily lacking the cold and hard sophistication that seemed so popular these days. Their unbridled and quite unconscious enthusiasm was hard to resist. He supposed that despite their eccentricities, they would all do very well with the *ton*.

He was certain Lady Rosalind would—she was looking particularly charming this afternoon.

That idea did not sit as pleasantly as he would have thought. Once another gentleman began to seriously court her, she would likely have little time or inclination to entertain him. He was becoming very fond of being entertained by Lady Rosalind.

The ladies Juliet, Cordelia, and Viola, along with Miss Mayton, hurried ahead. Balthazar walked with Lady Rosalind and Lady Beatrice.

He noticed Lady Rosalind leaned rather heavy on his arm. He could not say he was entirely opposed to it.

"I pray married life suits you, Lady Beatrice?" he asked. "If it does not, I shall put all the fault of it at Van Doren's doorstep."

Lady Beatrice smiled and said, "It suits me very well, indeed, Duke. And, I must tell you that I know of your helpful intercession in that particular matter. Van Doren confessed it all."

"I merely pointed out the truth to the viscount," Balthazar said.

"I wonder if I might return the favor someday," Lady Beatrice said. "Should you ever find yourself in love with a lady but hesitating to declare yourself."

"That is kindly offered, but I doubt it would become necessary," Balthazar said.

"I shouldn't think so, Beatrice," Lady Rosalind said. "The duke will declare his feelings at just the right time."

"That is correct," he said. "We will see where we are on that subject in a few years."

"A few years!" Lady Rosalind cried.

Balthazar had not expected quite such a reaction.

"What Rosalind means to say," Lady Beatrice said hurriedly, "is that one can never know precisely what the timing will be."

Balthazar nodded. "That is true, of course. The best laid plans of mice and men often go awry, as Robert Burns put it so eloquently."

They had come to the doors leading into the theater proper. Though Lady Rosalind's younger sisters and Miss Mayton had been well ahead of them, they came upon them just inside.

All four of the ladies were pale and their eyes wide.

"It is not fairies and woodland sprites, as we'd thought it would be," Lady Juliet whispered.

"It is people," Lady Cordelia said. "Dead people."

"Marie Antoinette, the King of France, Madame DuBarry…and others," Lady Viola said.

"And they can all see the model of the guillotine right in front of them!" Lady Juliet said.

"Yes, because they all seem alive," Lady Cordelia said. "But then somehow very dead too."

"Queen Marie Antoinette looks so angry, and she stares right at you," Juliet whispered.

"I thought Madame DuBarry looked very well, though," Miss Mayton said helpfully. "Almost cheerful."

"Cheerful?" Viola said. "How can she be?"

Balthazar pinched himself to stop from roaring with laughter. None of them had come with the first idea of what they were to view. They'd thought they would view a bucolic scene of wax fairies and wood sprites and had instead been faced with the Reign of Terror.

"Madame Tussaud!" Miss Mayton shouted, wildly waving in the direction of the stage.

Balthazar looked in that direction. A middle-aged lady, elegantly dressed, had picked up her skirts and was racing stage right toward the wings. She stopped in her tracks and Balthazar watched her slowly turn and very determinedly put a smile on her face.

My God, she'd spotted the Benningtons and attempted an escape. She would have got away too, had not Miss Mayton had a habit of calling out to people like a fishwife.

The lady walked over, though Balthazar might characterize it as dragging her feet.

"Our dear friend, Madame Tussaud," Lady Rosalind said. "We are delighted to see you again. Madame, this is my sister, Lady Van Doren, and this is the Duke of Conbatten."

Madame Tussaud curtsied low. "Your Grace, Lady Van Doren," she said.

"Madame Tussaud," Juliet said, "we were shocked to see your wax figures. We'd assumed they would be fairies and woodland sprites. Or perhaps squirrels and butterflies."

The lady's forehead wrinkled. "But who would wish to pay to see that?" she asked.

"*We* would," Lady Viola whispered.

"It looks to be a very interesting exhibition," Lady Beatrice said.

"The work is very exact," Madame Tussaud said. "The cast is taken from the actual face."

"The face…the dead face, you mean," Lady Juliet said.

"Naturally, the dead face," Madame Tussaud said. "You do not think the Queen of France would put up with it when she was alive."

Lady Cordelia staggered and her sister Lady Viola caught her arm and steadied her.

"Perhaps we ought to get Cordelia home," Lady Beatrice said, "she does not look at all well."

Lady Rosalind nodded and said, "Madame Tussaud, we must have you to dine. I am certain my father would like it."

Madame Tussaud appeared a little panicked over the suggestion. Then she recovered herself and said, "Je suis dévasté. My host has planned out my evenings for every night of the week while I am in London."

The Benningtons all nodded sadly at this news, though their acceptance of it appeared to cheer Madame Tussaud.

They took their leave of the madame. And King Louis XVI, Marie Antoinette, Madame DuBarry, and Robespierre too.

What an outing. Balthazar had not been so entertained in ages.

CHAPTER TEN

ROSALIND STARED STRAIGHT ahead in the carriage. "I am so confused," she said softly.

Juliet patted her arm. "We were all shocked, I know. But those people are dead, and we cannot help them. I think we ought to forget all about it and never go to another waxworks in our lives."

"No," Rosalind said hurriedly, "it was Conbatten. Beatrice, he said it would be years before he would declare himself!"

"What on God's green earth will he be waiting for?" Miss Mayton asked.

"Yes, why should he wait years?" Viola asked.

"Ah, I think I see!" Beatrice exclaimed. "That is probably it. Rosalind, he said it might take years because he presumes it will take that long to discover you in danger and rescue you from something."

"Do you suppose?" Rosalind asked. She desperately would like to hold on to that idea. She'd been going along assuming she and Conbatten were in absolute synchronicity with one another. After all, how else could it be?

Her heart beat faster at the sight of him. She wished to throw herself into his arms. She wanted to touch his lips with her own. His voice sent a shiver down her back. Did he not feel the same? If he did, how could he bear to even consider waiting years?

"You see, Rosalind," Cordelia said, "you've told him of your requirement. You did have only the one requirement, so he could not exactly ignore it."

"No, he really could not ignore *one* requirement," Juliet said. "It was not like Beatrice's so many requirements and then the fates just threw up their hands and said never mind, here's Van Doren."

Beatrice laughed despite herself. She said, "Perhaps you might modify your requirement. Perhaps you might hint that your requirement for a courageous act could be either before or after marriage. Just that it must happen sometime."

The carriage had been going for a quarter hour and now stopped in front of a small storefront with a blue sign above the door that read *The Tea & Tome*. They had planned the stop for their sister. Beatrice was determined to buy a book for the husband who had turned out to be the fates' final answer to her too many requirements.

"I shan't be a moment," Beatrice said. "I know precisely what I seek. Van Doren will be delighted with me as he very much wishes for a copy and I sent footmen out delivering notes everywhere so that I might find one and reserve it."

Beatrice was helped down to the sidewalk and disappeared into the shop.

After the carriage door closed, Cordelia said, "Beatrice is right, you know. Poor Conbatten thinks he'll have to wait years for his chance to rescue you. He doesn't know that we've got something already arranged."

"Neither does Beatrice, for that matter," Viola said.

"You know we would tell her in an instant if it were not for Van Doren. He would tell Papa and then it would be all up."

"We will tell her everything once we've done it," Rosalind said. "She won't mind it."

"Of course she will not mind it," Viola said. "And just think how happy Conbatten will be when you get robbed and he realizes he won't have to wait years."

"He'll be over the moon when he sees you getting assaulted

in the park," Juliet said.

"I hope so," Rosalind said. "Oh, it must be so. I shall die of a broken heart if it is not so."

Miss Mayton clucked sympathetically. "Now you understand what happened to all my poor gentlemen," she said.

"I do!" Rosalind said. "I do see how they did not view life worth living. I must have Conbatten—nobody else will do."

"Now Rosalind," Viola said, "do not ever lose hope. Beatrice was very sure Van Doren would propose to Lady Mary and she would go on to be a spinster. Then quite unexpectedly, he turned up at the door raging about his love for her."

"That's true, it was very sudden," Rosalind said. "And he was terribly intemperate."

"Wildly so," Viola said encouragingly.

"Rosalind," Cordelia said, "you are the most courageous among us, you must not wilt in the face of your current challenge."

"You are right," Rosalind said, taking a deep breath. "Rosalind Bennington does not wilt. Rosalind Bennington does not falter. Rosalind Bennington hires a pickpocket to rob her."

"That's the spirit, my dear," Miss Mayton said.

Beatrice emerged from the shop carrying a brown paper package tied with string. She clambered back into the carriage. "*The Battle of Camperdown* is now on its way to Van Doren's library."

"Beatrice," Juliet said, "Rosalind has reminded herself of her bravery and is determined she will not wilt or falter."

"Oh I am glad," Beatrice said.

"We reminded her that you were planning on being a spinster until Van Doren turned up and raged at the door."

Beatrice leaned back and smiled. "He did rage, did he not? He still does, I quite like it."

"You'll see, Rosalind," Cordelia said. "Conbatten will rage for you before you know it."

And so they went on very much cheered by the idea of the duke raging.

SHRIMPS FELT AS if his insides jiggled around all by themselves though his body did not move. He'd hid himself at the servants' entrance of Westmont House to wait for the ladies' carriage to come back.

They had tasked him with finding a pickpocket, and he had, though it had not been easy.

Barney had accosted him in the garden again, just like he'd said he would. He'd come back expecting Shrimps to hand over something valuable and had been very threatening when he'd got nothing.

Shrimps had told him of the opportunity for ten pounds. It had taken a lot of explaining.

"What are you tryin' to pass off?" Barney had said, grasping him by the coat collar. "I'm to go to the park and take a lady's handkerchief and then I'm paid ten pounds for it. Sounds like rubbish to me."

"I know it sounds…unusual," Shrimps said. "It has to do with some fella she likes."

"Right. More like set up poor old Barney to get took by a magistrate is what it sounds like."

"No, it really isn't. How would I do that? I don't know any magistrates and I don't want to!"

"Then what's the real game, mate?"

"The ladies, they're all sisters you see. And they are very strange sorts of people. They just want this duke to see the one of them getting robbed."

Barney had folded his arms. "I see. So the duke can act all hero-like and haul me off to the magistrate."

"No, they don't want that. When it happens, the other sisters will cause a commotion, allowing you time to get away. Then the one what was robbed, Lady Rosalind, plans on fainting in the duke's arms. Then they get married. That's my understanding of the thing."

"And they said they'd pay ten pounds," Barney said. "What if they go back on it?"

"I've seen the money, they've already put it aside. Anyway, they're as flighty as bees trapped in a bonnet, but they won't go back on a deal. They'd never do that—these titled people have codes they live by, you know."

Barney had looked as if he did not know that. Shrimps had not always known it himself, but he'd picked up quite a lot by listening at the servants' table. Lord Van Doren's word was good. Even if he changed his mind, he stuck to whatever he'd agreed to because he was a viscount and people expected it.

"Ten pounds," Barney said thoughtfully.

"Ten pounds. All you have to do is grab the lady's handkerchief and run. You do that every day anyhow."

"*If* I decide to go forward, and I said *if*, this is how it will go," Barney said. "I'm bringing my boys to watch. If it's a set-up and I get took, they're comin' for ya."

Barney leaned close and towered over him. "Comin' for ya in the permanent way, you understand. They'll drag you to the nearest bridge and throw you into the Thames. So think about whether your life is worth this scheme."

Shrimps had shivered over the idea of going over the side of a bridge, as he knew it was not an empty threat.

"Under those conditions, a drownin' in the Thames, you still say I won't get took?" Barney asked.

"You won't get took," Shrimps assured him. He just prayed there would not be some overenthusiastic hero nearby who would give chase to Barney and somehow catch him. It would look like a set-up, even though there was no set-up.

Shrimps told Barney everything he needed to know—where he was to go, what Lady Rosalind looked like, the three roses on the bonnet, and the signal.

Now, he just waited for the ladies to come back so he could tell them it was all arranged.

He peeked round the corner of the stairs at the carriage wheels that had just rolled to a stop in front of the house.

There was a great clamor and commotion of them getting out of the carriage, as there always seemed to be when they were together.

Lady Van Doren called her goodbyes as she made her way across the street and into the house.

"Lady Rosalind," he whispered.

She stopped and looked about.

"It's Shrimps, I'm down here."

<hr>

TATTLETON PACED HIS quarters. Atop having a pile of dogs in his servants' hall and the whole place taking on the smell of wet fur, there was a mystery going on under his nose.

What were the ladies up to? What did they want with Shrimps?

First, they had insisted that Shrimps come to see all those dogs that had sprung out so suddenly from the wretched cur. Then they'd gone down and sat with the boy. Why?

As if that were not mystery enough, not an hour ago he'd heard the carriage arriving, opened the front doors, and what did he find?

All four ladies on the servants' stairs with Shrimps, looking as if they were having some sort of confidential conversation!

Seeing his look of confusion over the scene, Lady Rosalind had informed him that Shrimps was out taking the air and they'd all agreed he looked tired and told him to sit on the steps and rest.

Was he to be taken as a fool? Was he expected to believe such a thing?

Then, he'd brought tea into the drawing room and heard the tail end of a conversation. As usual these days, they were discussing the duke. Now they had added in something about a pickpocket.

What was the connection between all of these things?

Tattleton sat down heavily. He was no Bow Street Runner and had not the first idea where to begin to unravel whatever was happening.

All he knew was that they were probably heading toward disaster by way of a duke, a boy, and now a pickpocket.

While he waited for the blow, whatever it was to be, to fall upon the house, there were nine dogs below stairs to think about.

They were contained now, but it would not be too long before they were up on their feet and chewing every leg of furniture in the servants' hall.

⟫⟪

BALTHAZAR HAD MADE his way into the park. Lady Crinkleton's charity picnic was on offer and he must turn up.

He really did not see why. The point of the thing was to raise money for orphans. He was happy to give her plenty of money and did not entirely understand why the picnic must take place at all.

If he were to guess, he supposed Lady Crinkleton enjoyed the accolades that could only be felt in person, with a crowd. And then he supposed she was always very happy to introduce the prince so that he might drone on for a half hour about how heartily he supported Lady Crinkleton's work.

The queen financed Lady Crinkleton's work more than anybody did, but that royal lady had somehow been clever enough to avoid making an appearance. He guessed it amused her to force her son away from his entertainments for an afternoon of charity work in her stead.

All of the inconvenience of it might be overlooked if the lady bothered to supply any sort of decent refreshment. Alas, Lady Crinkleton liked to make her point about the plight of orphans with dreadful offerings. Lemonade would be the only drink and it would be of such a dreadful quality as to make Almack's own insufferable lemonade appear the nectar of the Gods.

He steered his horse to the area that would house parked carriages of all sorts, and then paid a groom twice what he looked for, with strict instructions that his horse must be watered and kept in shade. It was a hot day and there was no reason Hades should also suffer on Lady Crinkleton's behalf.

Despite his careful arrangements, Hades looked entirely disgusted with his current circumstances.

As he approached the gathering, Lady Rosalind's party was immediately apparent. They were quite the crowd, coming all together. Not only was Lady Rosalind with her sisters and Miss Mayton, but the earl, Darden, Van Doren and Lady Van Doren were in attendance too.

Miss Mayton scanned the landscape like a hawk making lazy circles over a field. She spotted him and her attention grew sharper.

She waved. It was no delicate and subtle signal, but a full outstretched arm, as she was wont to do.

He nodded in her direction and told himself not to laugh.

Whatever long and boring speeches Lady Crinkleton had planned for them all, perhaps the Benningtons would alleviate the doldrums of it.

He made his way over.

After everybody was sufficiently greeted, Lady Juliet said, "Your Grace, if you have not been to the refreshments table yet, I do not advise it. It is all very dreadful."

"Ah, yes," he said, "Lady Crinkleton makes a point that orphans do not have the luxury of anything good, so neither should we."

This idea seemed to strike the younger girls very hard.

"Of course that is it," Lady Viola said. "The poor orphans, and here we were complaining of what must be very usual for them."

"Now I feel terrible," Lady Juliet said.

"I too," Lady Cordelia said.

"Do you suppose we ought to go back and get plates?" Lady Viola said. "So that we might suffer as the orphans do?"

Her sisters nodded. Miss Mayton said, "Very fine feelings, my girls. I will go and suffer with you."

The sisters made a quick curtsy and were off to suffer as the orphans did.

The earl only looked amused at this turn of events. Lord Van Doren was holding his lady's parasol and spent his time adjusting it so his lady would not feel the heat.

Darden had been corralled by his friends in the *Young Bucks Club* and they all surreptitiously glanced his way, no doubt still wondering if they ought to invite him to their club.

Lady Rosalind kept tugging on her bonnet, as if she were in some way uncomfortable.

"Does the sun get in your eyes, Lady Rosalind?" he asked.

"No, no, Duke, I adore the sun," she said.

She did some more tugging and he began to wonder if some unfortunate hairpin was digging into her head.

The younger sisters returned with plates of old, dry bread and glasses of the wretched lemonade.

Lady Cordelia sipped from her glass and shivered. "I cannot believe the orphans are allowed to suffer so."

Lady Rosalind nodded and tugged once more on the brim of her bonnet.

Somebody shoved him from behind, and as he turned to see who had caused such an affront, Lady Rosalind fell into his arms and cried, "I've been attacked and my handkerchief stolen!"

As if that were some sort of cue, the other sisters all managed to throw their plates and glasses into the air.

Balthazar looked over the heads of the spectators behind him and saw a boy sprinting away with Lady Rosalind's handkerchief. He was fifteen or sixteen and had a very distinct brown birthmark on his cheek. It was a wonder, with that distinguishing mark, that the fellow had not been taken in by now.

He very briefly thought of going for his horse and running the thief down, but it was never his interest to take in a boy such as that, only making off with a handkerchief that would buy him his dinner.

Instead, he found himself with a drooping Lady Rosalind, and covered in bits of bread and lemonade.

There was something strange here. The other sisters looked on with interested expressions, not seeming the least bit nervous though they had managed to lose control of their plates and glasses.

It was almost as if they looked upon a stage play.

The earl hurried over. "My dear," he said to his daughter, "have you been hurt? Come and lean on my arm."

"No, no, Papa," Lady Rosalind said faintly. "The duke supports me just now."

"Coming through," a voice said behind him.

Balthazar would recognize that voice anywhere. Lady Hightower.

"Conbatten," she said by way of greeting. "I saw it all, the wretched little blighter spotted a crowd and was determined to try his luck. Now, Lady Rosalind, breathe deep."

Lady Hightower had applied a vinaigrette to Lady Rosalind's nose.

Balthazar presumed it was rather strong in nature, if reactions were anything to go by.

The lady coughed and wheezed.

"You must be the Earl of Westmont," Lady Hightower said to the earl. "Your daughter graced my drawing room with her playing the other night. Miss Mayton, how do you do?"

Balthazar noticed the earl color at the mention of his daughter's playing, so he was not completely in the dark on such matters.

"This is Lady Hightower, Earl," Miss Mayton said by way of introduction.

"Lady Hightower," the earl said, "I thank you for your assistance just now."

"Never fear, Earl, there is more to come," Lady Hightower said. "Despite my vinaigrette, Lady Rosalind still droops like a tulip in the tropics."

Lady Hightower was, of course, correct. Lady Rosalind was still limp in his arms, despite the surprise vinaigrette.

"My carriage is just there, very close, as I do not enjoy slogging across hill and dale to attend one of Lady Crinkleton's self-congratulatory ceremonies. We all appreciate her efforts but I do not need to act the foot soldier to prove it. I will take Lady Rosalind into my carriage and give her a cool glass of ale. Conbatten? I do not imagine she can walk in her current condition."

Having given everybody their marching orders, Lady Hightower picked up her skirts and sailed off in the direction of her carriage.

Balthazar had no recourse but to sweep Lady Rosalind into his arms and follow.

"It is very good of you to carry me, Duke," Lady Rosalind said weakly. "You did catch me so quickly, it was very brave."

"Was it?" he said.

"Of course, had I not fallen into your arms, I am certain you would have caught the thief."

"Very likely," he said.

"Naturally, a lady cannot help but to be impressed with the bravery of it all," Lady Rosalind said with a deep sigh.

Balthazar pressed his lips together lest he laugh in the face of his drooping tulip. He had wondered if he watched some sort of stage play. Now he was rather certain of it.

Lady Rosalind was so intent on gentlemen displaying their courage and bravery that she'd begun to engineer opportunities for it. Who else had been a victim of her stratagems?

He could not imagine how in the world she'd done it, though. How had she gone about hiring herself a thief?

They reached Lady Hightower's carriage and Balthazar placed Lady Rosalind gently on a seat.

"You can stay upright, Lady Rosalind?" Lady Hightower asked. "I am certain you can if you put the effort into it."

Seeing that Lady Hightower insisted on it, Lady Rosalind *was* able to keep herself upright.

Of course she was, the little minx.

"Very good, Conbatten," Lady Hightower said. "You may be off."

"I bid adieu to my rescuer," Lady Rosalind said in a faint breathy voice.

Balthazar bowed. He closed the carriage door, turned, and got some way from the carriage before he allowed himself to snort with laughter.

CHAPTER ELEVEN

Rosalind had very unexpectedly found herself in Lady Hightower's carriage, sipping a glass of ale.

The lady had asked her an awful lot of questions! Did she often droop like that when faced with a trying circumstance? What was her opinion on Conbatten? How long had she known the duke? What were her ideas of a lady marrying for a title?

In between all the inquiries, she'd waved that awful vinaigrette under her nose.

Rosalind had answered the lady very vaguely, except for the last question. That one she answered very strongly—nobody was to imagine that Lady Rosalind Bennington cared anything for titles. Other young ladies might consider it good sense, but she viewed holding a title over love as the most foolish thing in the world.

Lady Hightower had seemed pleased to hear it, though Rosalind found the lady otherwise rather inscrutable.

Except for Lady Hightower's sudden appearance and having to leave Conbatten's arms for the lady's carriage, the plan had come off without a hitch.

She'd found herself in Conbatten's arms, and glorious arms they were. It had been heaven to collapse into them.

The memory of that had taken up all her thoughts until she was once more in her own carriage and on the way home.

She could not speak to her sisters about anything that had

happened, as Darden had insisted on riding with them.

As her brother went on and on about how Conbatten had handled the whole circumstance with such aplomb and how he really must seriously consider inviting him into the YBC on account of it, Rosalind's thoughts began to be less on Conbatten's arms and more on his words.

Or rather, lack of words.

Why, after she'd informed him in the clearest possible terms that he'd satisfied her requirement for courage and bravery, had he not declared his love for her?

What was he waiting for?

Rosalind once more got that sick feeling that perhaps he did not feel as she did.

But then, how could it be so? Why would the fates use her in such a manner?

It did not seem possible. Did he not always make a point of coming straight to her when they found themselves in the same sphere?

In all of the workings of the plan for a pickpocket to rob her, that had been the one piece of it that she had not been certain how to work out. How to be sure he was nearby and not off with another party and being distracted by them.

She'd not needed to arrange that bit of business at all. He'd come right to her on his arrival.

Her aunt had helpfully waved so that he might see them, and then he'd come straight over.

Finally, they arrived back to the house. Darden was still talking but, blessedly, her aunt interrupted him.

"I do think Rosalind still seems pale, Lord Darden."

"Oh, yes, of course, poor Rosalind," Darden said, seeming to finally remember that that situation had not *only* involved Conbatten.

"I think we shall take Rosalind above stairs and order a tea tray. Tea is always very reviving," Miss Mayton said.

"And we will keep her company while she revives," Juliet

said.

"Of course we will," Viola said.

"We will be right by your side, Rosalind," Cordelia said.

"I will help you up the stairs, Rosalind," Darden said.

"There is no need, Lord Darden," her aunt said. "We can manage very well. In any case, I am certain you wish to be off to your club to report the extraordinary events of the day."

Darden nodded vigorously. "That is true," he said. "The members must all hear of Conbatten."

THANKS TO MISS Mayton's good management, the sisters were secluded in Rosalind's bedchamber with a generous tray of biscuits and a pot of tea. There had been much assurance made to the earl that Rosalind was quite recovered and no damage done, she was only tired.

"Do say what is wrong, Rosalind," Cordelia said. "From my view, the thing went off wonderfully."

"Oh yes, our plan came off," Rosalind said. "But Conbatten did not declare himself. I made certain he understood that he had met my requirement as he carried me to Lady Hightower's carriage, but he said nothing."

"Perhaps it was too much of a surprise," Miss Mayton said. "After all, it was only *us* that were expecting a pickpocket. He knew nothing about it."

"He did not seem overcome with surprise, though," Rosalind said.

"What precisely did he say to you while he carried you to Lady Hightower's carriage?" Juliet asked. "It looked terribly romantic."

"It should have been everything romantic," Rosalind said, "and yet, he said so little!"

"What did he say, my dear," Miss Mayton asked.

"Well," Rosalind said, thinking back, "I said it was very brave to catch me as quickly as he did and he said, was it? Then I said that if he had not had to catch me, he would have set off after the thief. He said that was very likely. Then I said, very clearly, that I was impressed with his bravery and he said nothing at all!"

Slow tears had begun to roll down Rosalind's cheeks, as the more she thought back on it, the more a heaviness gripped her heart. He had not been at all as she'd thought he would be.

"I think I may have been wrong," she said. "I know I said I would not wilt, but I feel very wilted just now. I'm feeling exceedingly…unrequited."

Rosalind's sisters hopped on the bed and surrounded her. Finding herself enveloped in arms everywhere, all sorts of nice things whispered in her ear, and handkerchiefs dabbed at her eyes, she took a deep breath.

"Oh dear, what am I to do?" she whispered.

"Now, there, my love," her aunt said, "there is no reason to despair. It occurs to me that men are the less…perceptive sex. I think we have only been too subtle for him to comprehend."

"Really?" Rosalind asked. "A pickpocket was too subtle?"

"It appears so," Miss Mayton said. "I have been very foolish not to see it after all the experience I have."

"Do explain, Aunt," Viola said.

"Let us just examine the facts," Miss Mayton said, "Did not Phillipe hang himself because he did not have the foresight to wait until morning to hear if I received his note? Did not my Transylvanian duke mope about for years thinking I might come back and then when I very coincidentally ran into him again, throw himself off the castle walls? Did Hans perceive that his love could not be requited when I would not hold his hand? If he had, might he have stopped his growing love and not had to throw himself over the side of an Alpine cliff?"

"She makes sense, Rosalind," Cordelia said. "Men are not as clever as one would hope. I have a mind to make my own requirement physical strength and then my gentleman can leave the thinking to me."

"Examine the facts, my dear," Miss Mayton said. "Whenever we are in range of the duke, does he not come straight to you?"

"He does, I have noted it myself," Rosalind said.

"And does he not seem to hang on your every word?"

"I suppose so, at least it seems so."

"And most importantly, does he pay any other woman that sort of attention?"

Rosalind dried her eyes. She had not considered that aspect of things. He did not seek out any other woman. Only her. That much she was sure of.

"And finally, do you suppose it was a coincidence that you said we would go to Madame Tussaud's exhibition and then he turns up too?"

"That is so much evidence!" Juliet said.

"Our aunt must be right, Rosalind," Viola said.

"If you *are* right, Aunt, what are we to do?"

Miss Mayton tapped her chin. "We will have to think on it. Whatever it is, it must be a deal more direct."

"We'll think of something, Rosalind," Juliet said, patting her arm. "We always do."

"While we think," Miss Mayton said, "we ought to send flowers to Lady Hightower. She was very good to lend her carriage. Had she not, there would not have been the opportunity to be carried in the duke's arms."

Rosalind nodded. "You are right and I shall write a very nice note and not mention that vinaigrette at all."

⇶⫷

BALTHAZAR HAD LEFT the park and faced the wrath of Henri over the state of his clothes. After being apprised of the nature of the assault on fabric—plates and glasses thrown in the air on account of a pickpocket—Henri had pronounced the Bennington household an enemy to fine tailoring. And, therefore, *his* enemy.

He'd since sent a note to Lady Hightower to thank her for her assistance in the park and she'd responded with an invitation to dine. He was more than happy to pass up Mrs. Jenson's rout in favor of the peace of Lady Hightower's dining room.

She'd fed him an excellent dinner and, as was her habit, they'd spent their time at table discussing literature.

Balthazar was always amused at how bored Bellforce looked over it. He imagined the butler thought other butlers listened to scandalous gossip at table and all he got was information on the latest Royal Society paper.

Now though, the drawing room door was closed and brandy poured for both of them. This was always the moment when Lady Hightower got to business and he expected nothing less now. It was too coincidental that she wished to spend an evening with him just after the events in the park.

"Conbatten," she said, "I usually find my eyes very reliable. I see what I see. But there are occasions when I am not altogether certain of what I saw. First, I imagine I've seen one thing, and then I begin to think perhaps I have seen another."

Balthazar nodded, perfectly understanding her meaning. "You wonder precisely what it was that took place in the park this afternoon."

"Do *you* wonder about it?"

He nodded. "I do."

"I saw the whole thing you know. I had my eye on that scoundrel who made off with Lady Rosalind's handkerchief as he was quite obviously scanning the crowd. Then he raced to her when there were other potential victims far closer. I thought, why her? Later, I began to wonder about her tugging the brim of her bonnet and her sisters' seeming lack of surprise."

"You wondered if the tugs had been a signal," Balthazar said. "She was tugging like mad—I thought maybe a hairpin was digging into her head."

"But if it was not a hairpin, if somehow that farce was planned…"

"Lady Rosalind has made it abundantly clear that she expects any gentleman in her sphere to be ready to prove his bravery at a moment's notice," he said. "I believe she has now taken to engineering opportunities for such a display."

Lady Hightower's expression could not be read. Very suddenly, she roared with laughter.

"Oh goodness, that is too funny," she said, gasping for air.

"I was rather amused myself," Balthazar said with a smile.

She pointed to a vase of flowers. "Lady Rosalind sent them." She reached for a small card on the table and handed it to him. "The note."

He opened it.

Dearest Lady Hightower,

I and my entire family thank you for assisting me at my darkest hour.

Rosalind Bennington

"Her darkest hour," Lady Hightower said with a snort of amusement. "A person has not been on the earth very long if *that* was the darkest hour."

"She is rather dramatic, only rivaling my valet when he got a look at my clothes," Balthazar said.

"Poor Henri, did he threaten to throw himself into the Arno again?"

"And the Thames."

"What are you going to do about it?"

"Do about Henri?"

"Do about Lady Rosalind. This display, this playacting in the park, was set up for *your* eyes."

"I hadn't planned to do anything about it. I imagine Lady Rosalind will be subjecting other gentlemen to the same treatment. I do not believe I have been singled out."

"Oh you don't believe it? What were her parting words to you? Something highly ridiculous along the lines of, *Adieu, my brave rescuer.*"

Balthazar laughed despite himself. "I did think that was a

particularly inspired bit of nonsense."

"I asked her a lot of questions in the carriage and was able to ascertain one thing at least—she is not at all interested in marrying for a title."

"No, she never would be. She has not the temperament for such cool calculations."

"Just so. Therefore, it is you she is interested in. Not your title, not your standing, not your money. You, the person. Now, I find this young lady rather bizarre, but she has two things going for her—she entirely lacks sophisticated artifice and she likes *you*."

Balthazar set down his brandy. "Are you suggesting—"

"I am suggesting you examine your heart and see where you are. That is all."

Though Lady Hightower said that was all, it was actually quite a lot.

He had of course had a passing thought that had it been the right time for marriage, Lady Rosalind could certainly be a rather pleasant choice. More than pleasant, really. He'd not allowed his thoughts to go further, as it was not the right time for marriage. Though, sometimes they'd gone further of their own accord.

That marvelous hair, and her upturned face, and hazel eyes. And then, it was always so interesting to talk to her. It never felt constrained, as it so often did with other ladies.

He sometimes had the urge to loosen one of her curls and twist it round his finger. He had perhaps even allowed his thoughts to wander to if she would like to join him in a ninety-eight-degree bath with glasses of champagne. She was an irresistible creature.

However, it was definitely not the right time for marriage.

He'd laid out the facts very clearly for himself. A wife would be handwringing at the door every time he left on the queen's business. At first, it would be a mystery where he was going, dressed in black. Then her imagination would take flight and he would be accused of keeping a mistress or engaging himself in nefarious activities.

Eventually, he would have to tell her the truth to stop her from weeping or throwing things at his head. Then she would tell someone and the news would fly out the door like a murmuration of starlings at dusk. Finally, she would demand that he stop his forays into Rats' Castle.

She'd not be wrong in any of it, he'd not be wrong in any of it, and the queen would be enraged that her secret was out. Therefore, it was not the right time.

Especially not now, when it appeared the Mondrian was not dead after all and was currently building a mammoth housebreaking operation.

But then, Lady Rosalind was not exactly like the composite of the woman he'd had in his head. Despite her dramatic faint into his arms, she seemed rather stalwart. In truth, he doubted she'd ever fainted in her life. She was not the sort for handwringing or weeping.

And somehow, she'd managed to hire herself a pickpocket.

"All I say is, now that you are apprised to what lengths Lady Rosalind will go on your behalf, perhaps look at her with new eyes. I do not like to imagine what she might try next," Lady Hightower said. "She is frighteningly enterprising."

"I cannot think there will be a next," Balthazar said.

"Who knows? Maybe she'll decide to hire an army of pickpockets and run through handkerchiefs by the dozen," Lady Hightower said.

Balthazar drained his brandy over that thought.

"Now, I will kiss your forehead and you can be off while this old bat goes to bed."

Balthazar took his leave. He also decided that, on the off-chance Lady Rosalind was planning to hire an army of pickpockets to steal her handkerchiefs, he would send her a dozen embroidered.

After all, it did not say anything in particular. It was only a gentlemanly response to a lady's self-proclaimed *darkest hour*.

He found himself laughing all the way home.

>>>——<<<

TATTLETON PACED HIS quarters. There might be some individuals with a less incisive mind than his own that believed in coincidences. He did not.

It was his experience that when one viewed what might appear coincidence, if one brought a more critical evaluation of the circumstance to bear, one would discover it was not a coincidence at all.

Was it ever a coincidence that fires were started in the house at the same time that Lady Cordelia was leaping around lit candles as Desdemona? No, it was not.

Was it a coincidence when they had four young cats in the house last season and then suddenly it was discovered that some sort of animal had been into Cook's icing for a cake? No, of course it was them.

Perhaps it was only a coincidence that he'd overheard the ladies of the house mention a pickpocket, and then Lady Rosalind was accosted by a pickpocket.

He was very afraid it was not, though.

But if it was not, that would mean that the young ladies had some foreknowledge of Lady Rosalind's handkerchief flying out of her pocket. If they had foreknowledge of it, then it would mean they had arranged it.

That, of course, made no sense. One does not arrange to have oneself robbed. Nobody in the world had ever arranged to have themselves robbed. Even if one were to locate such a deranged individual who might arrange a robbery, Tattleton was certain to his bones that the deranged individual would not be a young lady.

And yet, had they not been in conference with Shrimps? If anybody in their sphere were to know a pickpocket, it must be him. Shrimps had probably been a pickpocket himself.

And had not that duke they talked about all the time, Conbatten, been nearby when the pickpocket had struck? Could he have been in on it too?

His instincts so rarely steered him wrong and his instincts were telling him that Lady Rosalind had wished to be robbed and then somehow found a way to be robbed.

But why?

If it were true, what were Shrimps' and the duke's involvement in it?

And even more spine-chilling, what was to come next?

As if he did not have enough to worry about! Those eight creatures below stairs were beginning to open their eyes. Sixteen beady eyes staring blankly. He could only imagine what they thought about. How to destroy the place, probably.

It would not be long before their legs started working and then, as far as he could see it, all would be lost.

CHAPTER TWELVE

ROSALIND HAD BEEN up in the middle of the night with a rather inspired idea. It had come to her suddenly, and she could not sleep for thinking of it. She had spent hours working out precisely how it could be done.

Now she and her sisters lingered in the breakfast room. She could hardly wait to tell them all.

"Tattleton," she said, looking meaningfully at her sisters and her aunt, "we will stay in here with our tea for a bit, but we do not require anything else."

The butler nodded, though he looked strangely worried about the idea of them lingering.

He retreated with the footmen and shut the door behind him.

"Poor Tattleton seems so nervous these days," Juliet said. "Do you suppose he worries over the health of Bess' pups? He shouldn't do, they are all getting on very well, but he does have such a soft heart."

"I am sure that must be it, my dear," Miss Mayton said, still working her way through a pile of toast.

"I've had an idea," Rosalind said.

Her sisters leaned forward. Miss Mayton set down her toast.

"What if some gentleman, some until now unknown person, a baron from the countryside, was to challenge Conbatten for my love?"

"That would be rather marvelous, but where are we to dig up

a baron willing to challenge the duke?" Juliet asked.

"He would not be real," Rosalind said.

"That's too bad—I should like to meet a baron willing to fight the duke," Cordelia said.

"So there would be no actual duel," Miss Mayton said. "Just the idea of one."

"Exactly," Rosalind said.

"Very sensible," her aunt said, nodding.

"You wish to have Conbatten accept the duel, though there is no duel," Viola said.

"Yes, we could invent some fellow from the countryside who has always been in love with me and has now followed me to London. He will challenge the duke and if Conbatten accepts, then I will know he truly loves me."

"And the duke will know that he has satisfied your requirement and can go ahead and declare himself," Cordelia said. "He must realize it—what could be more brave than a duel?"

Miss Mayton nodded her approval. "It certainly would be direct enough to penetrate his understanding. Though, we still must find a person to stand in for this lovestruck baron."

"I was thinking," Rosalind said, "that we look for a stand-in for the baron's *second*. The second need not look like a person willing to fight the duke."

"No, indeed," Miss Mayton said. "A second very sensibly stays out of those sorts of things."

"All the second need do is look like a man, deliver a written challenge, and wait for a verbal acceptance. The second need not even enter the house, but could stay on the street, inside a carriage, so he would not be viewed too closely."

"Do you suppose our pickpocket would do it?" Viola asked. "We could lend him the right clothes and hire a carriage."

"No, that won't work," Rosalind said, because of course that very idea had occurred to her during the night. "He won't have the right accent for a countryside baron or be able to carry himself with the right authority. The footman who took the note would notice, I'm sure."

"Wait a moment," Miss Mayton said, "you mentioned the second only need *look* like a man."

"Yes!"

"Well now, I suppose I could, if I were to get hold of the right clothes and pull a hat very low and stay in the carriage," Miss Mayton said. "Naturally, it would be unusual, but it *is* in the name of love. I could very easily lower my voice, say as little as possible, and sound very gruff."

"That is what I thought!" Rosalind said.

"It is rather genius," Juliet said.

"We could borrow some of Darden's clothes and make adjustments," Cordelia said.

Miss Mayton looked at her pile of toast, and then at her ever-expanding mid-section. "Or perhaps the earl's?" she said.

"Oh, yes, Papa's would do better," Viola said.

"He should not miss them, I do not think," Rosalind said. "Though he gets new tailoring every year, he holds on to the last year's just in case."

"And since Aunt will be in a carriage," Cordelia said, "all that will be needed is a shirt, neckcloth, waistcoat, and coat."

"And the hat," Viola said.

"Also, very bushy sideburns to cover her face," Juliet said. "We could snip off some fur from Bess, she shan't mind it."

"And glue it on," Rosalind said. "We could write out the challenge and so all Aunt would have to do is call a footman forward and say, 'This must be delivered to the duke at once. I will wait for an answer.'"

"This must be delivered to the duke at once," Miss Mayton said in a gravelly voice. "I will wait for his answer."

"Oh that's very good," Juliet said. "The footman will never know anything is amiss. He will be too busy thinking about the note that must be delivered at once."

"Then there is only the carriage to think about," Miss Mayton said. "We'll have to see how one goes about hiring one."

"We need not, though," Rosalind said. "Father's carriages have the coat of arms only on the right side. If we direct the carriage to approach the house from the left it could not be seen."

"What about Sandren?" Cordelia asked. "If we take our own carriage, he will be driving. He shan't like it, I do not think."

"We could tell him it is a game," Rosalind said, having already thought of how to get around the coachman. "We can say a Mrs. Ellington has set us all off on something she calls a goose chase. We are given clues and hints and must follow them to the letter. If we are successful at each stop, we finally reach her house and receive a prize. Then, after we leave Conbatten, we say we did not get the right answer and so must go home."

"That sounds wonderfully fun," Juliet said. "I wish there really was a Mrs. Ellington with such a good idea."

"Once we receive his answer, that he *will* meet my baron at dawn, we tell Sandren to speed away and around a corner," Rosalind said, the delightful scene playing out in her mind.

"But what then?" Viola asked. "You will have named the place and time for the duel and he will go and nobody will be there."

"He will think the baron has thought better of it and run back to the countryside," Rosalind said.

"And then he will come straight to the house and tell you that he's gone to meet the baron at dawn and the fellow never turned up," Juliet said. "*That* is the moment he will declare himself."

"I have to think so," Rosalind said. "I do not see why he would wait until the afternoon."

"Then we must all be up very early on the appointed day," Cordelia said. "You would not want the duke banging on the door and demanding admittance while you are still in curl papers and a nightdress."

"Good thinking, Cordelia," Rosalind said. "Now, we must just put this plan in motion!"

"You really have thought of everything, my dear," Miss Mayton said. "I do not see any aspect of it that could go wrong."

Rosalind sighed. Surely, this would do it. A man willing to fight at dawn for her must be a man who loved her *and* realized he'd displayed his bravery enough to declare himself.

The door to the breakfast room suddenly swung open, startling them all.

The earl came in waving a paper. "My old friend Lord Cannerly, you remember I met him at Almack's? He is having a dinner on the morrow. He's invited me, Rosalind, Darden, and you too, Miss Mayton."

BALTHAZAR PONDERED THE note that had just come from Hamill.

Conbatten—

We have discovered why Mondrian, and I am now convinced it is in fact Mondrian, has been searching birth records. He looks for a lad of seven or eight years named Henry whose birth would have been recorded in one of the poorer parishes. The surname remains unknown, but this Henry seems to be a high value target that can be used for something.

My guess is that this is why Mondrian's housebreaking operation has included making off with personal correspondence. He was hoping to uncover a scandal of some sort, and now he has done. I assume it is a child out of wedlock or one born with physical or mental deficiencies. If the child can be found, then the blackmail can commence.

This particular information Mondrian has got hold of was somehow uncovered in Kent, though we are not quite clear how or what house it was taken from. Though, it does indicate that Mondrian is on the trail of something he deems profitable if he has expanded operations outside of London.

Hamill.

That put a new wrinkle on things. Of course it must be Mondrian—your average thief did not have the wherewithal to search birth records nor know what to do with a letter outlining an out of wedlock pregnancy or a child born with an incurable malady. Mondrian understood who was who in society and what could be had with the right information in his pocket.

Mondrian also understood that the stolen letter as proof would not be enough, anybody could forge such a thing. No, he wished to get his hands on the boy, and likely prayed the boy was still alive and had not fallen prey to a childhood illness.

If the child were the offspring of a high-placed person, they would not have remained in the parish they were registered in.

An out of wedlock child would likely have been moved to the countryside somewhere and placed with respectable people. His school fees and upkeep would be paid through a solicitor. The boy would always be aware of the mystery of his past, but he would never discover the truth of it. Rather, he would go on to a trade of some sort, or perhaps become a schoolmaster or solicitor or physician.

If the child were afflicted with a physical or mental disability, then he was likely residing in one of the many private institutions set up to receive such children.

Whoever was involved in this, they would sleep well believing they'd done what was right. It was distasteful in the extreme, but not uncommon.

They would sleep a deal less well when they were black-mailed, though.

Balthazar had mixed feelings about working to thwart the matter. On the one hand, Mondrian must be stopped. On the other, a gentleman causing such a circumstance and farming its result out to somebody else to raise perhaps ought to be made to feel some pain over it. Or a lot of pain over it.

His cousin, Viscount Harebly, had been born with a terribly curved spine. He'd died of pneumonia at the age of twenty-three, but he had at least died at home. His father, the earl, had wished to place him in an institution as a baby. The countess had refused.

Though it was not talked about, and Balthazar only knew what had occurred from his father, when the earl attempted to take the boy, the countess had stopped him at the nursery door with a loaded fowling piece. She informed him that should he choose to take the boy when she was not there to protect him, the earl could be assured of being murdered in his bed.

That had been the end of the debate.

The countess had been right, of course. Harebly never rode a horse or boxed a match, but he was a keen mind and had been a great intellectual. He'd made vast improvements to his estate, leaving his younger brother in a very secure footing.

Henri bustled into his bedchamber carrying a coat and a box. "If you wish to wear the blue coat to Lord Cannerly's dinner, I believe I have rescued it from its recent state of assault. I am being optimistic that the garment will be safer there than it was at Lady Hightower's musical evening."

Balthazar laughed and said, "I daresay it will be safe enough to wear to Lord Cannerly's dinner."

Lord Cannerly had a neighboring estate in Essex and had been great friends with his father. He was a jolly old fellow and Balthazar liked him very much. He had further to recommend him that he maintained a longstanding correspondence with Lady Hightower, so she would also attend this evening.

"I only say," Henri said with a sniff, "will Mrs. Whirlwind of Crumbs be attending? I should like to know if this superb Italian wool is set to walk into imminent danger."

Balthazar did not have the first idea of whether Miss Mayton would attend. At Almack's, it had seemed as if Lord Cannerly had been delighted to encounter the earl.

He supposed it was a possibility. Then of course, if the earl and Miss Mayton were to come, Lady Rosalind probably would too.

Balthazar wondered what the chances were. If she did come, he wondered if he would be seated nearby.

Though, he really ought to stop wondering about such

things.

It was very hard to do, though.

As he did not answer Henri's wish to know if his coat were to walk into danger, his valet said, "The box of handkerchiefs for Lady Rosalind has come. The fabric is the finest lawn and the embroidery is superb. Though, Signor Ribaldi no doubt wonders why he is making ladies' handkerchiefs now."

"I suspect it is *you* who are wondering."

Balthazar took the box and opened it. The material was in fact the best. The embroidery was stitched very close and fine— two corners had a charming scene of the park's northwest enclosure and the other two that of the keeper's lodge. It was the very scene that had been the stage for Lady Rosalind's *darkest hour* in the face of a pickpocket. In the center were her initials—RB.

He laughed despite himself.

"Perhaps Henri does wonder over this," his valet said.

Balthazar presumed he was very put out about it, as when Henri referred to himself in that manner, as if he were King Louis, he generally was.

He walked to the desk and wrote out a note to accompany the box.

Lady Rosalind—

I pray you are sufficiently recovered from what surely must have been a terrible shock. Please allow this small offering to replace what was torn from you on that fateful day in the park. Conbatten.

Now, he positively guffawed.

"If only Henri could amuse his duke so well," his valet muttered.

"Not until you begin hiring pickpockets to rob you," Balthazar said.

He could see perfectly well that Henri did not know what to make of that. Who *would* know? It was entirely too absurd.

Though, it touched him in some way, too.

"WELL," MISS MAYTON said, as Lynette helped Rosalind into her dress, "it is very apparent that the duke cannot stop thinking of you being robbed in the park. Did you notice that the four corners of the handkerchiefs are embroidered with the very place it occurred?"

"I did indeed," Rosalind said, putting her arms through the sleeves. It was a lovely green silk and she'd almost hesitated in wearing it. It was the sort of dress she would wish Conbatten to see her in and there was no chance of that tonight.

Lord Cannerly's dinner was to be a small one, with only fourteen invited. They already made up four and Rosalind suspected the others would be as she was—a member of a family that had longstanding ties to the lord, just as her father did.

But then, Viola had pointed out that as so few people would see the dress, she might wear it again soon. She might wear it sometime when Conbatten would be able to view it.

"I suspect," her aunt said, "that he wishes these handkerchiefs to remind you of him carrying you to Lady Hightower's carriage."

"Do you think so?" Rosalind said, spinning round and annoying Lynette, who was trying to button her up.

Over the lady's maid's sigh, Miss Mayton said, "I cannot think what else he means by it."

The door flew open and Viola, Cordelia, and Juliet streamed in. "We've been sent to hurry you, Rosalind," Cordelia said.

"Darden is toe-tapping, Father is fretting that you will arrive late, and Sandren has been outside for ten minutes. You know how Sandren gets about his horses standing round waiting," Juliet added.

The sisters all looked to Lynette, who huffed and said, "Dressing goes very much faster when somebody is not twisting and turning all the time."

"Oh Rosalind, do be still for Lynette," Viola said.

Lynette gave a grateful glance to Viola and finished the buttons. She gave Rosalind's hair a few more adjustments and stepped back. "Done," she said.

The sisters and Miss Mayton all left the room together and flew down the stairs.

After much waving and wishing good luck, the carriage set off.

Rosalind leaned back in the carriage and said, "Goodness, that was a rush."

"Never mind it, my dear," the earl said, satisfied that they were finally on their way. "Sandren knows London roads like the back of his own hand and will get us there in good time."

"I wonder who else will attend the dinner," Rosalind said. "Darden, is there not some lady you wish to see?"

"Me? No! Well, as you know, my time is so very taken up just now…"

Though the interior of the carriage was dim, Rosalind was certain her brother had gone all shades of red. Beatrice was convinced that Darden wished to put off marriage until the last possible moment and she was beginning to think her sister was right.

"Darden knows his duty," the earl said. "He shan't let us down. While we wait for the lady he will walk through life with, I will employ myself by imagining the delights of grandchildren all round."

Darden did not answer, and Rosalind supposed he hoped that imagining grandchildren would be enough for his father for the time being.

"Perhaps there will be some fellow for you there, Rosalind," Darden said in an obvious bid to get off the subject of what he had been doing, or not doing, regarding his future prospects. "Perhaps that fellow you saw on horseback and fell in love with that we keep waiting to find out about."

"One never knows, of course," the earl said, "though he is

beginning to seem like a phantom. Perhaps that gentleman has been called out of Town."

"Perhaps," Rosalind said, glancing at Miss Mayton.

"Well, you shall not be entirely without entertainment," the earl said. "I imagine the duke will attend and he does seem to amuse you."

"Conbatten!" Rosalind said, a deal more enthusiastically than she meant to.

"Conbatten," Darden said reverently.

"I would think so," the earl said. "They are country neighbors and it would not be very neighborly to exclude him. Of course, I should not speak so precipitously. The duke likely has many engagements on his calendar and this invitation was rather last minute. He may had been invited, but that does not mean he will come."

Rosalind shivered at the very idea of it. She had not for a moment thought there was a chance that Conbatten would be met with tonight.

Her aunt reached for her hand and squeezed it. She squeezed tightly back.

If only he did not have so many invitations! If the fates were on her side, this would be a night he did not have any plans and he had accepted Lord Cannerly's gracious and neighborly invitation.

Goodness, she had been thinking of this dinner as only a duty to her father. Now she was feeling very kindly disposed toward Lord Cannerly, the dear old fellow.

CHAPTER THIRTEEN

BALTHAZAR WAS DELIGHTED to find Lady Worthington in Lord Cannerly's drawing room. He'd quite forgot that Cannerly had been a mentor of sorts to her late husband. Cannerly was such a good old fellow, of course he would wish to include Lady Worthington. He would not wish to think of a poor widow being forgotten about.

Of course, there was nothing particularly poor about the widowed Lady Worthington. She'd come through her mourning period and came out the other side her same gay and witty self.

Lord and Lady Mendover were also in attendance, and they were pleasant enough. They had brought along their daughter, Miss Jenson, who he considered a rather insipid specimen.

The young lady was pale in the extreme—pale skin, pale blue eyes with red rims, lashes so pale they could hardly be seen, and lifeless straw-colored hair. All of that could easily be overlooked, after all it was only a matter of taste, but her conversation seemed formed to match her looks and was equally pale.

She appeared especially pale standing nearby Lady Worthington, who was all vigor and life.

An old fellow named Lord Bentley from their neighborhood in Essex was there and Balthazar was surprised to see him as he did not realize the man was in Town.

He was an irascible creature who liked to challenge every idea. If one said the sun was bright, Lord Bentley would wonder if it had not been brighter on other days.

Lord Marlrymple and Lady Felicia were also in attendance and Balthazar was not surprised. They seemed to be everywhere together these days. It was presumed that the spinster and the widower were to be a match someday soon.

They were still missing four people and Balthazar had restrained himself from asking who they were. He was discomfited to examine how much he hoped Lady Rosalind was among them.

Somehow, Lady Hightower's counsel to examine his own heart would not leave his thoughts. He understood that his reasons for not considering marriage at this time were full of good sense.

However, other ideas that might be of equal sense had begun to present themselves. He was drawn to Lady Rosalind as he had been to no other lady, he could not deny that. If he were not carefully monitoring the direction of his thoughts, they often ran in her direction.

She was a stunningly beautiful and interesting lady. Not to mention original. There would not be a string of others like her coming to Town.

Was that not something to think about? What was he to do when he was ready to marry and there was not a Lady Rosalind in sight?

And then, the even darker idea of what *her* future would hold. She was not a lady who would drift from season to season. She would be snapped up as soon as a gentleman could manage it.

That vile gentleman, whoever he was.

How was he to like it then? Seeing Lady Rosalind as Lord Whoever's bride?

He would not like it. He had to face that fact.

So, he supposed the real question was did he dare place his own inclinations over that of the queen's? That was a question he could not yet answer, and until he could his hands were tied.

There was a commotion at the drawing room doors…and there she was.

Looking very smashing in a dark green silk, too.

Miss Mayton waved wildly in his direction. He pressed his lips together to stop from laughing.

Lady Worthington said, "Goodness, who is that alarming creature?"

"That is Miss Mayton and she is indeed alarming," he said. "She is a spinster in widow's weeds, is prone to saying off-putting and wildly inappropriate things, and I believe she has been a very unsteady guide to Lord Westmont's daughters."

"I see," Lady Worthington said, "I missed the eldest's debut last season, I assume that young lady just now coming in with the unsteady Miss Mayton is daughter number two. Darden has often mentioned his five sisters at home. Goodness, he is looking well."

"Do I detect some interest in Lord Darden, Lady Worthington?" Balthazar asked.

"No, you do not, you devil," she said laughing. "It is too soon for me to think of such things, and he is a little too boyish. I am sure he will age well, though. His father is a handsome old gentleman."

The family in question now approached, led by the intrepid Miss Mayton.

"Your Grace," Miss Mayton said, barreling forward, "we are still all aflutter about the attack in the park, though we do not forget your daring assistance."

"Miss Mayton," Balthazar said, determined to ignore the ludicrous reference to his daring assistance, "Lady Rosalind, allow me to introduce you to Lady Worthington. Earl, Darden, I believe you already know the lady."

"Indeed we do," the earl said. "I am glad to see you looking so well Lady Worthington."

Lady Worthington nodded graciously. "Now what is this I hear about an attack in the park?" she asked.

"It was nothing at all," the earl said. "Some young cur made off with my daughter's handkerchief."

"But it was not nothing, Father!" Lady Rosalind said. "It was very violent and the duke stepped in so bravely. That must be remembered."

"Indeed," Miss Mayton said, "we all witnessed the bravery. It was really something."

Balthazar felt he was very near losing the ability to control his laughter. The bravery, indeed.

This was made worse by Lady Worthington's raised brow. The lady was astute and not likely to believe in the frightening violence of losing one's handkerchief. He must just hope no mention was made of the circumstance being named as Lady Rosalind's *darkest hour.*

"His Grace was on hand at Lady Rosalind's darkest hour," Miss Mayton said, nodding.

Balthazar turned and coughed to hide his hilarity.

Thankfully, Lord Cannerly's butler found that fortunate moment to signal that the party was ready to go through.

It seemed Lady Hightower was to act as Lord Cannerly's hostess. "Conbatten, do take in Lady Rosalind. Lord Bentley, do the honors with Miss Mayton, if you would be so good."

And so, Lady Hightower paired off the couples, one by one.

Balthazar was certain she had a fine time doing it, too. He was not unaware that she'd very purposely paired him with Lady Rosalind. He could not say he was sorry over it, though.

Darden had been saddled with Miss Jenson. Lord Mendover would take in Lady Worthington, while the earl would guide Lady Mendover. Lord Marlrymple and Lady Felicia would go in together, naturally.

It was all done expertly and to everyone's satisfaction. That was, except Lord Bentley, who was never satisfied with anything.

Just wait until you actually talk to Miss Mayton, old fellow. Then you will really have something to complain about.

SHRIMPS HAD PAID off Barney and he had been very glad to see the last of the ten-pound purse that had been living under his mattress. He'd worried about it night and day. What if it were stolen? How would he ever explain it? Nobody would believe a wretch like him and he'd be off to the Old Bailey.

He'd also been glad to see the last of Barney. That fellow had seemed a little surprised that the handkerchief stealing had come off without a hitch and that there actually was ten pounds to be paid.

At least, he'd thought he'd seen the last of Barney.

But tonight, Barney had been back, waiting for him in the garden.

Why did Oyster have to go out at night? He didn't know, but he'd tried skipping it once and what he found on the floor the next morning had taken a lot of cleaning up. Cook claimed he could smell it all the way in the kitchens and if it happened again the dog would have to go.

So, there was nothing for it. They had to go out before settling in for the night.

If only Oyster did not need to make a full circle of the garden, sniffing at everything! He'd tried telling Oyster that there was no purpose to it, that it was the same shrubs as yesterday and the day before, but he would not be convinced.

Barney had come up behind him, silent as a ghost. Shrimps had almost jumped out of his clothes.

"It's only me, old mate," Barney had said with a laugh.

"What do you want?" Shrimps asked. "I gave you all the money."

"I ain't looking for money this time," Barney said. "I'm lookin' for information."

"I don't have information!" Shrimps whispered. "Nobody has less information than me! I can't even read."

"One of the bosses was wondering, what's your real name?"

Shrimps shuddered. His mother had told him that nobody must know it. He knew his given name, and she said his full name was contained in the letter sewn in his coat. But nobody must know it until he delivered the letter to some people in Kent. He was to find the Seven Oaks and ask to be directed to the Conroys.

Of course, he did not know how to get to Kent and he was not certain it would have been a good idea anyway. His mother had been delirious when she was giving him all those instructions. Most of it had sounded like she was dreaming or something.

Even if he knew how to get to Kent and even if it did seem like a good idea to go there, he would never be so stupid as to give up his current situation.

"You know my name is Shrimps," he said.

"I been told Shrimps ain't the sort of name what would be put down in a record. There's got to be another name. Like Johnny or Frederick or…Henry."

Shrimps felt the blood drain from his face. He knew himself to be Henry, but why did Barney want to know it?

"I've only ever been called Shrimps except when I was sick, then me mum called me Jimmy dear," he said, trying to sound as confident as possible.

"Jimmy, eh?" Barney said skeptically. "And the last name?"

"Black," he said. It was the name his mother had used, though she'd told him it was made up. She never had said the real one, as she'd been afraid he might tell it someday, as children were terrible at keeping secrets.

"Jimmy Black?" Barney said. "Not Henry Conroy?"

"I never heard of that person," Shrimps said. He was feeling worse and worse about this. His name was Henry and he was supposed to *find* the Conroys.

"You got anything written down that says your name is Jimmy Black?" Barney asked threateningly.

"Like what?" Shrimps asked, trying to sound like Barney had asked him a stupid question. "Do you think people write me letters? I don't know anybody who would write me a letter and I couldn't read it if I got it!"

"Ya better not be lyin' about it," Barney said.

"Why would I lie about my name?" Shrimps said. "I didn't do a crime, if that's what you think."

"Do a crime?" Barney said, laughing. "What crime would that be? The crime of being the worst pickpocket in London? Now listen here, the boss has sent word that he wants proof of your real name. If it is Jimmy Black, you best be able to prove it somehow. I'll be back in a week and ya better have something or else."

A light suddenly spilled out into the garden and Barney slipped behind some bushes.

Cook had opened the door and stood with a candle. "Shrimps! Tell that dog he cannot stay out all night. It's time to come inside."

"Coming!" Shrimps said. "Oyster, let's go!"

He ran into the house with the dog on his heels, leaving Barney in the garden to ponder if he were Jimmy Black or a person named Henry Conroy.

He wondered if he were Henry Conroy himself. He was Henry somebody, he knew that. And his mum had told him to go to Kent and find the Conroys.

It would add up that he was Henry Conroy, but he couldn't say what the significance of it was.

Why would Barney's bosses be looking for a Henry Conroy?

Whatever it was, it would not be good and he did not want to find out. He would stick to Jimmy Black. He just didn't know how he was to prove he was Jimmy Black.

Barney had said he'd have to prove it or else. What was the *or else*?

He hoped it wasn't going over a bridge and into the Thames.

ROSALIND HAD SMILED happily as she was led in on Conbatten's arm. It was just as it should be and Lady Hightower had been a dear to arrange it.

Apparently, Lord Cannerly had two dining rooms in his house and no breakfast room. Her father had told her that the fellow thought all rational people had their breakfast while still abed. There was not the smallest need to drag oneself downstairs for eggs.

Further, when he wished to have a small dinner, which this was and which he preferred, he did not like to have his guests in the proper dining room. Why be at a table so big that one was only constrained to talking to their immediate seatmates?

That was one point Rosalind must disagree with. She would have been immensely satisfied had she only to talk to Conbatten on her left, and then occasionally turn to Lord Marlrymple.

As it was, the table was not large, and much narrower than an average dining table.

"Now you see," Lord Cannerly said from the far end, "we are cozy as anything and will not need to shout across table should we wish to have a wide-ranging conversation among ourselves."

Rosalind was not at all interested in a wide-ranging conversation. Lady Hightower was on her end, with Lord Mendover and Lady Worthington across.

She would particularly wish Lady Worthington away. She was a young widow and there was something so confident about her. Conbatten seemed to admire it, so of course Rosalind could not admire it.

Nevertheless, she had a stage to set and she would not let Lady Worthington or anybody else get in the way.

A footman held forth a platter of roasted duck and Conbatten served it to her.

She sighed and murmured, "I wonder."

"Does something distress you about the duck, Lady Rosalind?" Conbatten asked.

"The duck? Oh dear, no. I have only let my troubled thoughts escape me. Do forgive me for it, very bad form."

"As they *have* escaped you, I rather think the cat is out of the bag, as they say," Conbatten said.

"You say I ought to unburden myself entirely?" Rosalind asked. Whether he meant so or not, she had every intention of unburdening herself.

"If you wish," the duke said.

"Well, since you would press me on it," she said, "I am troubled over a certain gentleman, a baron from my neighborhood, who is very rash. He is terribly in love with me though I have rejected him. Before I came to Town, he swore he would follow me here."

"Has he done so?"

"I cannot be sure," Rosalind said. "I have not seen him, but I get the feeling that he is here. I have felt he has been lurking around somewhere. Watching me and where I go and who I talk to. The problem is, what will he do?"

"What do you suppose he will do?"

"As I said, he is very rash. A duel with anyone he considered a rival would not be out of the question. He would probably bring his brother to act as his second."

"I see," the duke said. "So I will imagine, then, that this brother is either equally rash, or he is the younger and would not mind finding his elder brother dead on a green and he the new baron."

"Oh, I think the brother must also be rash."

"And if one were to keep an eye out for these two heroes, what would one be looking for?"

Rosalind felt a little confused over the invented baron and his brother being named heroes.

She said, "The baron is of course very handsome and strong. His brother, the second who would turn up with a challenge, if there was to be one, he is…less so. Archibald is his name. He is short. And a little fat. With a doughy complexion and very large sideburns."

"Poor Archibald. He will need to get hold of his brother's title if *that's* all he's got going for him," Conbatten said. "I imagine he is not as rash as you imagine, but is rather hoping his rash brother gets himself killed."

Rosalind glanced at the duke quizzically. Why should he worry about Archibald's motives or his prospects?

Lady Hightower interrupted their conversation. "Conbatten, I must have your thoughts. Lady Worthington says there is a wax figures display at the Lyceum that is positively fascinating. Ought we to go to it?"

"I have seen it, as have Lady Rosalind and her sisters," Conbatten said. "Certainly, Lady Hightower, if you wish to go, I will escort you there. It is very original."

"My family are great friends of Madame Tussaud," Rosalind said. "We met the lady while we traveled to London and of course promised her we would attend her at the Lyceum."

"Was not the figure of Marie Antoinette so lifelike, Lady Rosalind," Lady Worthington asked.

"Oh, well, I did not look very closely. You see, we had to rush out to take my sister Cordelia home. We had expected, well we thought…"

Rosalind trailed off. For some reason, she felt less than confident just now. It was as if everyone around her were somehow more sophisticated. Like perhaps she seemed a simpleton for rushing out of Madame Tussaud's exhibit.

"Unfortunately," Conbatten said, "the Benningtons had been under the impression that they had come to view forest scenes or wood sprites."

Lady Worthington nearly snorted with laughter. "Goodness, what a shock to be faced with dead royals instead."

"That must have been a dark hour indeed," Lady Hightower said, dabbing her napkin to her lips.

Rosalind did not answer, as she was not quite sure of their intent. Were they joking? Or making fun of her? She could not quite tell.

Whatever it was, she did not prefer it. Nor did she prefer

Lord Cannerly's overly narrow table. She would be quite satisfied if Lady Worthington would concern herself with entertaining Lord Mendover, or Darden on her other side.

There was no need to be talking across table to Conbatten.

BALTHAZAR HAD NEVER considered himself a person who laughed easily, but these days he felt like he was on the verge of laughter often.

Lady Rosalind's story about the lovesick and very rash baron was both hilarious and alarming. She was clearly plotting out some new opportunity for the gentlemen in her sphere to display their dedication and bravery.

How would it be done though? Where would she dig up a lovestruck and out of his wits baron and his short and fat brother Archibald?

He could not think she meant to try any such thing. Rather, she would go round the Town sighing and mentioning this problematic baron, waiting for someone to declare they would meet the fellow at dawn.

She was a daring and adorable creature.

Would she be daring enough, though, to be easy of mind if a husband left the house at midnight to venture into the Rats' Castle?

"I wonder, Lady Rosalind," he said cautiously, now that the other guests within hearing talked of some new play or other, "what your views might be on duty? Duty can sometimes be onerous, or even dangerous at times."

"If it is a duty," Lady Rosalind said, "then it must be done no matter how onerous or dangerous. Naturally, one would give all for one's family."

"Yes, I suppose they would. Unless it could be avoided."

"A person ought not avoid it if it is a duty, though," Lady

Rosalind said. "For instance, two summers ago my sister Juliet was stung by a hornet. She was in terrible pain over it. As I am known to be courageous in my family, it was my duty to approach the nest and knock it down so they never could sting her again."

"And so you did knock it down?" Balthazar asked.

"No, not in the end," Lady Rosalind admitted. "It turns out they build surprisingly sturdy nests and so after I climbed a ladder and hit it with a broom they got very angry and I was stung quite a lot. But still, it was a duty to try. In any case, my sister felt ever so much better knowing that I had answered their insult."

She paused, then said, "And Juliet could not feel too bad over her swollen arm when she saw what happened to my face."

Balthazar smiled. Lady Rosalind's battle with the hornets did not tell him much about how she would view his various forays on behalf of the queen, but it was engaging, nonetheless.

He had a great urge to trace his finger along one of her cheeks and gripped his napkin instead.

It was getting harder to resist those sorts of inclinations.

Perhaps he ought to consult with the queen. He felt the need to consult with somebody and she was the only person who could comment directly on whether he had the right to indulge his feelings.

His ever-growing feelings, it seemed.

In the meantime, he was happy to listen to Lady Rosalind very charmingly natter on about the battle of the hornets. It turned out that not only had her hornets built a very sturdy nest, but they were easily enraged, exceedingly energetic, and had chased her all the way back to the house. Some had even got into the house and the footmen chased after them with brooms while Lady Rosalind and her sisters hid behind curtains in the drawing room.

As dessert was served, his thoughts were brought back to the present and the very well-fashioned pianoforte he'd noticed in Lord Cannerly's drawing room. In a matter of a half hour, they would find themselves back in that room and opportunities for playing would present themselves.

He would consider it a success if he was able to keep Lady Rosalind and that instrument forever parted.

He would not like to view Lady Worthington's expression were she to be taken on a *travel through the world of music*. He certainly would not like Lady Rosalind to view such an expression. She may have been stung by hornets, but he would prefer she not be stung by Lady Worthington's or anybody else's looks of incredulity.

"Do you play piquet, Lady Rosalind?"

Chapter Fourteen

ROSALIND HAD FOUND her sisters all splayed on her bed and asleep when she arrived home. They'd since woken up and Miss Mayton had hurried in, dressed in her nightclothes and a nightcap.

She'd told her sisters all about the evening—how Conbatten had taken her into dinner and then urged her to play piquet with him, rather than entertain the party at the pianoforte.

Miss Jenson had played the instrument instead and once Rosalind heard her cautious and rather insipid stylings, she'd comprehended Conbatten's intent. The dear man had not wished for poor Miss Jenson to feel as if she could not measure up to a travel through the world of music.

Rosalind had not mentioned feeling a bit outclassed by Lady Worthington, as she did not like to think of it. And, after all, Conbatten had not urged *that* lady to piquet, had he?

"I have prepared him so when the carriage arrives and he receives the challenge to a duel, he will not be caught unawares, as it seems he was with our pickpocket," she said.

"Very good thinking, my dear," Miss Mayton said, helping herself to a biscuit from the glass jar by the side of the bed.

"By the by," Rosalind said to her aunt, "your name is Archibald."

"Specific," Miss Mayton said, nodding. "That adds a ring of truth to the whole thing."

"When will we go, though?" Juliet said. "I'm all jumpy about it and wish to set off at once."

Rosalind tapped her finger to her lips. "I was thinking we might go on Sunday, after church. We must make sure Conbatten is at home, and that is the most likely day."

"We might say to father that we wish to take some air," Cordelia said. "After all, it would be true. We always do like to take air."

"And there would not be room for Papa or Darden to come," Viola said, nodding.

"But what if Darden wishes to take his horse out and follow along with us?" Cordelia asked.

"We can say it would not be the right time," Rosalind said, "because we wish to discuss personal ladies' matters in the strictest confidence."

Juliet laughed and said, "Oh yes, there is no quicker way to make Papa or dear Darden run from a room than to mention personal ladies' matters. Remember when Papa was on the verge of scolding Cordelia about the second house fire, and she said she got distracted by personal ladies' matters?"

"I wonder what they think these matters are?" Miss Mayton asked.

"I think they are not certain and do not wish to find out," Viola said.

"Sunday is the day after tomorrow," Rosalind said. "That gives us a day to alter the clothes, snip off some of Bess' fur for sideburns, and find some glue we can use to put them on."

"I'll get the glue," Juliet said. "I'll tell Tattleton that I am making a collage of my poems."

"Good thinking, Jules," Viola said. "And we all have scissors in our sewing boxes so it will be no trouble to snip off Bess' hair."

"I really think we have thought of everything," Rosalind said.

"Of course we have," Cordelia said, "we've looked at the thing backwards and forwards."

The sisters sighed contentedly, as they always did when they had designed a foolproof scheme.

"Aunt, how did you make out at dinner?" Viola asked. "Who took you in and what were they like?"

Miss Mayton sighed and said, "An elderly gentleman named Lord Bentley took me in. I really do think the fellow suffers terribly from the gout or some other painful malady. He was very grim throughout and did not even seem struck when I told him of Gregorio and his unfortunate deadly blow to himself in the library just minutes before I arrived to tell him his love was requited."

"How could he not be struck by it, though?" Cordelia asked.

"Indeed, I found it very strange," Miss Mayton said. "I told him all the details, right down to Gregorio's parting words. All he said was, 'I've heard worse.'"

"What an odd fellow," Viola said.

"I think he must be terribly odd," Rosalind said. "I heard Conbatten ask him how his estate got on and he said as far as he knew the house was still standing, but there was every chance that a letter detailing its collapse had been delayed in the post."

Miss Mayton finished her biscuit and said, "Poor Lord Bentley. Now, I must chase you all into your own beds. It is late and we have much to accomplish on the morrow—we will wish to be rested."

BALTHAZAR HAD SENT a note to the Lord Chamberlain to arrange a meeting with the queen. Contacting Salisbury always proved the fastest route to an audience, rather than going through the usual channels and getting waylaid and delayed by petty functionaries who demanded their pound of respect for their authority.

Salisbury had come through and arranged an early meeting. The Queen liked to be up with the sun and though her ladies-in-waiting could not prefer it, she was generally dressed and at a tea tray by eight.

As so few other people in London wished for the queen's attention so early in the morning, she had been free and was agreeable to the meeting.

The ride through the streets was refreshing, as there were so few people about. Hades appeared delighted to be out in the air long before the usual time. Balthazar almost began to think Hamill was on to something with his early morning jaunts.

But then, he really did not like to rise early and Henri would be completely thrown off if he were to change his habits now.

He rode through the gates to Buckingham House and prepared to face down all the petty functionaries who would be lurking in the halls, wondering how he'd got past them. Not the least of which would be the dowager marchioness, who would no doubt spend the rest of the day complaining about him.

Balthazar was led into a bright and sunny anteroom overlooking the gardens. The queen was at her favored marble table, ensconced on a cream velvet settee. The dowager marchioness sat in the chair next to her, the lady's eyes narrowing in his direction.

He bowed low and kissed the queen's outstretched hand. "Your Majesty. Marchioness," he said.

"There you are, Conbatten. Well, I rarely see anything so youthful and full of life at this hour of the day," the queen said.

Balthazar kept his features strictly serious, though everybody in the room would know that particular comment was a little sting meant for the dowager.

"My dear Marchioness," the queen said, "you may retire. I will be quite safe with Conbatten by my side."

The dowager, having been dismissed, had no choice but to take her leave. She was, not unexpectedly, looking very sour over it.

"Do sit, Conbatten," the queen said. "I feel as if I am forever craning my neck to see who is talking to me."

Balthazar sat in the chair that had been recently vacated by the dowager in time to hear that lady huff as she made her exit from the room.

The queen smiled at the huff, and he got the idea that perhaps it was a sort of game they played between them. A one-upmanship of sorts. He also guessed the marchioness mostly found herself on the losing end of the stick.

The queen poured two cups of tea and said, "Salisbury tells me you wished to speak on a personal matter. I must admit to being intrigued—so few people ever tell me anything interesting. I trust you not to hem and haw and dance round whatever it is. Out with it."

She was direct. As always.

"Ma'am, I had firmly decided to put off marriage for the foreseeable future, believing such a union would not benefit the Queen's Knights' current activities."

"As I doubt you would arrive to tell me of that decision, I presume there is now a reason why you question it," the queen said.

"Yes," he said simply.

Queen Charlotte peered at him. "You've got to tell me more than that. Who is she? What is so remarkable about her, that she has stolen the duke's heart?"

"She is Lady Rosalind Bennington, the Earl of Westmont's daughter, and—"

"Wait a moment. Westmont. Is she the one who thrashes the pianoforte? I did hear a very amusing story about Lady Hightower's musical evening. Was that the girl?"

Balthazar nodded. "Lady Rosalind calls it a travel through the world of music. Personally, I do not believe she can read music and just stitches bits and pieces of what she can remember all together."

"I heard it was ghastly. She does not sound very accomplished."

"No, perhaps not in that particular area," Balthazar admitted.

"How does a girl come to be her age and not read music, or at least memorize a whole piece?"

Balthazar shifted uncomfortably. "I imagine she has not had the steadiest guidance. The earl's daughters have all been raised by an aunt of some sort."

"Oh yes, now it is all coming back to me. The lady spinster who goes round in black as if she's a widow. Mrs. Manton, or some such thing."

"Miss Mayton. Yes, she is a rather eccentric lady."

"Very odd."

"Yes, it is all very odd. And yet, you see, it is just that Lady Rosalind…"

"It is just that despite her coming with little to recommend her, you love her," the queen said.

Balthazar nodded. Of course, Lady Rosalind came with a great deal to recommend her, but her qualities were rather hard to explain. He did not think the queen would see the charm in a young lady having hired a pickpocket. Or telling him charming stories about a rash baron who might turn up for a duel.

"At least tell me she is a stalwart sort," the queen said.

"Very."

"She is not prone to fainting?"

"Not unless she means to," Balthazar said.

"I suppose only you know how she would receive the news of your activities on my behalf."

"I cannot know for certain, but I believe she would stand up to it."

Queen Charlotte fiddled with a fan and then laid it down. She sighed and said, "Naturally, there is everything against it just now. Lord Hamill tells me that Mondrian, that horrid creature, is not actually dead and up to all sorts of mischief. Yes indeed, everything is against it, but for one thing—were I to deny you, I would find myself resented over time."

Balthazar shook his head. "Certainly not, Ma'am, I—"

"Nonsense, of course you would resent it. You would do

your best to hide such feelings, but I would know it. I always know it. Do not I know that my dear marchioness has steam coming from her ears right at this moment? I am not supposed to care, you see, because I am the queen. And truthfully, sometimes I do not."

The queen had a far-off look in her eyes, as if recalling something.

"But then, sometimes I do. I am a person, though some would like to forget it. And then, you are a duke and must have an heir. If none of you in the Knights are to marry, what then? I think the king would begin to inquire why whole family lines were dying out for lack of wives."

Balthazar did not answer and let a silence hang in the room. When the queen was weighing a matter, it was best to just let her get on with it.

"All your fathers started this thing and they all had wives. How did the duchess, your mother, view it when your father left the house late at night?"

"She thought he was going to a club that only met at midnight," Balthazar said with a smile. "She thought it was something to do with Parliament and politics and viewed it a rather silly conceit. Though, I do not believe Lady Rosalind would be so fooled."

"Hmmm, do you suppose you could wed her and then leave her in the countryside? Just visit from time to time to get her with child? The house in Essex is very well turned out. You could leave her a pile of money to redecorate the place. That always seems to keep a lady busy, though I cannot fathom why."

His eyes widened at that prospect. Leave Lady Rosalind in Essex, alone on his estate? He imagined she'd be there for all of ten minutes before she'd designed some outlandish scheme to find herself in London. As Lady Hightower had already astutely pointed out, Lady Rosalind Bennington was frighteningly enterprising.

No, Lady Rosalind was not the sort who could be happily

locked away in the countryside, satisfied with choosing new drapes.

Nor would he wish to leave her there. What would be the point of marrying her if they were only to exchange letters? Not that she'd put up with it and nor would he.

"I see that would not suit," the queen said. "Well, I suppose we hope for the best then. Let us pray this not very accomplished young woman has at least possession of cool nerves."

Balthazar nodded. He was hoping the same thing himself.

TATTLETON FELT AS if he were a blind man staggering along the edges of a cliff. He would go over the side eventually, but he could not know when! Worse, how had he even got atop a cliff? What *was* the cliff, exactly?

The ladies of the house were up to something, that much he knew. However, he did not have the first idea of what it could be.

He was convinced the pickpocket in the park had been arranged and somehow that young ruffian Shrimps had been involved. Possibly the Duke of Conbatten, too.

He had almost managed to convince himself to forget about it. After all, whatever the purpose, there had not seemed to be any repercussions from it. Perhaps it had only been one of the ladies' ill-thought out schemes and now they had moved on to other ideas.

Tattleton had noticed that he'd not overheard anything further about a pickpocket, though Conbatten still appeared to be much talked about.

It had begun to seem as if he had worried himself for naught.

That was, until today.

The ladies and Miss Mayton had left in the carriage and there was something going on. They had left with a large sack. What was in it?

If that were not alarming enough, Charlie had come to him after the carriage had departed and informed him that Lady Viola and Lady Juliet had come down to the servants' hall and trimmed fur from the dog, carefully placing it in a small brown paper sack.

Lady Viola was overheard to say something about glue. Had he not just fetched glue for Lady Juliet the day before? She was to make a collage of her poems, though Tattleton had never heard of such a thing and had yet to see evidence of it.

Tattleton had told Charlie to forget what he'd seen.

If only *he* could forget it, too. Cutting hair from a dog sounded like some sort of witchcraft. Where were they taking the hair now? What else was in the bag? Fingernail clippings? Eye of newt? On a Sunday!

His boyhood in Penrith, not far from the stone monoliths of Long Meg and Her Daughters, came rushing back to him. Everybody had been warned never to try to count the monoliths twice. If the same number were arrived at both times, then either Long Meg would come back to life and kill them all, or something evil would happen to the ill-advised counter.

Had not Randall Blade been dared to do it? Had he not been stupid enough to do it? And then, what? Three months later he'd fallen under a cart's wheel and broke his leg. He'd walked with a limp forever after.

Over the years, Tattleton had convinced himself that it had been a coincidence. And then refused to look too closely at the fact that he did not believe in coincidences.

What else could taking a dog's hair be for, if not some sort of spell?

Should he go to the earl?

But then, what would he say? 'My Lord, I am afraid your daughters have taken to dabbling in witchcraft.' He would sound preposterous and be on his way to Bedlam shortly after.

Those wretched dogs. All those dogs! Dog hair in a paper sack would not have left the house had there been no dog in the house.

As it was, there were nine of them. One of them had just had a haircut and eight of them were on the move!

Oh, they were wobbly and falling down and not getting far, but that would not last. They'd get better and faster and then what?

Tattleton shut his eyes. There was nothing he could do about any of it but walk carefully along the cliff's edge and wait for the earth to crumble beneath his feet.

Hopefully, he would crash land on a ledge of some sort and live to tell the tale.

THE BENNINGTON'S CARRIAGE had set off at two o'clock in the afternoon. Both the earl and Darden had shuddered when they were told that the purpose was to discuss personal ladies' matters and had inquired no further.

As Conbatten's house on Grosvenor Square was too close by to give them sufficient time to prepare Miss Mayton to be Archibald, the lovelorn baron's second, they'd directed Sandren to drive to Piccadilly and then circle back around to the square. This would also ensure that they approached the square in the right direction and their father's crest would not be noted.

Sandren had not seemed to understand the point of it all, especially not when he was apprised of this "goose chase" they were supposed to be on, but he did not refuse either.

They had since closed the curtains on the windows and helped Miss Mayton into her clothes. It had been no great matter to do—though it was a tight fit, they'd wrangled her into a waistcoat and coat right over her dress and then covered her dress' neckline with a neckcloth.

"The knot in the cloth is perhaps not the most studied, but on the whole, the clothes look very good," Rosalind said. "Very good indeed."

"Agreed," Juliet said, screwing off the top of the glue pot. "Once we get the sideburns and the hat on, nobody would ever know that you are not Archibald."

"Good luck to them trying to guess it," Cordelia said.

"I'm beginning to even feel like Archibald," Miss Mayton said in a very gravelly voice.

"Viola," Juliet said, "you brought a paintbrush?"

"Just here," Viola said, handing Juliet the brush.

"I'll hold the bag of fur while you paint on the glue," Juliet said. "After all, you are the artist and must do it, just as I helped Rosalind with the demand note since I am the wordsmith."

"You all do work so very well together," Miss Mayton said. "Oh, that tickles!"

Viola had just painted a long stripe of glue from above the top of her aunt's cheek to her chin.

"Very good, Viola," Rosalind said, "make it very wide. We have piles of Bess' fur and we wish to disguise our aunt's face as much as possible."

Once the glue was on, Juliet handed clumps of fur to Viola, who applied it to her aunt's face in a very artistic manner.

"It's like magic," Rosalind said. "It really is turning our aunt into a gentleman!"

"And look, Rosalind, we even have enough to make Aunt's eyebrows bushy."

Viola painted glue over Miss Mayton's eyebrows and pressed tufts of fur over the lady's eyebrows.

Cordelia placed the beaver hat on her head and pulled it down to Miss Mayton's recently embellished brows.

Their aunt was entirely transformed.

"I'd not the first idea it would look this good," Rosalind said. "I think you could go into the house and sit in the drawing room and Conbatten would never suspect it was you."

"I think so too," Miss Mayton said, "though, ought we to tempt fate?"

"Oh dear no, the fates do not like to be tempted," Rosalind

said, nodding. "They begin to think you take them for granted and they never like it."

Cordelia handed her aunt a gentleman's cane. "I borrowed this from Papa," she said. "If one of the duke's footmen is looking at you too closely, you can wave it around to distract him, just as Grandpapa used to do when he wished to get his way."

"Goodness, he did like to wave that stick in one's face. Very good thinking, dear," Miss Mayton said.

"Here is your note, Aunt," Rosalind said, handing over the carefully composed challenge to a duel.

Miss Mayton looked it over. "It sounds so real!"

"I like that we made him the fourteenth baron," Juliet said. "It makes it sound as if the family has been around for ages."

"And then his brother Archibald is lame from being a soldier, which makes perfect sense and explains why he stays in the carriage," Cordelia said.

Juliet pulled open the front curtains and opened the little window to communicate with the coachman. "Sandren," she said, "we are ready to proceed to Grosvenor Square, number thirty-eight."

Sandren turned and nodded. Then his eyes grew wide and he reined in the horses.

CHAPTER FIFTEEN

S ANDREN HAD PULLED on the reins hard and maneuvered the coach to the side of the road. Settling the horses, who were entirely startled by it, he turned round again.

"Who—"

"It is only Miss Mayton," Rosalind said. "We are directed to use a disguise on this part of the goose chase."

Sandren narrowed his eyes. "Speak then, if you will," he said, staring at the hair-covered face before him.

"It is really me, Sandren," Miss Mayton said.

"But what is, I mean, your face, Miss Mayton? You look, well you seem as if…something has gone terribly wrong with you!"

"It's just some dog hair," Cordelia said. "There's no harm in it, Bess did not mind giving it over at all. We just snipped some and then glued it on."

"Why?"

"To look like sideburns," Viola said.

"Those are sideburns?" Sandren said.

Now the groom had dismounted and was looking in the side window. "Well I never," he said softly.

"Now, Sandren," Juliet said, "you are not to be alarmed about any of this. When next you look back here, we will have all disappeared under blankets, but for Miss Mayton. Do not concern yourself with it, it is just a part of the goose chase."

"I don't understand this goose chase!" Sandren said.

"Nobody does, Sandren," Cordelia said in a conciliatory tone. "It's the *ton*, they like strange amusements and Rosalind has to fit in, does she not?"

"I do not remember anything like this last season, when Lady Beatrice was fitting into the *ton*."

Viola shook her head. "No, you wouldn't have," she said. "Mrs. Ellington was in a confinement last year. Twins, we heard."

"Proceed, Sandren," Rosalind said, with what she hoped was authority. "We have little time to lose if we are to prevail on Mrs. Ellington's goose chase. We are determined to come out ahead."

Sandren nodded reluctantly and got the horses moving again. Rosalind breathed a sigh of relief, the highest hurdle had been cleared. Everything was falling into place.

She and her sisters wished their aunt good luck and arranged themselves underneath the carriage throws.

Were any footmen of Conbatten's to peer in and wonder about the blanket covered lumps, they would be told it was luggage.

⟫⟫⟫⟫⟪⟪⟪⟪

BALTHAZAR STOOD AT the window of his bedchamber, idly drinking a cup of coffee. The queen had sanctioned his idea of asking for Lady Rosalind's hand and it felt as if a harness had been thrown off him.

He'd been keeping his desires under a hard rein and now they only grew and bloomed. He thought he understood Lady Rosalind, at least partly. She was a complicated woman and that suited him just fine. Of what he thought he did understand would be required for her future happiness, she must be rescued from danger from time to time. It was a matter easily arranged and he would be happy to oblige.

Of course, he still must ask the question and there was always the chance she might decline him. He did not think so, but she could be a complicated and contrary creature. He would find out how it was to be for him at Lady Bloomington's masque in a weeks' time. They would both attend, and a masque was a perfect setting for stealing a lady away to a quiet corner.

Henri had taken the news of his plans as well as could be expected. The poor fellow had been fretting and muttering all morning—"Why? Arno! Happy as we are! Thames! Not too late!"

Balthazar had soothed his feelings just a bit by reminding his valet that he could have chosen someone who would be peering into the servants' business every minute. He was certain Lady Rosalind would not give a toss for how long they all lounged around or how much of his wine they drank.

Henri had a certain soft spot for his wine cellar, after all.

Balthazar was surprised to see Lord Westmont's carriage suddenly clatter to a stop in front of his address. He could not see the crest, but he would recognize that fine team of Hanoverians anywhere.

What was he doing here?

As one of his footmen ran toward the carriage, the window opened. An older gentleman who was certainly not Lord Westmont poked his head out. The fellow had the most alarming visage. Were those sideburns? Or a beard? Or something in between? Whatever it was meant to be, it was distastefully unkempt. An odd-looking fellow.

Perhaps it was not Westmont's carriage after all and there was another matched set of horses looking very like.

The footman was handed a note. The boy nodded and ran back into the house.

Strangely, the carriage did not set off, but remained where it was.

If it were an invitation of some sort, the fellow could not think to wait for an answer? What a strange thing to do, particularly on a Sunday.

There was a rap on the door and Alden came in with the note on a silver tray. "Your Grace," he said, "a Mr. Rimperton sends this. He informed Benjamin that he will wait for an answer and he demands the answer in writing."

"Does he?" Balthazar said.

"Naturally," Alden said with a huff, "Benjamin informed this gentleman that nobody but the king and queen was to demand anything from a duke. Mr. Rimperton then seemed distressed and cried that he was a war hero and had injured his leg and could not come into the house. Benjamin said the gentleman seemed quite upset."

Balthazar took the note. "Perhaps he has been damaged in the mind," he said. "He would not be alone in it. Let's see what the poor fellow wants. I suspect he finds himself down on his luck and there is some loose family connection he seeks out in desperation."

"Ah, that might very well be the case," Alden said. "Benjamin reported that the fellow's carriage is filled up with items covered in blankets. Perhaps it is all his worldly possessions."

Balthazar nodded. He would not think it at all unusual for a man facing poverty to hold on to his horse and carriage to the last possible moment. He'd probably been haunted by creditors, took what he could out of the house under cover of darkness, and set off.

He opened the sealed letter.

Sir—

I am a baron living nearby Taunton and have been near-engaged to Lady Rosalind Bennington for these past two years. Though the engagement has not been announced, as the lady has so far not accepted, I expect that circumstance to change once I dispatch all other suitors. I am a rash man, Duke, and have been informed that you are often in the company of my one and only lady love.

I will not stand for it!

I will meet you on the dawn of your choosing, on the green of your choosing, armed with the weapons of your choosing.

Please reply in writing posthaste to my second, my brother

Archibald who waits in the carriage. (He cannot come in, he is lame from the war)

Jonathan Rimperton, Fourteenth Baron of Leister

Balthazar dropped the letter. "No, it cannot be," he said, and then began to laugh. He could not stop laughing. His sides began to hurt from it, it was too absurd.

"Your Grace!" Henri cried, as if he was being felled by an illness.

Between guffaws, he said, "Read the note."

Henri picked it up and scanned it. "A duel! You must not do it! This fellow says he is rash, there is no telling what will happen! He will fire early, I know it. Do not answer this, Alden can say you are not at home and make this Mr. Rimperton go away."

"Your Grace?" Alden said. "Shall I tell Mr. Rimperton that you are not at home?"

Balthazar heaved in a breath to calm his laughter. "First, that person in the carriage appears to be fifty, if a day. He pretends to be the younger brother. How old is this rash and lovesick baron supposed to be? Second, I do not see why we should send poor Archibald away when he has traveled all the way from Portland Place."

Henri dabbed his forehead with a handkerchief. "You will answer this, then," he said, sounding very dejected.

"Oh yes," Balthazar said. "My coat, if you please."

"You will go out there?" Henri asked. "Why? Do you know this scoundrel?"

"I believe I do. Mr. Archibald Rimperton, otherwise known as Miss Mayton. I cannot wait to hear what she will have to say for herself."

"Miss Mayton?" Henri cried, grabbing a coat from the wardrobe and helping him into it. "What world am I living in, where everything is topsy-turvy and nothing makes sense?"

"In Lady Rosalind Bennington's world, it seems," Balthazar said. He left his butler and his valet pondering what Miss Mayton was doing dressed as a man with hair all over her face.

Balthazar jogged down the stairs. Benjamin opened the door for him, though from his expression it did not seem as if his footman felt at all positive about their recently arrived visitor.

As Miss Mayton saw him emerge from the house, and he was certain it *was* Miss Mayton, she waved her hand out the carriage window and shouted gruffly, "Halt! My brother insists on a written answer. Come no closer!"

Balthazar would bet she did not wish him to come closer. Nor would Lady Rosalind and her sisters, who were no doubt crouching under blankets.

He strode forward despite her wish to send him back into the house. "Now, Mr. Rimperton, do be reasonable. I am not going to kill your brother so that *you* can step forward as the fifteenth baron. Furthermore, it would take quite a lot to get me out of bed at dawn."

As he approached the window of the carriage, he saw Miss Mayton's eyes grow wider and wider. She waved a cane around and shouted to the coachman. "Drive on! Go! Drive on!"

The coachman appeared entirely at a loss, but he did start the horses and they went at a fast clip down the street and around a bend. The carriage trotted around the gardens to head in the opposite direction. In the distance, he saw the Earl of Westmont's coat of arms on the door.

Balthazar watched them go with his arms folded, laughing to himself. Lady Rosalind was an entrancing and bold woman.

"I suppose I'd better propose before she arranges her own kidnapping," he said to his startled footman.

ROSALIND SLUMPED ON the sofa. They had rushed off from Conbatten's house after he approached the carriage…and refused the duel.

Sandren had been in near apoplexy over the whole thing and not seeming very convinced that they had lost at Mrs. Ellington's goose chase and must now go round Piccadilly again before setting off for home. They had needed the extra time to get Miss Mayton out of her disguise.

Sandren was certainly relieved to be taking them home, but exceedingly suspicious over why they had to make an extended journey over it.

That, of course, was nothing. Conbatten had refused the challenge to a duel to win her and that was everything.

Since they'd arrived back to the house, the earl had come into the drawing room. Miss Mayton, seeing Rosalind was not yet up to facing anybody, had told her father that they were still engaged in discussing personal ladies' matters.

Her poor Papa had done an about face and hurried back out again, no doubt wondering if the black veil Miss Mayton wore had anything to do with it.

Rosalind sighed. It was all over. There was nothing further to be done. She'd given Conbatten every chance to come to her rescue and he'd refused.

She could not ignore what his feelings were. Or rather, what they were not.

"That's it then," she said softly. "Our Beatrice was once convinced she would be a spinster, but after all it will be me."

"Because you could never consider anybody but Conbatten," Juliet said.

"Never."

"Certainly," Miss Mayton said, "there must be some rational explanation for the duke's refusal to duel."

"Yes, there is," Rosalind said. "He does not have me in his heart as I do him. If I were the one being challenged, I should take up my pistols forthwith and race to the nearest green to win Conbatten. He only joked that Archibald wished to be the next baron."

"But wait, Rosalind," Viola said, "perhaps that is where it all went wrong. Sending Archibald, the brother, as the second. This led the duke to believe that Archibald wished to see his brother killed and perhaps had even urged him to it."

"That could be it," Cordelia said. "The duke might have felt he must put a stop to actual fratricide, despite his love for you."

"That makes sense," Juliet said. "If you had only said the second was a friend, then the duke would not have worried that he participated in some unsavory family plot."

Rosalind's mind grasped at what she knew to be a very weak straw. At Lord Cannerly's dinner, she had described Archibald in less than glowing terms. The duke had declared that a person such as that likely wished the elder brother dead and out of the way.

"I am certain that must be it," Miss Mayton said from under her veil. They had discovered in the carriage that while getting their aunt's sideburns on had been no trouble, getting them off again was near impossible. They did not know what they were to do about it.

"The duke would likely have agreed to fight the baron if the second had not been the brother," Cordelia said.

Just then, Tattleton had come in with the tea tray. As he laid the service, Juliet said casually, "By the by, Tattleton, you remember that glue you gave me?"

"Yes, Lady Juliet."

"Well, there have been some mishaps with my project to make a poem collage. So I was wondering—what can one use to get glue off?"

Tattleton appeared startled by the question. "I am not entirely certain," he said. "I believe the only thing that softens it is hot water. At least, that is what the carpenter who came to fix a chair joint last year told me. He had Cook boil water to get it loose."

"Excellent," Juliet said, nodding to Miss Mayton. "When we go above stairs, can you send a pot up?"

"Hot water. To use on a paper collage, my lady?"

"It will be tricky, no doubt, but I'll have to give it a try."

Tattleton nodded, though Rosalind did not think he looked at all enthusiastic over sending up a pot of hot water to Juliet's collage of poems. He was probably worried that she'd spill it all over.

The butler retired from the room and closed the door.

"There now, Aunt, we shall have Bess' fur off your face in no time," Juliet said.

Now that the problem of her aunt's sideburns had been resolved, Rosalind's thoughts went back to the duke. It was at once hopeless, and yet she found it very hard to give up all hope.

Were she to give up all hope, then she must proceed in misery forevermore.

But what else could she do? He would not be driven to declaring himself.

"I think what has happened," Miss Mayton said from underneath her ghostly veil, "is that we have executed a well-thought-out plan, but for one detail. We should not have made the brother the second, but naturally we could not see that at the time."

"But what now, Aunt?" Cordelia asked. "If we cannot drive him to a duel, what else could there be?"

"It seems to me that we have not boxed him in sufficiently," Miss Mayton said, bobbing her head up and down. "He imagined it safe enough to refuse the duel, but what if this lovesick baron were to pose some real danger to Rosalind?"

"That would be very good," Viola said. "We already have him believing in the lovesick baron, after all. No need to go inventing somebody else."

"Yes, and we have painted the baron as being very rash. He might do anything, who can say what a rash man might do?" Cordelia said.

"But what rash thing could he do?" Rosalind asked. "What could be more rash than a duel?"

"A duel would have only been dangerous to *him*," Juliet pointed out. "We need to think of something that would be dangerous to *you*. He could not ignore it if he loves you and he must love you."

"Hmm. What if…" Viola said, trailing off.

"What if what?" Rosalind said, leaning forward.

"Well, what if the duke was to think the lovesick baron had stolen you off and intended to take you to Gretna Green?"

"That would be marvelous!" Juliet said.

"Yes, it would be," Rosalind said. "Though I do not know how we would arrange such a ruse."

"It is a very good thought, though," Miss Mayton said.

"We just must think of how it could be done," Cordelia said. "This is a matter of love, and so there is always a way."

Rosalind sat back. It would give her a very definitive answer, whatever that answer was to be. If Conbatten were to imagine that she'd been carried off by the lovesick baron and did *not* follow her…then she would know that he did not give a toss that she was on her way to a marriage over the anvil.

How was it to be done, though?

"We'd better go up while we ponder it," Viola said. "We have to get Aunt's sideburns off before dinner, else I do not see how she is to eat under that veil."

CHAPTER SIXTEEN

BALTHAZAR, HAVING A firm idea of the token he wished to bestow on Lady Rosalind, had sent out inquiries in all directions. Mr. Rundell of Rundell and Bridge had written back describing a ring that was precisely what he looked for. A large red ruby symbolizing a red rose, surrounded by gold in an intricate pattern of Thyme. Passionate love and courage, in the language of flowers. It was precisely what he wished to say. It was precisely what Lady Rosalind would need to hear.

Hamill had arrived to his house unexpectedly, just as he was about to set off to the jewelers. He had told his friend of his errand and they had set off together.

As the carriage trundled its way to Ludgate Hill, Hamill said, "Well? Who is this lady that has conquered you and sends you running for jewelry?"

Balthazar gazed out the window at the passing scenery. "I'll keep that to myself until I am assured that I have conquered *her*."

"Gad, you think you might be turned down?"

"I think I cannot take an acceptance for granted."

"You really went to see the queen about it, and she was amenable?"

"I did and she was."

"Interesting," Hamill said. "I do not, as of yet, have a lady in mind for myself. But, it is well to know the queen would likely sanction it."

"You are only just twenty," Balthazar said, "far too young to consider such a step. Wait until you are twenty-five and have burned off some of your alarming energy. When you find you are no longer racing out of your house at dawn, off on a series of physical pursuits, you may have settled enough to consider a marriage."

"Why do you say so? Do you say a lady would not prefer my mode of going on?"

"I suspect not, it is exhausting just to hear about, never mind witness. Don't you ever pause and read a book?"

"Bah, I hate books. My sister is always spouting off about something she read. There is some Wordsworth fellow she is enamored with and we never hear the end of it."

"He is a poet, very well known," Balthazar said drily. "Now, I know you did not come to me simply to ride along to the jewelers and tell me of your disdain for books," Balthazar said. "What news?"

"Crosby writes that the boy Jimmy has finally been prevailed upon to give up where he was living in the Rats' Castle. We have the location of the room, we know there were five boys living there, including the one that got away. That was Shrimps, you remember, the one that now resides in Van Doren's household. And, we've got a description of the leader of that room. He is the eldest and largest of them all and his name is Barney Mudbetter. He can be recognized by a brown birthmark on his cheek."

Balthazar suddenly rapped his cane on the roof to stop the carriage. As the horses slowed, he turned to Hamill. "A brown birthmark on his cheek? If that is so, then it is the same who pocketed Lady Rosalind's handkerchief in the park. I do not know if you were aware of that circumstance."

"Everybody is aware," Hamill said. "Darden has gone round the town, spouting off about the alleged aplomb of your actions on that exciting day. We all wish you would put that gentleman out of his misery and just barge into his club and say you will join it."

"Yes, I am sure you do. However, I doubt Darden knows as much about the circumstances as I think I do."

Hamill looked at him expectantly.

"You are going to find this hard to believe, but I believe Lady Rosalind arranged for herself to be robbed."

"What—"

Balthazar held up a hand. "Let us not delve into that fact just yet. I had been wondering how she managed to hire her own pickpocket. How stupid that I did not see it before! Of course, the only way she could do it was to work with someone who would know a pickpocket to hire—Shrimps."

"So this Shrimps character is living in Van Doren's house and still working with Mondrian's gang."

"Or at least he is in some sort of contact with them."

"Should we pay Shrimps a visit?"

"No, not yet. There would be too much to explain to Van Doren and then we would likely only scare the boy off and he'd disappear. Rather, I think we might pay a visit to Barney, who will not know that *we* know there is a connection to Shrimps."

Hamill nodded. "We ought to go very late. Pickpockets will not be at home before the crowd of theater-goers is long abed and every drunk gentleman has staggered through his door."

"We should go after Lady Bloomington's masque. "We will already be dressed in dominos, we only need wear dark clothes underneath."

"Are you certain you will not be too taken up with your soon to be bride?" Hamill asked with a smile.

"I do intend to conduct that business at the masque, however it may go for me. But if I am successful, I will not approach the father until morning."

"Well, if she's managed to hire her own pickpocket, I dare say she'll be stalwart enough to accept *you*."

"You do not know who I plan to propose to."

"Of course I do," Hamill said, laughing.

ROSALIND AND HER sisters had gone above stairs very early to dress for dinner, as they still had the matter of Miss Mayton's sideburns to contend with.

Tattleton had sent up the hot water and then there was no hiding the matter from Fleur.

Fortunately, Fleur was very loyal to her mistress and would not breathe a word of the startling sight. At least, she would not speak of it in English. And, as nobody else in the servants' hall spoke French, that was deemed sufficient.

Fleur dabbed and rubbed and indeed the glue softened and a lot of the hair was slowly and painfully parted from Miss Mayton's cheeks.

Not all of it, though. There were scraggily bits that appeared glued on forever and they found they could go no further when Miss Mayton's skin began to get very red from all the rubbing and pulling.

Fleur had taken sewing scissors and trimmed what was left as close as she could. They found that if Miss Mayton wore her veil draped on either side of her face it was really not that noticeable.

To Fleur's credit, she did not inquire as to how the sideburns had come about in the first place and only said, "La tonne est excentrique."

That matter sufficiently concluded, they set to thinking of ideas on how to make Conbatten believe the rash and lovesick baron had stolen Rosalind off to Gretna Green.

Nobody really had anything much concrete as to how to do it. All they could really think of was how they would like it to seem.

Rosalind was certain that the duke would attend Lady Bloomington's masque, so of course that was the ideal setting. If he were to see her driven off there, it would be most perfect. Whoever was driving her off could just drive to the end of the street, then seeing they were pursued, leap out of the carriage and run off into the night. Then, Conbatten would find Rosalind alone in the carriage and he would have rescued her. That would be the moment when he could profess his true feelings in the privacy of the carriage after her aunt had quietly stepped out to give them privacy.

It was a lovely scene, but how in the world would they arrange it?

For one, where was her father in all this? Where was Sandren? Neither of those two people would ever agree to such a thing.

In truth, Rosalind would not dare propose such a thing to either of them.

Juliet did have the idea that they might dissuade their father from going at all. He never really liked those sorts of things.

But then, what to do about Sandren?

To be at all successful, they'd have to leave him behind too.

Viola wondered if they might not hire a carriage and say that Lady Hightower was determined to escort them.

That might work, of course, but they did not have the first idea how to go about hiring a carriage and hiring a coachman who would agree to their rather unusual plan.

It was finally decided that they must consult with Shrimps. He was the only person they knew who might have the sort of contacts to arrange such a thing. They would invite him over to see Bess' pups again and see what he would say.

They did not have a plan, per se, but they had at least determined something they might do.

Rosalind felt as if everything hung in the balance. As if her very life hung in the balance. She must have an answer. Would Conbatten come after her, or would he not?

If he did not pursue the carriage, then she would go home to cry her eyes out. But if he did, then all would be right with the world.

She did not know how on earth they would arrange such a scheme, but in her heart she knew it must be arranged. She must know, one way or the other. Whatever the truth was, she wished to face it head on. She could not drift from season to season, wondering and pining.

No, she absolutely refused to live in a gray uncertainty. She would be always nervous, always waiting for the crushing blow—the news that he would marry another.

If there were to be a blow, let it come quickly. Let it be a clean and swift guillotine cut and not death by endless small pricks.

They had since gone down to an early dinner, and as it was Sunday, Beatrice and Van Doren, and even Darden, had gathered too.

The earl had instantly noticed Miss Mayton's close-held veil round her face, which was a style he had not seen her wear until this night.

Before he could inquire, she had only shaken her head sadly and whispered, "Personal ladies' matters."

There had been no further inquiries about it.

At table, Rosalind had said, "Beatrice, would you mind sending Shrimps to us tomorrow morning? We wish him to see the pups' progress. Their eyes are open and they are struggling to their feet in the most charming manner possible. They are full of hi-jinks in the mornings and I think he should really like to see it."

"That is very kind, Rosalind," Beatrice said. "It is so thoughtful of you to remember Shrimps."

"He is rather hard to forget," Van Doren said. "As is his dog."

"Now, it is true, he is of a nervous disposition," Beatrice said. "Then, of course, Oyster naturally follows him in it. But Cook says he is a hard worker."

"Yes, I know," Van Doren said in a conciliatory tone. "I hold nothing against him, I just live with the hope that he eventually calms down."

"As *we* have always lived with the hope that *you* would eventually calm down," Juliet said.

"A hopeless sort of hope," Viola said, nodding.

"Just a shred of hope, really," Cordelia said.

"I will point out," Van Doren said, "that I have not lectured you even once since I have come to Town."

"And yet," Juliet said, "it is always on the horizon."

Beatrice was doing her best not to laugh. "Aunt," she said, in a bid to change the conversation, "shall you read to us tonight?"

"Oh, she must!" the earl nearly cried. "I have been thinking about it all day."

"I'm sure we all have, Father," Darden said, in his usual agreeable manner.

"Thinking about it, dreading it, it is all the same," Van Doren muttered.

Beatrice gave him a sympathetic glance.

And so they went on as they always did these days—Van Doren teased and then soothed by his wife's sympathetic glances.

❧❧❧

TATTLETON STOOD BY the sideboard as he did at every dinner, monitoring the work of the footmen and ensuring that the earl's wine glass did not become empty.

His expression would be inscrutable, he well knew. Nobody looking at him would guess at the turmoil roiling round his breast.

Every new piece of information coming to him painted a worse picture.

How foolish he had been to fear that it was only a dabbling in witchcraft going on under this roof!

That would be nothing compared to what he now suspected.

The dog hair that he had feared was a part of some dark ritual had in fact been glued onto Miss Mayton's face!

He may have come across that information in a less than usual manner, having listened at the door after he left the drawing room this very afternoon. Was he not to have noticed that Miss Mayton wore a black veil, as if she'd come from a funeral? And then, what could he do after Lady Juliet had requested hot water to unglue a paper collage?

He'd felt, for the safety of the house, he ought to know what was really going on.

The last thing he had imagined was that it was wanted to soften the glue that held dog's fur to Miss Mayton's face!

There was only one conclusion to come to—Miss Mayton had disguised herself as a man.

What could be the purpose? What had they been doing?

He knew that something had been strange when they left in the carriage with a sack of some sort. Fleur had later told him that he should not inquire, as it had to do with personal ladies' matters.

Well, he could not say he knew very much about personal ladies' matters, or wanted to, but he could not see what dressing as a man had to do with it.

Now, they were intent on having Shrimps back in the house. Was it connected? Should he go to the earl?

As always, when he thought of going to the earl, he was forced to put his wide-ranging thoughts into some sort of coherent paragraph he might communicate.

It never did sound coherent though. "My Lord, it seems that these personal ladies' matters that have recently been mentioned include Miss Mayton gluing dog hair on her face and somehow Shrimps is involved."

It made no sense!

Whatever was going on here, Tattleton was very afraid for the day when it *would* make sense.

What was he to eventually discover?

Whatever it was, he must know. He felt certain that there was some disaster barreling down the road toward them.

He could not stand idly by, allowing the disaster to barrel unimpeded. He must know more. He must talk to Sandren.

The coachman could at least say where they had all gone

with a sack and a pile of dog hair plastered on Miss Mayton's face.

HAROLD MONDRIAN SURVEYED his rooms with a satisfied eye. The neighborhood was not ideal. In truth, it was a particularly dangerous neighborhood. But then, that was what made it so safe for him.

He was never in fear of being chased by criminals, he paid off the right people to avoid it. He feared being chased by those who lived in the better neighborhoods.

Mondrian had taken the top floor of one of the few buildings on the street that did not appear to be ready to collapse. The layout was secure—one front door and one back door with stairs that led to an alley should one wish to depart in haste.

The rest of the rooms ran one into another. The outermost room that connected to the front door was well protected by men he employed. Anybody wishing to rush him would find themselves out of luck.

He was so close to his goal.

Mondrian paused, reminding himself that he'd come close before. So close.

He'd posed as the heir to the Dedmont barony, successfully convincing that family that their son was dead and he was the only living cousin of James Conroy.

He had assumed the son really was dead and had since confirmed the truth of it. However, at the time, he'd forged the manifest of the *Louisa*, a ship that had gone down, to prove the fellow had gone down with it.

If it had not been for that nosy old dowager and all her questions, he'd be living as a baron even now.

He had every right to! He was the son of a lord long since dead. That he had inconveniently been illegitimate did not mean he did not have the same rights as a gentleman. He had a gentleman's blood running in his veins.

Perhaps that blood was mixed with a tavern maid's blood, but it was there all the same.

His mother had told him all his life that he had a right to it. She'd even taken him to the estate in Yorkshire three times in his youth to present him to the family.

They'd been thrown out on their ear every time.

They'd nursed that bitterness between them and, over time, began to think of how they might take what would not be freely given.

His mother had not lived to see that day. But he had.

That marvelous day when he'd read in the papers that Mr. James Conroy of Kent had run off with Lady Edna Edenborough and the family asked anybody with information to come forward. Apparently, the families of both involved had tried to keep the whole thing quiet, but when the couple appeared to be missing for a matter of six months, they were terrified that something had befallen them. All was forgiven, if they would just come home.

Mondrian had been waiting for such an odd circumstance to come along. He began to look into it, and it grew more and more promising.

There was no young brother to step in if James Conroy had perished. Eventually, the courts would declare him dead, which of course would take years.

However, the legal heir would live as a baron until the day the courts confirmed he *was* the next baron.

More looking into, more research. Where was this legal heir?

More good news. The fellow was a ship's captain, sailing somewhere in the West Indies. He'd be gone for years, most likely. If he even came back at all. So many of those fellows died before getting home. And even if he did get home…well, Mondrian would deal with him then.

It had all gone along so well. He'd ingratiated himself to the family by showing them the manifest and expressing his grief.

He'd fooled them all, using the usual ways of fooling people.

They were complimented and kept in the highest regard and continually assured that what had happened to James Conroy and Lady Edna was not really their fault.

Fooled them all except that dowager.

She watched him like a hawk. She asked a lot of questions. She commented on his manners, his speech, his very way of being.

She told him, one rainy afternoon, that she did not believe he was a gentleman.

He'd really thought to strangle her then and there and had set himself to finding a way to be rid of her.

He'd not done it fast enough, though. She'd exposed him to all the family by hiring a solicitor who got a copy of the *real* manifest of the Louisa.

Their hope that James Conroy and Lady Edna still lived bloomed once more, he was condemned, and promptly thrown from the house.

To escape arrest, he'd faked his death by leaving his overturned sailboat in the channel.

Since then, he was able to discover that James Conroy and Lady Edna were in fact dead, though not by a ship's sinking.

Apparently, they'd tried to make a go of supporting themselves, which had gone as well as it ever was going to go for two people who had never worked a day in their lives. Conroy worked himself into a grave and Lady Edna landed herself in a workhouse.

Mondrian could not care less. That was, until it came to his attention that a boy had been born.

If that boy still lived, *he* was the heir to the Dedmont barony.

If Mondrian himself could not be baron, he could at least ransom the real one. He could extract a pile of money and then slip away. He could be off to America, where anybody with money could live as a gentleman and where his accent would be held in high regard, rather than scrutinized and sniffed at.

Now, he was rather sure he'd found the boy. He went by the

name of Shrimps, no doubt to hide his real identity.

He could not fathom why the boy did not claim the title, but then, that was not his problem. If this Shrimps really was the boy he sought, he had to irrefutably prove it, and then demand a fortune for his return.

He'd been gathering evidence ever since and he was very close.

CHAPTER SEVENTEEN

BEATRICE HAD BEEN as good as her word and sent Shrimps over in the morning. Once apprised of his arrival, Rosalind, Miss Mayton, and her sisters had hurried down to the servants' hall.

There, they'd found Shrimps fairly cowering under Tattleton's stare and seeming as if he did not know what he was doing there.

"Tattleton," Rosalind said, "you may go about your duties. We will stay with Shrimps."

"I do not mind staying, my lady," Tattleton said.

"Oh, we cannot keep you," Rosalind said.

"And I am very sorry to say it, Tattleton," Juliet said, "but the pups do not play as much when you are watching. I believe they might be intimidated by your presence."

"That is very true," Viola said. "They do not know you are the kindest most wonderful butler living."

"They only see your imposing looks, Tattleton," Cordelia confirmed.

Their poor butler looked at once discomposed and flattered. He turned on his heel and climbed the stairs.

Viola tiptoed to the door to confirm he'd gone up, and then quietly shut it.

"How do you do this morning, Shrimps?" Rosalind said.

Shrimps bowed. "My lady, I am a little shaken. I do not believe Mr. Tattleton wished me to be here."

"Oh, never mind Tattleton. He is our butler, all the really good ones have moods," Cordelia said.

"Do they?" Shrimps whispered.

"Were you not pleased that we wished you to see the pups, Shrimps?" Juliet asked.

Shrimps appeared to think this over. Finally, he said, "They're grand, I'm sure. It was only that I was rather nervous that you'd want…another pickpocket."

"Goodness, no," Rosalind said, in what she hoped was a friendly and encouraging tone. "We are quite done with that idea."

Shrimps appeared very relieved to hear it.

"This time," Rosalind went on, "we only require a coach and coachman to drive us not so very far to Lady Bloomington's house and then drive down the street while a duke runs after it, and then leap off and run away."

This seemed to stagger Shrimps and he collapsed into a chair.

"It is not nearly as complicated as it might at first sound," Cordelia said.

Rosalind nodded and proceeded to acquaint him with the plan. The coach would seem to be Lady Hightower's. She and Miss Mayton must simply get in and get away before Tattleton looked too closely. Then, on to Lady Bloomington's masque and slowly driving round until the duke was spotted. Then Miss Mayton would get out and wave to him and tell him what had happened. A rash baron was stealing Rosalind away to Gretna Green.

The coach sets off, the duke sets off, the hired men run away, and the duke declares his undying passion.

Rosalind said, "Shrimps?" The poor little fellow's eyes were glazing over. She supposed that could not be helped—he was prone to unsteady nerves.

"Now Shrimps," Miss Mayton said, "I have been frugal all my life and the earl has been generous. I am prepared to pay twenty pounds. I am sure some of your interesting friends would leap at the chance to take this on."

"But I—"

"I fear we've made it more complicated than it need be," Rosalind said. "All you really need do is talk to your friends and explain that you need a fine-looking carriage and a coachman in livery, and perhaps a groom to go on the back. We can direct them what to do on the night."

"For twenty pounds, Shrimps," Cordelia said.

"Will you be seeing any of your acquaintances soon, do you think?" Viola asked.

"Um, well," Shrimps said, "One of them said he would be back, but I really do not think—"

"You must ask, Shrimps," Rosalind said. "You must see what he will say to twenty pounds."

Shrimps nodded sadly. Rosalind was quite buoyed by the arrangement. Naturally, a young man of Shrimps' delicate temperament could not be expected to participate in such a scheme, but she had every reason to hope that the people he knew would be very happy to. It was a fine amount of money for very little work.

SHRIMPS HAD STAGGERED across the avenue of Portland Place and run to his room. In a shaking voice, he'd acquainted Oyster with the latest developments in his very frightening life.

It was never a good idea to go and see those pups! First a pickpocket, now a carriage, coachman, and groom.

He did not even understand the plan the ladies had. Driving the carriage down the street and then jumping out and running away so the duke could profess undying passion to Lady Rosalind?

If that duke was dying of passion, why couldn't he just say so?

It was madness, but what was he to do about it? They'd pretty much taken his stunned silence as agreement. They expected him to make inquiries.

Then there was Barney expected back at any moment, sneaking up to him in the garden. He'd come back to be convinced that Shrimps' real name was Jimmy Black. How was he to prove it?

The walls were closing in. He began to wonder if he ought not just pack his few things and run away from it all.

Oyster laid his head on Shrimps' lap and his underbite chattered.

He could not bear to leave Oyster behind. And yet, he had no right to take the poor dog into the streets to starve when he had a very comfortable situation in Lord Van Doren's house.

Shrimps did not want to leave that comfortable situation either!

If everybody would just let him be, he'd be very content to chop onions and knead bread for all the rest of his days.

"What am I to do, Oyster?" he whispered.

Oyster did not answer, though Shrimps was convinced that if he *could* speak, he would probably have very sage advice. Oyster's primary concern, outside of food and the garden, was safety. Did he not always sleep under Shrimps' bed so as to be well hidden if an intruder stormed in?

Shrimps had slept under his bed a few times himself and it was very comforting.

Just now, he felt almost paralyzed by fear. He could not make a decision. He did not know which way to turn or which thing to do.

⟫⟫⟩✳⟨⟪⟪

BALTHAZAR HAD TASKED Henri with determining where, if anywhere at all, the Benningtons might be found this night. Unless it were a small dinner they attended, he was certain he might crash his way in nearly anywhere.

He'd thought he might wait out the week until he met Lady Rosalind once more at Lady Bloomington's masque. The token ring was being reset with a larger ruby, as the one the setting had housed had not been deemed sufficient for Lady Rosalind.

He'd chosen a large and brilliant stone and it would be ready by the night of the masque. He would bide his time until then.

Biding his time had turned out to be a foolish idea. He could not wait a week—he must see her.

Since he'd determined that he would ask her to marry, his thoughts had spun out and around in every way possible. Pictures of her, waking by his side. Pictures of her during the night that preceded waking.

Thinking of her upturned face, her laugh, her perfect delicate features.

Imagining her directing his household, and the delightful mishaps that were bound to be a result of it. Seeing himself not at all concerned with it and buying her a necklace when it seemed she'd somehow massacred the accounts and caring no more about it.

After all, how else could it be? Certainly, Miss Mayton would not have prepared her for anything at all practical. He did not care.

He would move the pianoforte out of every house he owned and claim the instrument gave him a headache. Not her travels through the world of music of course, which were charming, but the instrument itself.

Balthazar could not help but think of the absurd lengths she'd gone to. A pickpocket. A rash baron, indeed.

He did not plan to tell her he suspected anything untoward about those ruses. She would not like it and he was determined that she would like everything round her.

He'd thought of calling to the house, but their at-home day had passed.

Where would she be?

Henri, his clever valet, had made contact with a grocer who served the house, who had struck up a conversation with the Cook, who had apprised him that there was to be no family dinner this evening, but for the youngest ladies.

The earl was off to cards with Lord Cannerly. Lord Darden was, the cook presumed, going to his club. Miss Mayton and Lady Rosalind were to attend Lady Rawley's theatrical evening.

Balthazar had inwardly groaned at hearing it. He had, of course, received an invitation to the evening. It occurred each season and he'd even gone once, some years past.

It was a ludicrous display of Lady Rawley and her friends acting out some scene or other to great acclaim. False acclaim, in his opinion. In fact, he was certain some of the people who attended every year went for the sheer mirth of it.

The one time he had gone, the scene they'd played out had been the end of Romeo and Juliet. Lady Rawley had been, quite naturally, Juliet. Her friend, Mrs. Robinson, had done the duty as Romeo.

As if the general idea were not absurd enough, they had added to Shakespeare's words and changed the ending. The apothecary, played by the ludicrous Lady Agatha, did not sell Romeo poison in this version, but only a sleeping draught. So then, both the couple were only sleeping in the tomb.

The sleeping went on for some time and the audience began to wonder if it were the end and ought they to applaud.

Quite suddenly, Lady Rawley's Juliet shot up out of her doze. Seeing Romeo looking dead but only asleep beside her, she railed against his stupidity at being dead, took his dagger, and knocked him on the head with the hilt, waking him up too.

It all ended happily and Romeo and Juliet lived. Of course, Mrs. Robinson's Romeo had been knocked on the head rather hard and had required medical attention after the theatrical was over.

At the time, Balthazar had silently vowed that he'd never subject himself to another of Lady Rawley's theatricals in his lifetime.

Now, however, he dug out the invitation for it.

It was to be *Cymbeline*, of all things?

Certainly, Lady Rosalind must comprehend the depth of his devotion if he were willing to subject himself to Lady Rawley starring in *Cymbeline*.

He scanned the description of the evening.

In this exciting new idea of Cymbeline, as Imogen pretends to be the boy Fidele, Fidele then pretends to be the lady Astra, who finds herself forced to play the boy Romero. (A lady who plays a boy who plays a lady who plays a boy—heads are spinning!) Romero is friends with the God Jupiter, that God being all along fond of Imogen who is of course Romero-Astra-Fidele. Jupiter will reveal all to King Cymbeline in the most dramatic terms in a final revealing moment.

Cast: The God Jupiter played by the incomparable Lady Margaret Rawley

Imogen-Fidele-Astra-Romero played by the indomitable Mrs. Jemima Robinson

King Cymbeline played by the indubitable Lady Agatha Montfried

Balthazar laid the card down. It was preposterous.

He wrote a note to Lady Rawley, saying he would come.

MONDRIAN HAD JUST been informed that Barney had finally turned up to his rooms. He was anxious to hear the news he wished for—the boy Shrimps could not at all prove he was a person named Jimmy Black.

Mondrian was certain he was not Jimmy Black, that he was in fact the Dedmont heir named Henry Conroy. But he must be certain there was no Jimmy Black before he could proceed.

Barney was led in.

"Well?" Mondrian said. "What did you discover?"

"He ain't got no proof of his name, or so he says. I threatened him with going over the side of a bridge and into the Thames so I think he don't got it. He had another of his propositions though."

"Another ten pounds for a handkerchief?" Mondrian mused. "Take the job if you like, but if you're caught don't bother turning to me."

Barney shuffled his feet. "It ain't no handkerchief this time. You'll hardly believe it, but Lady Rosalind Bennington what lives across the street wants to be kidnapped and she'll pay twenty pounds for it."

Mondrian paused. "Did you say she *wishes* to be kidnapped?"

Barney nodded. "These society people have some wild ideas. Shrimps says it's all to make a duke run after the carriage and profess his undying love. At first I thought he was makin' the whole thing up, but she *did* want to get robbed so that fella could see it. That little set-up was supposed to drive 'im to the altar but he's kept out of her net so far."

"Which duke?" Mondrian asked.

"He didn't say, all I know is he's tall."

"Tell me the whole of the scheme," Mondrian said, beginning to get an idea. He was planning to take Shrimps, otherwise known as Henry Conroy, and ransom him anyway. Why not take Lady Rosalind too, if she were determined to have herself kidnapped?

A duke, or her father, or both, might pay a nice purse to get her back. If he were very smart, and very lucky, he might someday soon find himself living in New York as a gentleman prince. The idea suited him very well.

"Sit down, lad," he said to the boy. "I want you to take your time and relay absolutely everything you know about this Lady Rosalind and her interesting plan."

ROSALIND WAS LOOKING forward to the evening as much as she could to any evening that she did not suppose she would see Conbatten.

She and Miss Mayton were to go to a private theatrical.

Of course, they had such things in their own neighborhood from time to time, and then they were so often entertained in their own drawing room by Cordelia's Desdemona. However, this was to be another thing entirely.

This theatrical evening was to be put on by three influential ladies of the *ton*. Lady Rawley would host the evening and her particular friends, Mrs. Robinson and Lady Agatha, were to be her supporting actors.

They were to do a scene from *Cymbeline*, which Rosalind must admit was not her favorite Shakespeare play.

But favorite play or not, what a joy it would be to describe to Cordelia how it had all been staged and how it had come off. It was said that Lady Rawley put on the event every year and Cordelia was already thinking about how she might befriend Lady Rawley and become one of her company when it was her time to be out in society.

When Rosalind and Miss Mayton had left the house, Cordelia had a stack of books in her arms, determined to read over all of Shakespeare's plays so she could be ready to tread Lady Rawley's boards if such an opportunity were ever to present itself.

They found Lady Rawley to be a charming woman, though she greeted her guests in rather outlandish attire. She wore flowing white robes and carried a gold staff with an eagle fashioned atop it.

Lady Agatha was also dressed for the occasion. She was to be Cymbeline, the king, and was garbed in a heavy gold doublet over her dress, a gold crown sitting atop her head.

Mrs. Robinson's bottom half was enormous and was arrayed

in layers of removable skirts, as she explained to Miss Mayton. There was an overskirt, then a skirt made to look like trousers, then another skirt, then another skirt made to look like trousers, then a final skirt. She would not say why all these layers were necessary, but she hinted that there were many twists and turns to their version of the play.

Miss Mayton had been intrigued to hear of the skirts made to look like trousers and Mrs. Robinson had explained they were just usual skirts, but brown fustian cut out in the shape of trousers had been sewn on the front to give the idea.

The drawing room had been set up as a theater and it was very well done. A wood stage two feet high had been built and installed at one end and velvet covered chairs in rows formed a semi-circle round it.

At the other end of the drawing room were a series of sideboards heavy with all manner of food and drink.

"I think Papa would have enjoyed this," Rosalind said. "But then, he was also eager to challenge Lord Cannerly to another game of piquet. I suppose one cannot be everywhere at once."

"It is for the best, I think," her aunt said. "After all, if your father had been bowled over by Lady Rawley's performance, then Cordelia might have wondered if he liked it better than Desdemona and we should not wish…oh my goodness."

Miss Mayton had paused. She grabbed Rosalind's arm. In a whisper, she said, "The duke. He is here."

"Conbatten? Here?" Rosalind whispered back. She could hardly believe it. Though she had a great confidence that the fates smiled kindly upon her, how had they managed it? She had never thought to find the duke at such an evening. She had been certain she would not see him until Lady Bloomington's masque.

She slowly turned as her aunt waved to him. Having caught his eye, he smiled and made his way over.

What a man. Just look round you, world—was there anybody finer? Of course, there was not. Nobody could approach Conbatten.

"Lady Rosalind, Miss Mayton," he said with his ever-elegant bow. He rose and seemed to peer at Miss Mayton's veil, still wrapped tight round her cheeks on account of the stray dog hairs that remained glued on.

"Toothache," Miss Mayton said by way of explanation. "Now, Rosalind, you did say you were hoping for a glass of wine, if only you could view what was on offer?"

Rosalind nodded. She'd not said so, but her aunt was so perceptive as to see it would calm her nerves over the sudden appearance of Conbatten.

"Might I escort you to the sideboard, Lady Rosalind?" the duke said.

She nodded and put her hand on his arm. "Duke," she said.

"You should probably take to calling me Conbatten," he said, leading her across the room. "I imagine you were heading in that direction anyway."

"Yes, I was hoping to," she said. How interesting that he wished to be styled as Conbatten, though she had not the social standing to do it. It must mean something.

He showed her the selection of wines and she chose a Canary. As a footman poured her a glass, Conbatten said, "I must put you on your guard, Lady Rosalind. Archibald, the brother of the rash Baron Leighton, has paid me a visit."

Of course she knew it, as she'd been there. But what would he say about it?

"It is as I feared," Rosalind said.

"Indeed, yes," Conbatten said. "I found it very disturbing that a brother was urging another brother to get himself killed, as certainly he would be. I declined to assist Archibald in his schemes. One hopes he's resigned himself to living as the younger brother and taken his older brother home."

Rosalind sipped her wine to give her some time to parse his speech. Was it as her sisters thought? Had Conbatten only refused the duel because he would not act as the means of a brother disposing of a brother?

"I cannot say what the baron will do next," Rosalind said. "If Archibald is to be considered rash, then the baron must be considered even more rash. I doubt he will be turned from his purpose so easily."

"I see," Conbatten said thoughtfully. "If he does not go home, then what does he do next? Do you have a list of various houses he might stop at to issue his challenge? It may be wise to alert other gentlemen of the circumstances of the case."

Other gentlemen? What other gentlemen? Did he think there were other gentlemen? Why would he think so?

"Well," she said slowly, "I can think of no one."

"Ah, just me, then," the duke said. "I wonder if he will reapproach me with some new idea."

Rosalind wrinkled her forehead, thinking of how to hint at what the baron might do. How to hint at an attempted kidnapping to Gretna Green?

"I cannot know, of course," she said, slowly. "I am only certain that he wishes to marry me and once he gets an idea into his head, it can be very hard to get it out again."

"A determined fellow, then?"

"Oh, yes, very."

The room had been filling and just then a glass dinged. A gentleman Rosalind did not know said in a loud voice, "Charming ladies and esteemed gentlemen, if you will be so kind as to find your seats, we will commence with the theatrical!"

Rosalind looked toward the chairs and saw her aunt waving. The dear lady had commandeered a chair and then leaned over two more as if she would guard them from all comers.

"I believe my aunt has secured a seat for you too, Conbatten. Unless you are with a party you would sit with?"

"I have come alone and would be delighted," the duke said.

He was delighted, he said. Surely there was something in that.

They made their way over and Miss Mayton said cheerfully, "There you are, sit between us, Your Grace."

Rosalind's aunt was balancing a glass of wine and a plate of cake.

"Lord Harvey was so kind as to fetch me a drink and this wonderful orange cake," Miss Mayton said.

For some reason, Conbatten stared at her plate and sighed. "*Iced* cake, I see."

Rosalind did not know what to make of it, other than Conbatten seemed to have an aversion to iced cake. Well, she supposed there was no end of things she would find out about him that she did not yet know.

And then, he would find out things about her too. He probably had not the first idea of what her opinions were on fried kidneys. She ran opposed to the general consensus, as she was very much against them. He also could not know that she did not read music, as she was so very adept at hiding that fact by taking her listeners on a travel through the world of music.

Would he consider that a fault, she wondered.

She supposed he must have faults too, as every person had. But what could they be? It seemed unfathomable that he had any. Perhaps the worst of it was that he did not like iced cake.

"Ladies, gentlemen," the same man who'd directed them to be seated said, "we are encountering a slight difficulty and delay. We pray for your patience, if you please."

Rosalind looked to the stage and saw Lady Rawley and Mrs. Robinson deep in a hurried conversation.

Lady Rawley stepped forward. "My dear guests," she said, "we find that Lady Agatha has come down with a rather virulent distress of the stomach and cannot perform. Rest assured, we have no intention of being defeated by this blow!"

Rosalind peered round her and it was true, Lady Agatha was nowhere in sight. Her gold doublet rested forlornly on a chair near the stage.

"I wonder," Lady Rawley continued, "what lady would be brave enough, kind enough, to step forward in Lady Agatha's stead? It is no complicated matter, a willingness is all we require."

There was a silence in the room. Oh, if only Cordelia had been here! Her dear sister would have leapt at the chance to put herself into the play.

Miss Mayton rose, and her cake slipped off its plate and into Conbatten's lap. "Fear not, Lady Rawley, we will not allow you to be let down," she said. "If you will direct me, I am at your service."

There was a gentle applause all round and Rosalind thought most people looked exceedingly relieved that they were not to find themselves upon the stage. She was rather relieved herself. She was not shy, but she was not the actress that Cordelia was.

Miss Mayton handed her empty plate to Conbatten and squeezed past him, seeming not to have noticed that her slice of cake was no longer upon it.

Her dear aunt. Naturally, she would not allow Lady Rawley's theatrical to be ruined and had been in too much of a hurry to rush to the breach to notice her cake had gone astray.

"Very well done, Aunt," Rosalind whispered as Miss Mayton moved past her.

"Never mind it, you just stay here and entertain the duke, my dear," Miss Mayton whispered.

As her aunt made her way to the stage, Conbatten's brows knit. He slowly picked bits of cake from his trousers and deposited them back on the plate.

Goodness, he seemed as if he *really* did not care for iced cake.

CHAPTER EIGHTEEN

T HE THEATRICAL HAD not even started yet and Balthazar felt as if he'd already been through a rather full evening. A rather interesting one at that.

Lady Rosalind was resolute in her story of the rash baron who had followed her to London, which he found charming in the extreme. As he did not wish her to imagine he would turn down a duel to win her, he claimed he'd only been held back because the matter seemed to involve a brother who wanted a brother dead.

Though, if he *had* accepted that duel so ridiculously posed by Miss Mayton in the guise of Archibald, what would they have done then? He could not imagine.

Now, apparently, the rash baron would be determined not to go away.

Let him stay on if he liked. A figment of a baron was nothing to him. In fact, he was very cheered by the idea that this figment had no other gentlemen to visit with outlandish challenges to a duel. Only him.

Balthazar had dared to suggest to Lady Rosalind that she call him Conbatten, rather than Duke, and she had. There had been something in it, the way she said it…he was glad he'd thought to do it.

So few people called him Conbatten and she must be one among them.

Lady Rosalind was everything charming and lovely and he would sit through no end of hours of *Cymbeline* or any other ridiculous thing Lady Rawley thought to bring forth. Who cared, when he had Lady Rosalind by his side?

He had supposed he would be working hard all evening to keep his expression neutral, or approving even, in the face of the farce that was to be shortly before his eyes. Now though, it seemed it was to become even more ridiculous than he could have foreseen.

Lady Agatha had been struck down with an illness and Miss Mayton had courageously stepped forward.

And courageously thrown her cake in his lap while she was at it. Henri would have a collapse over it, as this time the icing had spattered both his coat *and* his trousers.

Lady Rawley was giving direction to Miss Mayton, while Mrs. Robinson helped her into Lady Agatha's gold doublet.

"My dear Miss Mayton," Lady Rawley said, "you are a treasure to exert yourself on my behalf. Now, it is the simplest thing in the world—I, as the god Jupiter, will appear later in the play than would be usual. It will be I, Jupiter, that will reveal all of the real facts of the case to Cymbeline! All you need do is look surprised at each new revelation. Dear Mrs. Robinson here will unmask herself as Imogen one skirt at a time. First as Romero, then Astra, then Fidele, then finally Imogen."

"Goodness that is a lot of people," Miss Mayton said. "I do not recall Romero and Astra from the play."

"No, you would not," Lady Rawley said, nodding. "We've added them for excitement."

Mrs. Robinson nodded. "Indeed, there are quite a lot of people in my outfit, but I do not have any lines. I just must follow along with Jupiter's revelations and reveal my new identities as we go."

"And you, dear Miss Mayton," Lady Rawley said, "remember you only need look surprised at every turn of events."

"Well, I suppose I will be, in any case," Miss Mayton said.

Conbatten bit his lip. It seemed wherever Miss Mayton would go, absurdity would follow. How predictable that she would just now be poised to play King Cymbeline.

"Cordelia will be stunned to hear what is transpiring this night," Lady Rosalind said. "She is so well versed in her Desdemona, but to imagine our aunt on the stage as one of Shakespeare's kings!"

"A very surprised sort of king," Conbatten said drily, "if I understood Lady Rawley's stage directions."

"Oh she will do it marvelously, I think," Lady Rosalind said. "Our Miss Mayton has such steady nerves, you know. I have always thought she got them from all her romantic heartbreaks. It must toughen a person up, I imagine."

"Do you anticipate any of your own heartbreaks, Lady Rosalind?"

She seemed to become very pensive over the question and sighed. "I dearly hope not," she said softly. "I would not hold up to it as my aunt has been able to. I should become a spinster and be very bitter."

Spinster, indeed. Not if he had anything to do with it.

"My wonderfully patient guests," Lady Rawley said from atop the stage. "We are ready to begin, and I as Jupiter will reveal all to Cymbeline!"

So proceeded one of the most bizarre hours of Balthazar's life. Lady Rawley had composed herself a never-ending speech full of drama and pathos and waving her staff this way and that and occasionally marching across the stage as if she would be off to somewhere else, only to turn round again and keep talking.

Mrs. Robinson did her duty by ripping off a skirt, only to reveal another skirt. Some of them had the pattern of trousers sewn on to indicate that Imogen was now pretending to be a boy again.

Miss Mayton was…well, what was she? He could not find the precise word for it, though whatever it should be called, it was taking all his self-control not to collapse with laughter.

For one, with all the handwaving and clutching at her heart she did, her crown slipped off and clattered to the floor, taking her veil with it. This revealed what looked to be the remnants of some very badly composed sideburns. Lord Ravensby helpfully fetched it for her amongst pitying glances. Balthazar presumed everybody else in the room would think Miss Mayton had some sort of unfortunate condition.

He had a great urge to stand and say, 'Just to clear things up—whatever is on Miss Mayton's face, it was put there purposefully for her moment as Archibald, the rash baron's brother, and now she cannot get it off.'

Getting her crown back on and her veil securely tied again, Miss Mayton took to staggering at each new surprise Jupiter dramatically revealed.

Toward the end, it seemed Miss Mayton must have come upon the idea that each new surprise must be more shocking to her than the last. Cymbeline had just fallen onto the floor upon being informed by Jupiter that the boy-girl-boy-girl-again was in fact his daughter Imogen.

If Shakespeare had been allowed to rise from his grave to view this concoction, he would have jumped back in it again and slammed the coffin shut.

Balthazar pressed his lips together to retain some composure. When had his life got this absurd?

He glanced at Lady Rosalind and her rapt expression. She leaned forward, her slender neck exposed. *She* was when absurdity and improbability had marched into his sphere.

He could not be sorry over it. He had once imagined a very staid sort of life with whatever duchess he ended up with. He'd imagined polite courtesy and formal manners. He'd imagined a lady quietly playing an instrument or sewing or having somber meetings with his doleful housekeeper to discuss the practicalities of the house.

He would get none of that, if he had his way.

A life with Lady Rosalind was likely to be akin to a wild ride through a fog-filled forest, never knowing what would come next and always surprised at what was around the bend.

It was also likely to be full of laughter, as he had not laughed so much in the whole of his life.

She would just have to say yes, and she would hopefully not be too disturbed over his occasional forays into the night, in service to the queen.

However she viewed it, he would not take the queen's advice and lock Lady Rosalind away on his estate. Not unless he was locked up with her.

SHRIMPS DREADED HIS trips into the back garden at night. He never knew exactly when Barney would turn up again.

Barney had already been to demand proof that Shrimps was in fact Jimmy Black, which of course he had none. He had not proof he was anybody! A fellow like him didn't go round carrying proof of who he was. He did not even know what the proof was supposed to be.

Of course, there was the letter sewn into his coat, but he did not know what that said. He would never know, as he could not read and he would never allow anybody else to see his mother's words to him. They were personal words, just between them, even if he never knew what they were.

To distract Barney from his lack of proof, he'd told Barney of the new venture for twenty pounds. A carriage, a coachman, and a footman. A pretend-kidnapping for Lady Rosalind.

Barney had been skeptical over it, as he said nobody, not even a swell, wanted to be kidnapped. Shrimps had done his best to explain that it was all about the duke declaring his passion, though he personally didn't understand it himself.

Barney had finally said he'd talk to somebody knowledgeable about those sorts of arrangements.

Who the somebody was or how that somebody would be knowledgeable on the subject, Shrimps did not have the first idea. Maybe it was a coachman down on his luck who might take the job?

He was hoping not. He was hoping that what Lady Rosalind wished for was not possible. He could say he tried, but it could not be done. He might even hint to her that there were faster ways to get married than pretending to be kidnapped. As far as he could see, people did it every day with very little trouble.

Oyster was doing his usual surveil of the garden, though Shrimps never knew what he was looking for. Whatever it was, Oyster must confirm it was either there or not there before doing his business.

"Hey, mate," Barney said from behind him.

Shrimps jumped. He had not expected that Barney would be back so soon!

"Why do you always have to sneak up on me?" he said.

"I'm a creature of the night," Barney said, "I move in the shadows."

"It's scary."

"I don't care. Now, listen up. I talked to my associate what knows these matters and he says a feint of a kidnappin' is very common among the swells."

Common? Cook was right—these lords and ladies really did have too much money for their own good.

"So, I'm gonna do you the favor of comin' up with a coachman and a carriage for Lady Rosalind's stab at the thing. I'll go as the groom myself. And guess who else is going? You!"

Shrimps felt a trickle of ice slip down his spine. It was frightening enough to arrange these odd things Lady Rosalind wanted done. But to be there!

"Me? Why? I don't need to go," he said. "What use would I be? I'm terrible under pressure and everybody knows it!"

"Yeah, we all know it, but my associate who's arranging the carriage wants a little insurance that it ain't some sort of trap."

"Lady Rosalind doesn't set up traps," Shrimps said. "Not for you, anyway. The whole thing is for the duke. What would she want with you?"

"I'm tellin' ya how it's gonna be. At nine o'clock on the night, you're gonna go to the end of this street and get in the carriage, then we go forward and take in Lady Rosalind."

"And Miss Mayton," Shrimps said resignedly.

"Who is Miss Mayton?" Barney asked, grabbing him by the collar. "You didn't say there was another lady involved."

Shrimps wriggled out of his grasp. "She's the older lady what goes with her everywhere. You don't think a proper young lady just ups and goes out of her house by herself, do you?"

Of course, he could see that Barney had not ever considered the matter. Nor had he, until he began living in Lord Van Doren's house. He'd seen quite a lot of their habits. He'd even found out that all ladies had a maid to get them into their clothes!

He'd thought, considering how much they practiced dancing and playing music, that somebody would have shown them how to get dressed in their own clothes.

Those that lived rich had very mysterious lives.

"This Miss Mayton," Barney said, rubbing his chin, "she's all for the other one getting kidnapped?"

That *was* a sticking point. Shrimps really did not know why Miss Mayton had thought the pickpocket was a good idea. It seemed the sort of thing that an older person might have looked down on.

"Miss Mayton is an unusual person," Shrimps admitted. "I can't say why she is, only that Cook says these kind of people marry all their relatives and it makes for weak breeding stock, as anybody with hunting dogs would know."

"Right. So she's gone funny in the head."

"Something like that."

"But she won't cause no trouble?"

"No, she never does," Shrimps said. "She's very cheerful."

"Right. And who's this duke the whole palaver is done for?"

"His name is Conbatten. He's very tall. That's all I know about him!"

Barney leaned over him. "That's enough to know. Be at the end of the street at the appointed hour. If ya don't turn up, it's all off and my associate will be informing your lord of where that pickpocket in the park came from—hired by his very own servant."

With that, Barney slipped out of the garden.

Oyster had been very sensibly hiding under a bush. Now he crawled out and gave a little wag and a very big chatter of teeth.

Shrimps sighed and patted his head. "I wish Lady Rosalind would stop having so many ideas!"

THE YOUNGER LADIES had gone above stairs and everyone else was still out. It presented the perfect opportunity Tattleton had been waiting for.

He had announced he was going out to take the air.

There were, of course, a few surprised looks among the staff. He was not known for his fondness for either walking or outdoor air. It mattered little—they could not have ever guessed his real destination.

The stables.

He tiptoed down the mews and let himself in.

Tattleton found Sandren directing the hands on whatever he did with the horses. As far as he could tell, the beasts were to have oats before they retired for the evening.

Did horses retire? Did they lie down with a blanket over them? He really did not know.

Sandren had, naturally, been rather surprised to see him. Nevertheless, he led Tattleton into his private chambers.

The butler was taken aback about how neatly put together the whole thing was. There was an antechamber with comfortable chairs and then he could see a tidy bedchamber beyond. The floors were tiled and scattered with rugs, and there were paintings of horses on the walls. Somehow, there was not a speck of dust or hay to be seen.

It was a very comfortable sort of place.

Sandren poured him a brandy and motioned for him to take one of the chairs.

"I won't kid ya, Mr. Tattleton, I'm surprised to see you here."

Tattleton nodded. Of course, he would be. The butler had never set foot inside the stables either in Town or in Somerset.

"In general, Mr. Sandren, I prefer us all to stick to our natural milieus. I don't expect to find you serving dinner in the house and you do not expect to find me wandering round your horses."

Sandren nodded.

"But I fear we are approaching some sort of crisis situation and I would be remiss if I did not take steps."

"Steps?"

"The very steps that have led me to your door," Tattleton said, sipping his brandy. "I wished to ask you about a certain carriage ride that seemed most unusual. A certain carriage ride in which I believe Miss Mayton saw fit to glue dog hair on her face."

"Aye," Sandren said, nodding. "That was a strange one."

"But am I correct in thinking that Miss Mayton disguised herself as a man?"

"Right you are. And a strange-looking man at that."

"Why? Do you know why? This all seems very irregular!"

"That's what I thought myself," Sandren said. "It was a shock when I turned round and there is this fella sitting in the carriage with rather wild-looking sideburns. Then the fella speaks and it's Miss Mayton."

"Where did they go? What did they do? What was the purpose of this strange behavior?"

Sandren held a hand up. "Whoa, that's a lot of questions. Give me a moment and I'll tell you how it was."

He drained his brandy and poured himself another one.

"I was told to go to 38 Grosvenor Square. The Duke of Conbatten's residence. Then Miss Mayton attempts to sound all gruff and manly and hands the footman coming out to the carriage a note. She tells him she will wait in the carriage for a written answer. Oh, and the other ladies were all crouching under blankets."

"Crouching!"

"Aye, hidden away if you like. Anyway, who comes out but the duke himself and Miss Mayton is waving her hands around and telling him to go back but he don't pay her mind. He says something about Archibald—"

"Archibald!" Tattleton cried. "Who is Archibald?"

Sandren shrugged. "Some fella who wanted his brother dead, as far as I could gather."

Tattleton drained his brandy.

"Anyhow, the duke says he won't oblige. Something about not helping this Archibald become the fifteenth baron and that duels were held too early in the morning."

"A duel!"

"Yep, so the duke keeps coming toward the carriage and Miss Mayton waves a cane at him and shouts to me to be off. Off I go and have to drive to Piccadilly so Miss Mayton can get out of her men's clothes and then I drive them home."

Tattleton hardly understood what he was being told. Some strange man named Archibald, a challenge to the duke, Miss Mayton dressed as a man?

"I can hardly comprehend...why on earth...what does it add up to?"

"It was all to do with Mrs. Ellington's goose chase is what they said."

"Who is Mrs. Ellington?" Tattleton whispered.

"How should I know?"

"But did you not think to speak to the earl about this circumstance?" Tattleton asked.

Sandren shook his head. "They was all led forward by Miss

Mayton and I don't know nothing 'bout goose chases. What would I have said about it?"

Tattleton saw the point. He had not, himself, approached the earl. What was he to say?

Was there something called a goose chase?

He might think so, as the *ton* was forever inventing bizarre notions, but for one very important point. Had there been such a thing as a goose chase, it would have been the topic of conversation at dinner. If it had all been a hi-jinks bit of nonsense, they would have talked of it endlessly.

Not one word had been mentioned and Miss Mayton had taken great pains to hide whatever dog hair was still left on her face.

No, that story of a goose chase that Sandren had been told was all stuff and nonsense.

Tattleton staggered out of the stables more alarmed than he'd been going in.

CHAPTER NINETEEN

ROSALIND ADMIRED THE folds of her draping white gown while Lynette tied on the gold braided belt under the bodice and held out the wonderful velvet floor length cape that that would go over it. The velvet was a very dark red shade and it had gold braiding running along the edges.

She was to go as Boudicca to Lady Bloomington's masque—warrior queen of the Iceni, leading her people to victory.

This was the night when everything would be decided.

Rosalind had approached her father and told him that Lady Hightower was delighted to escort her and Miss Mayton to the masque.

As she had suspected, the earl had been equally delighted to bow out of the masque. Had he gone, he would have worn a plain domino, as he was not over-fond of that type of party.

He'd already left to meet Lord Cannerly at White's, and Darden had gone off to his own club. Darden was to meet some of his friends at the YBC, and then they would proceed to Lady Bloomington's house.

Beatrice and Van Doren would go as well, and that had been a trickier matter to arrange. Beatrice thought they all ought to go together. Rosalind had been forced to explain that Lady Hightower was the sort of person who did not like her favors refused. She and Miss Mayton must go with the lady.

If only she could tell Beatrice the truth! She could not,

though. A husband had inserted himself between the sisters and that husband was Van Doren. He would shut down their plan the moment he got wind of it.

It was no matter, she assured herself. Beatrice was always running late and they would be well away by the time she exited her house. Darden would also tarry and her kidnapping would have already occurred by the time he arrived.

She would go in her hired carriage and make circles round Berkeley Square until she saw Conbatten. *He* would not be late, he never was.

Rosalind suspected that while some gentlemen might be able to slip in late without too many frowns from a hostess, a duke had not the luxury. After all, his attendance would be a thing the lady would like to mention in the following days. 'Yes, I suppose you noticed the duke was there—he attended me early so we might have a conversation before it became too crowded.'

And what duke did they all wish to talk about? Conbatten.

She would see him dismount his horse and she would rap on the carriage roof and then they would be off. She would finally know—did Conbatten love her or did he not? Would he chase the carriage, or shrug his shoulders?

It made her feel sick to think of what the outcome might be. If he did not come after her, she would be devastated.

He must come after her.

Miss Mayton came into the room. "Goodness, Rosalind, you look smashing."

Miss Mayton was once more dressed in her full regalia of widow's weeds, her ghostly black veil brushing the hem of her bombazine skirt.

"Darden was a dear to arrange for me to go as Boudicca," Rosalind said, "though he could not have imagined the significance of it. Boudicca was brave, and so must I be."

Lynette's forehead wrinkled over the idea of requiring bravery to attend a masque.

"I wonder if something might be said to me this night,

Lynette," she said by way of explanation. "Something said that could change the course of my life."

Lynette's brow cleared and she nodded knowingly.

What she'd told her maid was true—she had just left out the means she and Miss Mayton would employ to get to the important moment.

"We ought to go down, Rosalind," Miss Mayton said, giving Rosalind a certain look. "We would not wish to make Lady Hightower's carriage wait."

Rosalind nodded and Lynette added the final touch—a gold crown. She would carry Boudicca in her heart as she faced the most momentous circumstance of her life.

Everything hung in the balance. Joy or despair. A happy future or gray shrouded years rolling one into the other like fog on the hills. Love, or lack of it.

"I am ready," she said, throwing her shoulders back.

"WHY TAKE THE ring with you?" Henri asked, looking critically at Balthazar's coat.

He had just tucked Lady Rosalind's spectacular ruby ring into his inside coat pocket. The stone was one of the best he'd ever seen—the queen herself would be happy to own such a gem. It was set securely in a hinged, oval red leather box, the inside lined with white velvet to allow the ruby to shine.

"There is a lump!" Henri cried. "It ruins the line of the coat! It is not perfect. Everyone will see it is not perfect and wonder what has happened to Henri. Why does not Henri produce perfection, as he has always done?"

It amused Balthazar that his valet imagined he was a rather regular topic of conversation amongst the *ton*.

"First, I am wearing a domino over it so nobody will see the devastation of my coat. Second, I am hoping the ring does not remain in my coat overlong and speedily reaches its destination on Lady Rosalind's finger. Then, all perfection will be restored."

"This is all very hasty," Henri fretted.

"What am I to do?" Balthazar asked. "Am I to allow Lady Rosalind and Miss Mayton to plan more and more bizarre schemes?"

"That is just it!" Henri said. "Elle est aussi folle qu'un chat sur des charbons ardents."

Balthazar suppressed his laughter. As mad as a cat on hot coals indeed.

"Which one is the cat on coals?" he asked. "Lady Rosalind or Miss Mayton?"

"Both! Ce sont des fous. I only say, what is the rush?"

"I see. You are determined, then, to wish for a more usual lady. Perhaps a grim lady who will look at the wine receipts and wonder where it is all going, and then she might make surprise visits to the servants' hall to see what you are all doing down there."

"Surprise visits?"

"And a cut down of wine."

"But I am French!"

"Yes, you do mention that often."

Henri sighed. "Alas, if you must have a woman in the house…then I suppose…you say she will not look at the wine receipts?"

"I highly doubt she will look at any receipts whatsoever. Lady Rosalind Bennington should not be troubled by such pedestrian matters."

Henri nodded and Balthazar thought he was once more mollified that his rather relaxed lifestyle was not set to come to an end.

Balthazar only hoped his own bachelor lifestyle *was* set to come to an end.

Really, if she refused him, what would he do? There was not going to be another Lady Rosalind coming along.

"Wish me luck," he said to his long-suffering valet.

"Bonne chance," Henri said softly.

Bonne chance. Yes, that was what he needed. Bonne chance.

ROSALIND AND MISS Mayton had gone down to the great hall early, in anticipation of the hired carriage arriving. They'd told Tattleton all sorts of frightening things about Lady Hightower. She must not be kept waiting even a moment. As her carriage pulled up, they must be running out with nary a pause. Tattleton and the footmen were not to disturb themselves over it.

Their poor butler had seemed very nervous over these ideas and had paced the hall and peered out the windows.

Finally, the carriage arrived. Shrimps had really done it. There it was, a hired carriage. The coachman was lanky with dark hair and very pale skin. His groom was rather heavy-set, had a very unfortunate birthmark on his cheek, and was squeezed into near-bursting livery. Neither of them had the bearing of a real coachman and groom, but who was to notice that? The carriage itself was very good-looking. Aside from no coat of arms on the door, nobody would guess it was not Lady Hightower's coach.

They'd raced out of the house and into the carriage.

As the carriage turned itself round and barreled out of Portland Place, leaving a disgruntled looking Tattleton at the door, Rosalind was rather surprised to find who else was in the carriage.

"Shrimps!" she said, "what do you do here? And who are you?" she asked the young man sitting next to him.

"Well, I was told I ought to come," Shrimps said, "so I did."

"And you?" Rosalind asked the young man.

"Mason."

"Why are you here, though?" Miss Mayton asked.

"To make sure it all goes smoothly."

Rosalind looked at her aunt and they both shrugged. It must

be admitted by them both that they did not know the ins and outs of a false kidnapping. Apparently, these people did, though.

"Very well, Mason. Shrimps. Now, what is most important about all this is the moment Conbatten catches up to the carriage. You must be well away by then. I would not wish him to be distracted and wondering if he should try to catch you. As well, if things go as I hope, I am to be told things that would be for my ears only."

Shrimps' brow wrinkled. "Is Miss Mayton to run out of the carriage too, then?"

"Oh dear," Miss Mayton said, "I am not much of a runner."

"My aunt will delicately step away. She need not go far, after all, Conbatten will not think to chase after *her*, will he?"

"That lady," Mason said, pointing at Miss Mayton, "will get out at the door. We got spies everywhere. That duke is already inside the house so she'll have to go get 'im."

"Already in Lady Bloomington's house?" Rosalind said. "We come so early, how is he already there?"

Shrimps shook his head sadly. "There's no accounting for rich people," he said softly.

"It don't matter," Mason said. "She goes in and gets 'im."

Rosalind nodded. Of course, in this sort of an operation, she must be willing to adjust and change course as necessary. She should have anticipated that it would be so.

"Very well," she said. She squeezed her aunt's hand. "We are so close," she said. "Just a few more steps to take."

"Never fear, my dear. I shall march into Lady Bloomington's house and find him in a trice. He is so very easy to spot, towering over everybody as he does."

That was true. It would not take her aunt but a moment to locate Conbatten and apprise him of the circumstances. Then he would rush out to save her.

"I await your rescue, my dear, darling Conbatten," she whispered.

The young man who sat across from her snorted.

Rosalind ignored it, she could not expect that person to be struck with the finer feelings that just now permeated her thoughts.

BERKELEY SQUARE BEING so nearby, Balthazar had reached Lady Bloomington's house in under five minutes. He'd almost thought to walk, so easy was the distance. However, Hades seemed to always know when he'd been left behind and would be impossibly rude the following day. Whether he went near or far, Hades wished to go. Balthazar had often thought that Hades' inclinations were less about the exercise and more about what other strange horses he might encounter at the destination.

Later, he would return Hades home and Hamill would take them both into the Rats' Castle for their foray into it to collar a few of Mondrian's boys and find out what they knew. They would take his carriage to their destination in case they wished to remove the boys to another location.

Hamill's carriage had been specially built. It was larger than most and a veritable fortress. Underneath the polished paneling, it was lined in iron sheets to stop any bullet wishing to make its way through. There were two large foot irons on either side of the coach and four heavily armed men to ride upon them.

On the inside, each seat lifted up to reveal a compartment filled with weapons, and there were compartments overhead as well.

Hamill could wage a war, just himself and his carriage.

There was so much to be done before that little adventure, though. His future must be secured, and his future was Lady Rosalind.

As he entered through the doors of Lady Bloomington's house, he wondered what Lady Rosalind had dressed herself as. He also hoped she was not *too* well disguised. He would like to pull her away into a corner before the ball began.

"Lady Bloomington," he said, bowing to her Egyptian queen.

"Conbatten," she said, "excellent to see you."

Very suddenly, Lady Bloomington's butler raced to her side and whispered in her ear.

Whatever the fellow said, it seemed to discompose the lady.

"Oh dear," she muttered.

"Lady Bloomington?" he asked. "May I be of service?"

The lady seemed to consider the offer. Then she leaned close to him. "Perhaps you might. Cahill has just told me that a certain Mrs. Mayton appears to have gone mad in the ballroom and is rushing here and there…looking for *the duke*. Do you suppose it's you?"

Balthazar pressed his lips together to stop from laughing. He could not fathom what Miss Mayton was up to this time. Perhaps he was to be told that Lady Rosalind had been stolen off to the garden by some rogue and he'd better go rescue her.

He would be delighted.

"I suspect it is indeed me that she seeks. Never fear, Lady Bloomington," he said. "Whatever bee is in the lady's bonnet, I will take the sting out of it in all haste."

Lady Bloomington looked exceedingly relieved to hear it.

Balthazar strode toward the ballroom and went through the doors.

The scene that confronted him was not exactly what he expected. The gathering of guests had seemed to shrink to the edges of the ballroom to escape the madwoman in the center of it. There were vicars and jesters, pirates and queens, all pressed against the walls and looking exceedingly alarmed.

In the center of the floor, Miss Mayton darted here and there, looking like a ghost who was forever searching.

She was garbed in the full regalia of her widow's weeds, her black lace veil trailing on the floor and smearing Lady Bloomington's chalk design.

"Where is he? I must find the duke at once!" she shouted at

the frightened guests.

"Miss Mayton," he said loudly, to gain her attention.

"Your Grace! There you are! Finally!" she cried, racing to him.

As the crowd looked on, she grasped at his domino. Then she paused and took a deep breath. "Lady Rosalind, well you know about the rash baron, I'm afraid he's kidnapped her. To Gretna Green!"

Gretna Green? This was too much. How was he not to start laughing and never stop? He had jested with himself that he ought to propose before Lady Rosalind arranged her own kidnapping. Apparently, he'd not been quick enough—she'd actually done so.

That charming, mad lady.

"I thought I should find you in here right away," Miss Mayton said breathlessly, "but it has been some time, a quarter hour, I think."

Balthazar peeled Miss Mayton's fingers from his domino. He folded his arms. "I see. And you think I ought to go racing after her to save her from the rash baron?"

Miss Mayton looked perplexed over the question. "What else would you do?"

"Very good. Now where do you suppose I might find this carriage heading toward Gretna Green, as it has been a quarter of an hour already. How shall I catch up with them?"

Miss Mayton appeared to be thinking hard. Balthazar dug his nails into his palms to stop from laughing.

"Perhaps they have not got too far," Miss Mayton said. "I believe the horses were rather slow."

Slow horses to Gretna Green? What an idea.

"Now, Miss Mayton, the time has come for all ruses and schemes to come to an end. They have been exceedingly charming and entertaining, but you must come clean."

Miss Mayton looked as if she might counter the idea. He held his hand up. "No more obfuscations, if you please. I am not an idiot. I was not fooled by either the pickpocket or the remarkable *Archibald*."

"You were not?"

"Certainly not."

"Oh dear, Rosalind was so hopeful…you see she just wished…her poor heart shall be broken…"

"I do not see why it should be," Balthazar said. "I have every intention of proposing this night and no intention of ever telling her I know the truth of these ruses."

The relief that flooded the old girl's face was profound. She was an eccentric creature, but she most certainly did care for her charges. Of course, she did—what other middle-aged matron would go to such ridiculous lengths?

"That is very good news, very good indeed."

"Now, where is she?"

"Come," Miss Mayton said, "she will be just down the street. It has been all arranged. The coachman and the footman will run off and I will delicately step aside and you may say your piece."

What a mad world Lady Rosalind's was. What a mad world he was intent on joining.

Balthazar led Miss Mayton to the great hall. Catching Lady Bloomington's eye, he said, "I am just taking Miss Mayton out for some air."

Lady Bloomington appeared grateful to hear it.

Once out of doors, Miss Mayton peered down the avenue. "Well," she said, "I think they must be just now going round the square to pass by again."

There were various coaches on the move round Berkeley Square, most of them stopping at Lady Bloomington's house. He supposed he must wait for one that did not stop. If he understood Lady Rosalind at all, she would helpfully indicate which coach she rode in by poking her head out the window and forlornly waving her handkerchief.

"I will assume I do not need my horse, Miss Mayton," he said. "They will pass by rather slowly with their slow horses and I might pursue on foot."

"Oh I imagine so," Miss Mayton said. "After all, the coach-man and footman will wish to run off, and then Shrimps and Mason must get themselves out too."

Balthazar felt the back of his neck go cold at the mention of Shrimps.

"Why is Lord Van Doren's servant with them?" he asked.

"Shrimps? Do you know him? He was the one who helped us arrange…things. He has associates who do these sorts of…things. Though, really, I was rather surprised to see him—I had not known he would come along."

Balthazar was well aware of Shrimps' associates. They were Mondrian's boys.

"Miss Mayton," he said sharply, "what did the coachman look like?"

"Him? I didn't get such a good look. He was rather thin and pale, though, with very black hair."

Mondrian.

"Was there anybody else?"

"Well, yes, of course there was a groom. A fairly large boy, I'm afraid his livery did not fit as one might have wished."

"Did he have a mark on his cheek?"

"Oh, you know him?"

The boy who worked for Mondrian. There could be no doubt now. Lady Rosalind had put herself in the hands of a very dangerous man.

Balthazar searched the street for any carriage that might be coached by Mondrian. Though he wished to be hopeful, the facts would not be subdued by hope. If Mondrian was the coachman, he did not do it for a lark. He did not do it for whatever few pounds Lady Rosalind had paid.

He did it because there was a greater prize to be had.

Demands for payment would be even now delivered to the earl's door. Lady Rosalind had managed to arrange her own *real* kidnapping.

How foolish he'd been to allow this nonsense to proceed! He should have put a stop to it at the pickpocket!

"Miss Mayton, you are to go home at once. When you get there, you must tell the earl everything."

"The earl! Oh, he will not like it, though," Miss Mayton said.

"No, he will not. But at least it will explain why he has just received a ransom note for Lady Rosalind's return."

Miss Mayton staggered.

Just then, Balthazar spotted Van Doren and his bride descending a carriage. And there was Darden too, on his horse.

"Go, Miss Mayton," he said firmly. "Ask Lady Van Doren to take you home."

He strode away from her. "Darden, Van Doren, step over here a moment." To a footman he said, "Go inside and find Lord Hamill, get him out here. Have another lad call Lord Hamill's carriage. Do so in all haste."

CHAPTER TWENTY

THE CARRIAGE BARRELED down the road. Rosalind held on to steady herself.

"Why are you continuing on?" Rosalind asked. "You are meant to go round the square. How is Conbatten to find us if we are not nearby?"

"Nobody's meant to find us," Mason said with a laugh. He pulled out a pistol and rested it in his lap.

Rosalind felt a stone sinking in her belly. What was happening? Why did that young man have a pistol?

"Mr. M said I was to keep you all calm-like," Mason said. "Just don't make a fuss and all will come right in a day or two."

"A day or two!" Rosalind cried.

"I said," Mason said, fingering his weapon, "stay all calm-like."

Shrimps' eyes were wide as saucers.

"You are frightening poor Shrimps," Rosalind said, determined not to mention that she was rather terrified herself. "He has very delicate nerves."

"So I heard," Mason said. "Now listen, there's no reason to not be all calm-like. We hide you away, we get money from your pa and some other fella, we leave you where your people can collect you again. Simple as daylight."

"Simple as daylight!" Rosalind said. "We paid twenty pounds to have a straightforward task performed, I really do not understand…"

Mason snorted, as he seemed to be in the unpleasant habit of doing. "Right, well I would say this is a matter of the boss shootin' a bit higher than twenty pounds."

"But, but it's criminal!"

"They *are* criminals," Shrimps whispered.

"Wait," Rosalind said, having a moment to parse what this person had just said. "You mentioned my father and…some other fellow? What other fellow?"

"A great muckety-muck, a duke of something or other."

Shrimps slid down in his seat as if he might be able to disappear into it.

"Conbatten?" Rosalind whispered.

"That sounds about right." Mason snorted again. "It's pretty funny if you think about it. One person kidnapped and two people payin'. I 'spose that don't happen every day."

"I should think not! Well, I never really understood how people ended up hanged. I really thought, it must have been a mistake, they were blamed for something they did not do because how could anybody—"

Mason leaned forward and put the pistol to her face. "Don't you never mention hanging again, miss. Never again."

Rosalind took in a long and slow breath to calm herself. If ever she needed her steady nerves and courageous nature, it was now. She must learn and think as she went. Lesson one—do not mention hanging.

How could she escape these people? She might throw herself out of the carriage before that temperamental fellow could fire his pistol and then run.

But if she did that, she'd be leaving Shrimps behind.

Why was Shrimps here anyway? She'd asked and he'd only said he'd been told to come and so he'd come. She had not thought much of it at the time.

"What does Shrimps have to do with your very unsavory scheme," she asked, attempting to sound as courageous as possible. "He only made the arrangements and he certainly would not have known your real purpose."

She paused, and then looked at Shrimps. "You did not know their real purpose, did you?"

A teardrop rolled down the boy's cheek. "'Course I didn't," he whispered. "All I ever wanted was to be left alone to chop onions, peel potatoes, knead bread, and take Oyster into the garden!"

Rosalind felt a pang then. A pang of guilt. It had all seemed so safe, somehow. Just a bit of hi-jinks to give Conbatten his opportunities. But it was not safe, and she'd dragged Shrimps into it.

Mason hooked a thumb at Shrimps. "Him? I got no idea why we got him. I don't suppose his lord will pay to get him back."

Van Doren. What would Van Doren have to say about this? He *would* pay to get Shrimps back. He'd be mad as a hornet, but he'd pay because he would consider it the honorable thing to do.

Then, he'd spend the rest of his life lecturing her about how she'd endangered a young boy.

And for once, Van Doren would be right.

She shouldn't have done it. She shouldn't have done any of it!

What had she been thinking? It was as if she'd been in some sort of dream state.

What would her father think? Would he throw Miss Mayton from the house for being part of it? He couldn't, could he? She was family. Rosalind could hardly imagine he would blame Miss Mayton...if this had been less serious.

She suspected her dear, steady father would be far less steady in the face of this disaster.

What would Conbatten think? He was meant to only gallantly chase a carriage halfway down a street. Now he was to pay a ransom?

And then, should she survive this very grave mistake, it would all come out. It would be known that she'd very foolishly arranged her own kidnapping!

Even if Conbatten loved her now, he could not love her when he understood what she'd done. No duke would ever countenance having such a duchess by his side. He was indulgent of her, she'd sensed that all along. But he would not go so far as to accept this.

This was no lighthearted peccadillo. This was rash and unthinking, and very grave.

She would deserve whatever was to come her way. Should she come out on the other side of this catastrophe, she would deserve the gray days ahead.

IT WAS NO easy matter to explain to Darden and Van Doren how it was that they must set off in a very heavily armed coach. Nor was it straightforward to explain how Lady Rosalind had been kidnapped.

That part was not particularly understandable to Hamill either.

Of all of them, Darden was perhaps the least surprised. "Five sisters," he'd muttered. "When they get together, they have the worst ideas."

"Do not forget Miss Mayton," Van Doren said gruffly. "She is their principal, always bravely tearing forward to ever more dangerous notions."

"The point is," Balthazar said, hopeful of bringing recriminations to an end, "I believe I know who has taken her. Somebody with connections to Shrimps."

"Shrimps!" Van Doren said. "I knew I should not have taken in that boy and his dog. Beatrice was so insistent, though."

"Yes, well, this person has got Shrimps too, though I am not altogether sure why," Balthazar said.

"You think they've been taken to the address we recently became aware of?" Hamill said, handing out pistols and swords from a seemingly never-ending supply in a wood box at their feet.

"I do not think they will have gone there, actually," Balthazar said. "But I am hopeful we can corner one of the boys in that room and wring another address out of him."

Hamill nodded. Darden said, "Where are these addresses?"

"Nearby the Seven Dials," Balthazar said, hoping they wouldn't get too squeamish about it.

Van Doren leaned his head back. "Of course. Where else would we be going? Carlton House?"

"My own sister, in the neighborhood of the Seven Dials," Darden said, quietly.

Van Doren patted Darden's hand. "We'll get her out," he said. "We have to. I could hardly face Beatrice otherwise."

"We *will* get her out," Balthazar said. It was not even a question. They must get her out.

⇒⟫⟪⟸

MONDRIAN LEANED BACK and laced his hands behind his head. Everything was going according to plan. Lady Rosalind and the boy he was now certain was the young baron, Henry Conroy, had been spirited away as easy as you like. Of course, it *would* be easy when the lady had actually paid to make it happen.

They were just now locked up in a room in his apartments. Mason had informed them that if they shouted for help, none would come. Some of the closer neighbors might yell back that they'd better shut their traps, though. They were guests of the Rat's Castle now.

Two ransom notes had made their way to their destinations—one to the Earl of Westmont and one to the Duke of Conbatten. Of course, he could not be certain the duke would actually pay, but it was worth trying out. He had ears everywhere and it seemed Lady Rosalind was in some way favored by the great and powerful duke. As for the father, he was quite sure he'd come up with ten thousand to retrieve his daughter.

The boy could be dealt with after he'd returned Lady Rosalind to her own hearth.

If he were able to squeeze another ten thousand from the duke, and then yet another ten thousand from the Conroys, he would be a rich man. He could live on percents, just as a gentleman ought to do.

He'd thought of going to America, but then, could he not just take on another identity and set himself up somewhere far from London and the Conroys? He might go up north, Scotland even. He could buy himself some land and live as a merry English squire.

His sons would grow up as gentry. They would be handsome and marry into families placed higher. His line would be on the move, creeping up the rungs, and nobody would ever know how it all started.

Yes, that was feeling like the better idea. He *could* go to America, but was that really where a gentleman of the blood belonged? Was it an accomplishment to find oneself highly placed in a society such as that? His father was an English aristocrat.

He began to very much feel as if America should be beneath his notice.

Mondrian drained his ale. He was an English gentleman, and he was poised to take his rightful place.

ROSALIND HAD WATCHED with trepidation as the carriage drove into a neighborhood she had never traveled to before. It was a neighborhood she had not ever imagined possible.

Of course, she did not know so much about London as to know all of its locales, but this was of the type that Sandren would have never taken her into.

The stench coming in, though the windows were closed, was

overwhelming. The houses leaned over the road as if they wished to swoop down and swallow it up. Or perhaps they would just give up attempting to stay upright and collapse in a heap.

The sounds drifting in were frightening—shouts here, laughter there, broken glass behind them, a scream somewhere else.

Where did all these sounds come from? All she saw out the window were shadows in doorways. A window up above might have a lone candle, but they were few. Most were dark. Who was behind those dark windows? Did they not light a candle because they did not wish to, or because they did not have one?

Shrimps had sunk into himself and Rosalind occasionally heard him mutter to himself. "I don't like this neighborhood. I never did. Oyster will wonder where I've gone."

The carriage had finally stopped, and she and Shrimps had been prodded down an alley and into a dingy building. Then, up three flights of stairs to a set of threadbare apartments.

Mason had rudely pushed them into a room with the dim light of the moon coming through a small and dirty window.

The room was bare and the hearth cold.

With a warning to stay quiet and "all calm-like" or he'd have to come back and shoot them, the door was closed and the lock turned.

Rosalind sank down to the floor. Shrimps sat down next to her.

"It's all my fault," Shrimps whispered. "I should'a told you they weren't to be trusted. Criminals never are, but you couldn't know that!"

"Oh, Shrimps," Rosalind said, "I absolutely could have known that. I should have known that. For heaven's sake—I *did* know that. I just chose not to examine that fact too closely."

"Do you reckon your pa will pay to get you back?" Shrimps asked.

"Of course he will," Rosalind said. "And then I shudder to think what he will say about it."

Shrimps' thin shoulders shrugged. "Words can't hurt you

though."

Rosalind was not so sure about that. Her father's words, Conbatten's words, whatever they were to be, they would cut deep and be well-deserved.

"Lord Van Doren will dismiss me, I know he will. I'm surprised he hasn't done it already," Shrimps said sadly. He sighed deeply, as if all the world's ills were held in his breast. "I'm a troublesome sort of creature and he doesn't like Oyster very well either. Even if I do chop onions faster than Cook has ever seen, he'll throw me out."

"Shrimps, Beatrice will make Van Doren keep you. I'll see to that. But I still do not understand what they want from you. I cannot think it usual for these types of people to kidnap a junior servant in the hopes that their employer will pay to get them back. I've never heard of such a thing."

Shrimps was silent.

"There is something else," she said. "I can tell there is."

He twisted his hands together. "I'm not exactly sure, only that I'm afraid there might be something else. See, Barney, he was the pickpocket in the park and the groom tonight, he's been coming to see me at night when I take Oyster out. I don't want to take Oyster out in the dark, but it turns out to be terrible if I don't. The mess, you see."

"Yes, I can imagine. But what does this Barney come to see you about?"

"He's been demandin' proof that my name is Jimmy Black."

"Is it?"

"No. I know my given name is Henry, but my ma told me to never tell anybody about it. I don't know my surname, as she said that was an even bigger secret and children are bad at keeping secrets."

"But you did keep the secret of your given name."

Shrimps brightened. "I guess I did. Until now, anyway."

"Why was it a secret, though?"

"I'm not sure. My ma told me all sorts of things before she

died—she knew she was going, you see. But none of it made sense. I was to go to Kent and find the seven oaks. Then, I was to ask around for the Conroys."

"What were you to say when you found them?"

"I was to give them a letter."

"What does the letter say then?"

"I don't know, I can't read. I've just kept it safe, sewn inside my coat. I thought, someday I might learn to read and then I could read my mother's words she set down for me."

"Do you wish me to read the letter for you?"

Shrimps seemed pensive. Then he said, "All along I thought I wouldn't let anybody read it. They're my mother's private words to me. But now I'm to be dragged back into my old life. Lady Van Doren will never be able to convince the lord to keep me, not after this. So, if I'm to come back round here to live, I probably won't live long enough to learn to read."

He opened his coat and in the dim light Rosalind could see some large and very clumsy stitching in an awkward square. Shrimps broke the thread and pulled out the seams.

He took out a tightly folded stack of papers.

The first read only—

My dearest son Henry, take these proofs of your parentage to the Conroys in Kent. Find the Seven Oaks and ask for direction, they are not far off. Your father and I will watch from heaven to see that you do so. All my love—Baroness Dedmont, née Edna Edenborough.

"Lady Edna!" Rosalind said.

"Who is Lady Edna?"

"It seems she is your mother, Shrimps," Rosalind said.

"She never went by that name," Shrimps said.

"Then perhaps that was a secret, too."

Rosalind hurried to look at the next paper, and then the next two. One was a marriage record, the next a birth record, and the final was a letter to the Conroys and Lady Edna's parents, outlining everything that had transpired after they'd run off together.

And what a sad account it was.

It seemed James Conroy and Lady Edna had been determined to make their own way. They did not see how either set of parents would ever be reconciled to their marriage, and the baronial estate was not entailed. They might not be able to take his title from him, but they could take everything else. Mr. Conroy had set out to do day labor and Lady Edna had taken in laundry.

They had gone forward, unafraid of what they must face. Then, they had been shocked at how difficult the work was and how little it paid. All they could afford was a single room in St. Giles. They had been terribly naïve in thinking it might be done, but they struggled on as all they cared for was each other.

The work had worn James down, but he'd been stoic about it. Even after he came down with a terrible chest, he'd refused to stay abed and left early every morning.

Until one day, somebody came with the news that James had perished where he stood. They said he'd gone very white, and gasped for breath, and then he was gone.

By then, Lady Edna was with child. She thought of going home, but she'd seen in the newspapers that another heir had been located and installed. Worse, she read that she and her husband had supposedly died in the sinking of the *Louisa*.

For some time, she had been near paralyzed with grief and fear.

She knew Henry was the rightful heir, but how was she to prove that he'd not been born out of wedlock? She did not have the papers to prove it. James had managed all of that.

Lady Edna had finally emerged from her daze and determined to work and put away any spare penny she could. Then she would pay someone to gather the papers.

Once she had them, she would return and face them all down. She cared little how they would rant and rave at her—her son would have his proper place.

This packet was the result of her efforts to gather proof. She'd written this account as she knew herself to be gravely ill. If she did not survive, Henry must know who he really was and be able to prove it.

"Shrimps," Rosalind said quietly, "how long have you been carrying this around, not knowing what it said?"

"Almost three years now," Shrimps said.

"Goodness," Rosalind said. "Shrimps, you are the son of Mr. James Conroy and Lady Edna Edenborough. They ran off together to Gretna Green. It was in the papers at the time. I remember because Miss Mayton found it very romantic and used to read us all the reports of it."

"Gretna Green," Shrimps said thoughtfully. "My ma used to talk about Gretna Green. She said there was a blacksmith's shop there and my pa called it the place where dreams are made of. She used to talk about it to soothe me to sleep when we didn't have enough to eat."

"Of course it would be the place dreams were made of, for them at least—it was where your parents married."

"That's a nice thought," Shrimps said, nodding.

"Shrimps, I do not think you understand the implications of these papers. You are the rightful heir to a barony. You are a lord. Lord Dedmont, to be exact."

Shrimps snorted. "I ain't never."

"According to these papers, you are." Rosalind paused, then she said, "And now it makes a deal more sense why they've taken you, too. You were asked to prove you really were the name you gave out because they were certain you were not. They *knew* you were Henry Conroy."

Shrimps appeared near overwhelmed by the information.

Rosalind said, "Put those papers away. It cannot do any good for these men to see them."

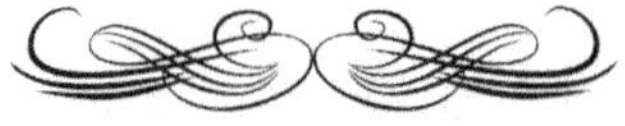

CHAPTER TWENTY-ONE

Hamill's coachman slowed the horses and Balthazar, Hamill, Van Doren, and Darden scrambled out of it. They were armed with everything they could carry.

They would go on foot down an alley to the building they sought.

As always happened when he entered the Rats' Castle, the few lights in windows went out, people slumped in doorways suddenly revived themselves and stumbled away, women pulled children inside, and gin shops slammed their shutters.

Darden looked about him at the scattering of people. "Do they know you?"

"Be quiet," Balthazar said. "Follow me."

The alley was close and reeked of urine. From the description, they were going four doors down on the right-hand side.

He paused in front of it. The door into the building hung loosely on its hinges, so no break-in was required.

The rent must be the lowest to be found if there was not even a locked door to protect its inhabitants. That made perfect sense—Mondrian would not outlay any unnecessary money for the maintenance of his gang of boys and they would not know they deserved better. As well, a thief was likely to pass by a building such as this. After all, what could possibly be in there to take?

According to their information, they were going to the second floor.

Balthazar prayed the information was correct. If it was not, he'd personally ride to Crosby's estate and strangle the little rogue who had given it out.

Everything hung on this one piece of information being right.

They moved single file up the stairs, pistols drawn.

On the second-floor landing, Balthazar held a hand up to stop their progress. In the silence, he listened.

There were only sounds coming from one room, and it sounded like boys.

He stealthily moved forward and pressed his ear to the thin door.

"You never saw anything so funny in your life. They think we're gonna act out some kind of love charade, we drop the older one at the party, and then off we go!"

"You stole a lady though," another voice said. "Ain't you gonna get hanged if they catch you?"

"I ain't gonna get caught. Mr. M says there's no way we get caught, he's got them locked up right and tight at his own place and nobody knows where he lives."

"You know."

"'Course I know, you puddin' brain. Nobody what's not in on it knows. Anyhow, me and Mason are gonna get paid five pounds. Five pounds each, mind."

"Five pounds," the other voice said in some wonder.

Balthazar had heard enough. He examined the door, which seemed more like a suggestion of a door than anything solid.

He used his shoulder to crash through it and raised his pistol before either one of the boys could try for a window.

"Don't make a move," he said, as Hamill, Darden and Van Doren piled in after him, weapons raised.

By the looks on the two boys' faces, he did not think they imagined fighting off four armed men who were twice their size.

"Where has Lady Rosalind been taken?"

"I don't know," the first boy said.

"Just tell 'im, Barney, afore he kills us both!" the other boy said.

"Shut it!" Barney said.

"A little late for that," Balthazar said. "In any case, I was listening at the door, you little braggart. Where does Mr. M live?"

The boy named Barney paled, only the birthmark on his cheek not losing color.

"I can't tell ya. He'll murder me," he whispered.

"Yes, I suppose he would, were you to remain here. But this is your lucky day. You'll be joining your friend Jimmy at a friend's estate."

"Jimmy? He's still alive?" the younger boy asked.

"Very alive and working an honest living as a stable hand. You've got yourself into something far bigger than you know. Your Mr. M is a man named Mondrian, and he is very dangerous."

"What do you reckon?" the younger boy said to Barney.

"Don't be daft, Sam," Barney said. "They're lyin' to us. Ain't nobody gonna take us anywhere nice. Jimmy's dead, just as we'll be."

The younger boy wailed.

"I suppose you'll have to see for yourself," Balthazar said. "Die where you stand or take your chances."

"I'll shoot them myself," Darden said. "Lady Rosalind is my sister."

This seemed to strike Barney fairly hard, and Balthazar guessed he'd not thought of Lady Rosalind as having a family. Oh, he'd know that she did, but it would have seemed a far away and not particularly real idea to a boy like that.

Now he'd just been faced with a very real brother, in the flesh and itching to blow his brains out.

"All right!" Barney cried. "I'll tell ya."

ROSALIND HAD LOOKED out the window to see if there were any chance of going out that way. There was no chance whatsoever. It dropped down three stories with no ledges to hold on to.

"It's hopeless," Shrimps said. "There's no escape."

"There must be something we can do," Rosalind said. "There is always something to be done."

Shrimps shook his head, defeated. "What could we do? Fly out the window? Crawl up the chimney? Hit them over the head with the fire poker?"

Rosalind whipped around. In the back of the cold hearth, there was indeed a fire poker left behind.

But actual combat with her attackers? With only Shrimps for reinforcements?

It did not seem at all feasible.

But what about the chimney? They were, after all, on the top floor. It could not be so very far to the roof.

Rosalind silently moved to the hearth and got on her hands and knees. She peered up the flue.

Far above, she could just see a few stars winking and blinking.

"Shrimps, I think we could get to the roof."

"The roof? The roof is very high. I don't like the roof."

"You're afraid of the roof?"

"No, I'm afraid of how high the roof is."

"We have to try though," Rosalind said. "If I can get up there, then you can too and I will hold your hand while we find a way down."

Shrimps sighed. "What way down from a roof?"

"There might be an attic, or something like that," Rosalind said. She squeezed herself into the rather small opening and was able to stand up.

Perhaps she could jimmy her way up. Certainly, that was how a sweep would get up there.

She braced her hands on either side, then raised her foot and pushed it against the side.

It promptly slid through soot and she landed in a heap.

Shrimps had been right, it was impossible.

Rosalind crawled out again. Shrimps looked at her with sympathy, her poor Boudicca robes now filthy and black from that unsuccessful venture.

Fire poker it must be, then.

If there was one thing running in her favor, it was the folds of the costume. She could hide the poker until she was ready to clobber her kidnappers over the head.

She crawled back over to Shrimps. "Have you ever done any fighting? You must have before you came to live with Van Doren. There must have been times when you had to fight."

Shrimps looked at her as if she'd lost her wits. "Fight? Look at the size of me! I'm a runner, not a fighter."

It was true, Shrimps was on the small side. Still, he must be ready to do his best.

"Now listen here, Henry Conroy, Baron Dedmont," she said sternly, "you are a lord and must begin to move through the world as one. You must be brave."

"Oh no," Shrimps whispered, "am I to have some kind of code or something, like Lord Van Doren does?"

"Just so," Rosalind said, nodding. "It occurs to me that we should not wait to see what happens to us. We must take the reins. We must take our fate into our hands."

"Fate?" Shrimps said. "Fate has never had anything good for me."

"Do not be ridiculous," Rosalind said with a smile. "You have just found out you are a baron. The fates must be very fond of you."

BALTHAZAR WAS CERTAIN they had got Mondrian's location from the boy, Barney. He'd given it, then Darden had threatened him with blown-out brains if he was lying, then Hamill mentioned they'd be taking both boys with them and would find out soon enough.

Barney had stuck to the information he'd given and Balthazar was confident it must be right. It was also not far. He'd put Barney and the younger boy in the coach, sufficiently guarded from the outside in case they had the idea to run off.

He, Hamill, Darden, and Van Doren went at a jog until they were quite close. Barney had described the building, and described the stairs that ran down the back of it into a narrow alley.

They would split—Hamill and Darden going in the front and he and Van Doren going up the back stairs.

He was certain there would be no escape for Mondrian. He just must be certain the desperate rogue did not harm Lady Rosalind in some bid to elude them.

As they wished for the element of surprise, and wished to make the intrusions simultaneously, they had agreed to wait for the first church bell to ring at eleven o'clock.

Then they would strike.

The quarter hour wait was beginning to feel like an eternity. Lady Rosalind was up there somewhere, no doubt frightened out of her wits.

She would have reckoned with how far out of control her little ruse had spun. She would wonder if Mondrian ever planned to let her go alive.

The poor darling. *His* poor darling.

He would get her out. Of course he would. Then, it would be time to construct some sort of story to explain what had occurred. Nobody could know the truth of it—Lady Rosalind would be notorious as the lady who had arranged her own kidnapping.

Balthazar did not think she could bear the scrutiny and the laughter over it. It had been a harebrained plan, but it had also been an earnest one.

Softly, he said to Van Doren, "I think after we retrieve her, we simply say that Mondrian was all along looking for a kidnap victim. Miss Mayton stepped out, and the carriage took off."

"The earl thinks his daughter left in Lady Hightower's carriage," Van Doren whispered. "How do we explain that?"

Good Lord. She'd involved Lady Hightower!

"Lady Hightower is a friend of mine, I will talk to her. We'll say something. She was taken ill and sent a note that was intercepted by Mondrian so it could be Mondrian himself that arrived. Nobody will believe *his* outlandish account of it."

"Of course they won't," Van Doren whispered heatedly. "They don't know the Benningtons like I do!"

Balthazar smiled to himself. No, the *ton* certainly did not know what a Bennington lady was capable of, and that was well.

The first church bell rang eleven o'clock.

They raised their pistols and raced up the rickety stairs to Mondrian's lair.

⫸⪻

ROSALIND PACED THE room, fire poker in hand. She'd tried to use it to break the lock on the door with no success.

Very suddenly, she could hear noise. A lot of noise. Glass breaking, wood splintering, shouts. What was happening?

She ran to the side of the door, pressing herself against the wall. Should one of her kidnappers burst in here, he would find himself whacked to the ground.

"Shrimps, I mean Lord Dedmont, come next to me. We must be ready to fight and run."

Shrimps hauled himself up and trudged over. "I'll only promise I can run. I never fought anybody in my life."

"Neither have I, but I'm willing to try."

She could hear pounding feet running through the apartment. Then a shout. Was that Darden? She could not be sure, but it sounded like his timbre.

A key rasped in the lock, the door handle turned, and the door swung open.

Rosalind raised the fire poker. The coachman came through the doorway and she brought her weapon down as hard as she could.

The coachman staggered. He turned, looking dazed. Then he fell to the floor.

Pounding feet. Another person was coming. Rosalind positioned herself again. She brought the iron down as soon as she saw his shadow.

A second man was felled.

"Rosalind!" she heard from another room.

"Darden!"

Her brother raced into the room, almost tripping over the two men who lay on the floor.

He grasped her and hugged her. "Thank the lord. You are an awful lot of trouble," he said, holding her against his chest.

Darden called out the door. "Hamill! We're in here—bring light!"

Lord Hamill rushed in, shading a candle. He looked around and said, "What happened to Conbatten?"

"Conbatten?" Rosalind asked, pulling away from her brother.

"Darden," Hamill said, "Find some rope or something to tie up Mondrian. I'll see to Conbatten."

In the dim candlelight, Rosalind saw Conbatten's lifeless body lying next to the coachman's. Lord Hamill bent down and held his hand over Conbatten's nose and mouth.

"I've killed Conbatten?" Rosalind shrieked.

"That would be very bad," Shrimps said. "He's a duke, you know."

"No, he's not dead. You just knocked him silly it seems," Lord Hamill said.

Van Doren came in and took in the scene. Then he glared at Rosalind.

She ignored him. She had no time for Van Doren's lectures

just now.

Shrimps was not so capable of ignoring Van Doren. He let out a sudden wail. "My lord, I didn't know anything about it! How was I to know I was a baron?"

Van Doren appeared mightily confused at that pronouncement.

As Rosalind raced to Conbatten's side, she said over her shoulder, "Shrimps is Henry Conroy, Baron Dedmont. We'll talk about it later. Do take him to get a glass of ale or some other restorative—his nerves are quite rung out."

Van Doren stared at his kitchen boy. Shrimps shrugged.

"Come on then," Van Doren said, grabbing Shrimps by the coat. "At least you didn't bring the dog."

Rosalind sat down next to Conbatten and raised his head to gently rest in her lap. She brushed his hair from his closed eyes. His wonderful hair. His wonderful face that looked so peaceful just now, as if he were asleep.

Hamill rose and said, "I'll get some cold water. That ought to rouse him."

Darden had come back with a length of rope and set to tying up the coachman.

Conbatten had rescued her. He had come.

Of course, there were several unintended circumstances surrounding the rescue, not the least of which was that the kidnapping was not ever meant to be real and she certainly had not planned on hitting him over the head.

He slowly opened his eyes.

"Conbatten," Rosalind said. "You have rescued me."

"He had some help, you know," Darden said, tying up the coachman.

Rosalind ignored him. Who cared if he had help? He had done it, she was sure he had managed the whole thing.

"I am very, very sorry about…well, all of this," Rosalind said.

Conbatten laughed and then clutched his head where the iron had struck him.

"*Are* you sorry?" he asked her.

"Very," Rosalind said.

"You ought to be," the duke said. "You entirely disrupted my plans for this evening."

Rosalind's heart, which had been so buoyed up at seeing him, began to sink. What did he mean? That he'd missed a card game or some other engagement?

"You had more important plans?" she asked. "More important than coming for me?"

"Rosalind!" Darden said. "You've just knocked out His Grace after he's been kind enough to lead us here. Perhaps do not commence an interrogation of his calendar."

"Rosalind Bennington," Conbatten said, "I intended to pull you aside at Lady Bloomington's masque, mention the idea that I am entirely besotted by you, and inquire if you would consent to marry."

"What?" Darden said softly.

Rosalind sat back. The hand that had been holding the duke's head on her lap went slack and his head smacked on the floor.

She quickly repositioned it back on her lap. "Really?"

"Indeed," he said, wincing at the latest assault on his head. "And yet, what did I find upon arrival? Miss Mayton racing round the ballroom, frightening Lady Bloomington's guests, and shouting for me."

Rosalind sighed. "Yes, that did go awry. But you did think that you would, what I mean is, you were certain, I suppose what I want to know is you would not change your mind over what was really only…an accidental kidnapping."

The duke began to laugh, and he laughed for quite some time.

Rosalind was not sure what his laughter meant, nor did it seem that Darden knew either, as he looked a bit terrified over it.

But she must find out. She must know.

"If you are to change your mind," she said, peering at him, "then you must tell me straightaway. I must know if I'm to become a bitter spinster for all of my days."

"Is that what you would do?" Conbatten asked. "You would not be swayed by some other fellow coming along?"

"Certainly not," Rosalind said, a little affronted that such a circumstance could possibly be considered. "It is Conbatten, or it is no one."

"Lady Rosalind, I cannot imagine spending my days with anyone but you. You are a confoundingly lovely and interesting woman coming with some of the worst ideas in the world and I have been under your spell since first we met."

"Have you?"

"Entirely."

Rosalind glanced about her and found Darden sitting next to the tied-up coachman, seeming rapt by the exchange.

"Darden, do drag that person out of here," she said with what she hoped was a voice full of authority. "And shut the door behind you."

"Well I—"

"You'd best do as she asks," Conbatten said.

"Your Grace, yes, of course!" Darden said, hopping up. He grabbed Mondrian's feet and dragged him toward the door.

In the silence they were left with, Conbatten said, "Now if you would reach into my inside coat pocket, I imagine you would find the token I wished to put on your finger at the masque."

"A ring?" Rosalind said, reaching into his pocket.

She drew out a lovely little red leather box and opened it.

The ruby picked up the moonlight and glowed in the dim room. "It is glorious!" she said, slipping it on.

"A ruby for passion and a pattern of thyme in the gold setting for courage."

"It is perfect. So very perfect." She paused. "Goodness, so none of this was necessary at all? I might have just gone to Lady Bloomington's masque as a regular lady going to a regular party?"

"But you are not a very regular lady," Conbatten said, "and I do not suppose I would have it any other way."

Rosalind, feeling very bold after that statement, bent down to kiss his lips. They were both firm and soft and positively glorious.

He reached his arms round her and pulled her down to him.

Rosalind was quite sure that she ought not be rolling round the floor with Conbatten. But how could she resist? His arms were just as she'd imagined, strong and wrapping round her tightly.

He whispered in her ear, "We'd better marry soon, I think, or I shall disgrace you."

"Very soon, or I am sure you will and I would not stop you," Rosalind said softly. "Should we think about running off to Gretna Green?"

"We absolutely ought not, you little minx. We've already got quite a lot to explain to your father."

"Oh goodness, my father."

"Do not fret over it, I'll smooth everything over," he said kissing her neck.

"Will you?"

"Now, and for all your days."

"How odd that I am to be a duchess."

"You never did care for such things, did you?"

"Never. You might have been a grocer for all I cared about it."

Conbatten laughed and rolled her over so she lay on top of him. "Lucky for you I am not."

"Lucky for me."

Then Rosalind kissed him again. And then again and a few times more. Time became a thing that did not harry, and she entirely forgot where she was.

Alas, Van Doren, that absolute wet blanket, barged in.

Fortunately, Conbatten was able to stop her brother-in-law's outraged sputtering with the news that they would marry.

They would marry. She and Conbatten. What a thing.

The fates had come through for her after all.

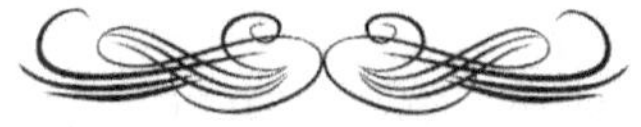

CHAPTER TWENTY-TWO

W HEN BALTHAZAR HAD set off for Lady Bloomington's masque, he'd imagined that were he to garner Lady Rosalind's consent to marry, he would approach the earl the following morning.

Circumstances dictated otherwise, though.

The explanation for this entire ridiculous evening must be made swiftly. And then preferably never mentioned again.

Fortunately, after Miss Mayton had told Lady Beatrice what had occurred, or at least as much as she knew of it, Lady Beatrice had kept her head. She'd taken Miss Mayton to her house to await the outcome. In the meantime, she walked over to the earl's house and inquired if any letter had been delivered to her father.

It had, and it waited on a silver salver for the lord. He was already abed and would receive it with his breakfast tray.

Lady Beatrice explained to Tattleton that it was a note long expected and she would answer it for her dear papa.

Tattleton, much to her surprise, clutched the letter and refused to hand it over. He rambled on about Miss Mayton posing as a man, and how he'd thought it might be witchcraft, and how he was determined that no more underhanded dealings were to go on under his watch. He would not be a party to giving away the lord's personal correspondence.

This meant it would be impossible that the earl would not read the ransom note eventually. It was impossible that the entire thing could be squashed.

Lady Beatrice had a footman standing outside to watch for any signs of her sister and brother, having every faith in Van Doren to bring them home safely.

When the carriages rolled up, she quickly motioned them in, hugged her sister tightly and called her the worst goose in the world, then explained that the ransom note had arrived and Tattleton had gone mad and refused to hand it over.

Everyone had speedily agreed that the earl must be told some facts, but he was not to be disturbed with too many facts. At least, they'd all speedily agreed, but for Van Doren, who Balthazar was beginning to think was a bit of a stick. However, as much of a stick as the fellow might like to be, he could not hold up against his wife's wishes. He was brought to heel by her soft and soothing voice as she talked him round.

They arrived to the house en masse, all prepared to tell the same story. Lady Hightower had sent a note that she was ill and could not take Lady Rosalind and Miss Mayton in her carriage. Mondrian had intercepted it and come instead. Darden, Van Doren, and himself had speedily rectified the matter. The fewer details conveyed, the better.

Poor Tattleton had been taken aback to see all of these people piling into the drawing room, and perhaps shocked to see Lady Rosalind's hand in Balthazar's. Then still more stunned that he was to wake the earl to attend this unexpected party.

He'd staggered off to do it, though Balthazar thought he'd rather hang himself than wake his lord. No matter, the thing must be done quickly, and it was best that the earl would not be at his sharpest after having been woken from sleep.

The poor earl. Him in his nightcap, attempting through a sleepy haze to take in that his daughter had been kidnapped, but only very briefly and all was well. As he attempted to parse that information he whispered, "My dear Rosalind! First a pickpocket, now a kidnapper? What is London coming to?"

Balthazar thought it well that the earl did not dwell on the circumstance too long or look at it too closely. As soon as the facts, such as they were, were relayed, he announced his wish to marry Lady Rosalind.

The earl was further staggered. "But I thought," he said rather unsteadily, "Rosalind dear, you did say, there was the fellow on horseback as we came into Town, you seemed quite set on him…"

Lady Rosalind hooked her arm through her father's and led him to a chair. "Indeed, I am set, and have been since that moment."

Balthazar did not have the first idea of what she was talking about. He only knew he did not like it. Who was this fellow?

"Do you remember, Conbatten?" she said. "You swept up a little girl who had run into the road."

He nodded. He did remember that, though he'd not had the first idea that he'd been observed by Lady Rosalind.

"But why didn't you say it was the duke?" Darden asked his sister.

Lady Rosalind looked quite exasperated, as if it were the simplest thing in the world to understand.

Miss Mayton said, "Rosalind required that the duke prove his courageousness on her behalf. Now he has."

"He certainly has," the earl said softly. "Well, Your Grace, if Rosalind is for it, then I have nothing to say against it. We can discuss the details in the morning."

"I am all for it, Papa."

"Earl, you'd better call me Conbatten," Balthazar said.

"Look at this," Lady Beatrice said cheerily, "it's all ended very happily."

"I don't know how," Van Doren muttered.

Lady Beatrice patted Van Doren's arm. "I will take my curmudgeonly husband home now. By the by, on the morrow, we'd best talk about what to do about Shrimps."

"Shrimps?" the earl asked.

"Shrimps, Papa," Lady Rosalind said. "He is a long-lost baron."

"Shrimps?" the earl said, entirely befuddled.

"Send Shrimps to me in the morning," Balthazar said. "I know quite a bit about that particular case. If he is indeed James Conroy's son, I will see that he is properly installed in that household."

"The kitchen boy?" Van Doren said. "Are you certain? I do not mind it, of course, as long as the dog goes with him."

"The duke will be delighted to take charge of Oyster too, I am certain," Lady Beatrice said with a laugh.

Balthazar nodded, though he thought Henri would be in a state of collapse were he to be discovering dog hair on various items of clothing.

Lady Beatrice and Van Doren took their leave. Lady Rosalind said, "Papa, be off to bed now or you shall be very tired tomorrow. You too, Darden."

The earl rose. "Well, I suppose if Miss Mayton stays it should be all right."

Darden dragged his feet a bit, and mumbled something about how pleased he was that His Grace should be his brother-in-law, but he finally did go.

They had not been gone a minute when Miss Mayton rose and said "Goodness, I believe I will retrieve my book. Of course, I cannot recall where I left it so I might be quite some time at it."

After the door closed behind her, Lady Rosalind threw herself into his arms and they fell on the sofa together.

He traced his finger along her cheek and kissed her lips. She was rather enthusiastic in the kissing back. Balthazar should not have been surprised. Lady Rosalind was no delicate flower on any matter.

She *looked* as if she would be, with her elegant and very perfect features, but she was not.

"So, my courageous darling, what next?" he asked. "Shall you be employing highwaymen to pursue us on our wedding trip?"

"What an idea," she said, giggling. "I still think we ought to set off for Gretna Green and then we can find some cozy cottage somewhere in the highlands. My father will not mind it."

"Your father has been pushed to the brink of incredulity, let us not push him any further."

"I suppose you are right," Rosalind admitted. "But perhaps you can get a special license? Else I do not know how we are to keep our hands to ourselves."

Balthazar laughed, rich and deep. "That will indeed be a challenge that will require all of our combined courage. I will certainly obtain a special license. However, my lovely Rosalind, I am a duke. The queen herself will wish to attend the church. The thing must be done right."

"How soon, do you think?"

"I will consult with Lady Hightower, she will know how to arrange it speedily."

"Lady Hightower," Rosalind said thoughtfully. "Do you suppose she will approve the match?"

"After discovering you employed her name in this shocking series of events by claiming it would be her carriage to collect you? Probably."

Rosalind kissed his lips gently. "She is a dear, then."

Balthazar undid the pins in her hair and pulled her down to him.

As it happened, Miss Mayton had terribly misplaced her book and was gone from the room for nearly an hour.

Balthazar had told no tales—it would take their combined courage to avoid compromising his dear Rosalind. Or perhaps whatever could be scraped together of *his* courage alone, as she did not seem very steadfast in the effort.

ON THE NEXT morning, Rosalind's sisters had of course been told of the terrible circumstance of Rosalind being kidnapped. At least, they were told the version their father understood. They were further informed that Rosalind had engaged herself to the duke and they did a remarkable job of seeming as if they'd not seen it coming.

They of course knew there were a heap of facts missing from this recital and waited until the earl and Darden had departed the breakfast room. The earl was to meet his friend Lord Cannerly for coffee at Whites. Conbatten was to join him there later for a private audience on the marriage settlement.

Darden was, quite naturally, on his way to the YBC. He was bursting to tell the news of the engagement to his friends at his club, and Rosalind thought he very much seemed as if it were *he* who had become engaged to Conbatten.

He'd left muttering, "This must tip the scales. Certainly, we must ask him to join our club, as he is now to be my brother-in-law."

Tattleton and the footmen had since been sent out of the breakfast room. Though, as always seemed to be the case these days, their butler appeared very nervous about leaving them alone there.

The door closed behind him.

"Well?" Juliet said.

"It was both terrifying and marvelous," Rosalind said. "The people Shrimps got in touch with, well, it seemed they decided that if I wished to be kidnapped, they might as well get a ransom. The carriage got to the end of the street and just kept going. Then, it turns out they were after Shrimps too, because he is the son of James Conroy and Lady Edna Edenborough."

"Goodness, I remember the news reports of them running off together," Miss Mayton said. "It was very romantic."

"What a night!" Cordelia said. "We tried and tried to stay awake, but we could not do it."

"It was just as well," Rosalind said. "By the time Conbatten left, it was near three and my head was all dreamy—I could barely speak."

"Does he make you dreamy?" Cordelia asked.

"Very dreamy."

"But tell us," Viola said. "Tell us of the moment Conbatten finally confessed his love."

Rosalind sighed. It really had been the most romantic moment in the history of romantic moments. There he'd been, lying on the floor with a head injury, telling her he'd been besotted from the moment he saw her.

"It was for him just as it was for me," Rosalind said. "He was in love with me from the very first. He thinks I am an adorable minx and he could not imagine living without me."

Rosalind's sisters all sighed contentedly, while Miss Mayton nodded and buttered another piece of toast.

"Let us see that ring again," Juliet said.

And so they went on very merrily, each of them trying on the ring and approving of the idea that Rosalind was an adorable minx.

All along, Rosalind had been determined to only recall what was happy about last evening. After all, it had worked so well!

In the end.

However, looking about at her sisters' bright faces and Miss Mayton's satisfied expression, she did feel compelled to say something of a warning.

"Now, all of my dear sisters," she said, "I must acquaint you with one other idea that is perhaps not as pleasant to consider," she said. "I did find, after getting myself into such a dangerous situation, that I had to reflect on how I got there."

"It was all that fellow Mondrian's fault," Juliet said. "Darden told us of him. Terrible man."

"Yes, he is indeed a terrible man," Rosalind said. "But I invited him into my life, and it might have ended very badly for both myself and Shrimps. I only say, I do not know what adventures might be coming for all of you, but have a care. Do not be as foolhardy as I have been."

"This must be laid at my door, I think," Miss Mayton said. "I am older and more experienced and should have seen that something would go awry. But then, the pickpocket came off so well…"

"Nobody can blame you, Aunt," Rosalind said. "I am a full-grown lady and it was my idea. Only, it turns out that Conbatten was planning to propose at the masque, so the whole thing was unnecessary. It was a danger that should never have happened."

The sisters, being of a practical mind and perfectly willing to take on advice from Rosalind's recent experience, vowed that whatever was to transpire in the coming years, a fake kidnapping was firmly off the table. Miss Mayton was also quite agreeable to the idea, as she said the shock of last evening's goings-on was still with her.

Having made that happy decision, quite naturally their minds turned to a trousseau.

TATTLETON SAT AT the servants' table, staring at the cur that was just now biting and tearing at the hem of one of his pant legs. There was not even a point in complaining about the dogs. There were too many and they were everywhere. The house was like a besieged castle that had been overrun by enemy forces.

Charlie had set up a barricade of sorts around the hearth, using wooden crates from the grocer. That had held them back for all of a day.

Tattleton ignored the cur's growls, as if his pant leg were some sort of prey that must be dispatched. His mind was far too full of more weighty matters.

There were so many ideas to take in and none of them went together to make any sort of sense. The ladies had talked of a pickpocket, and then a pickpocket turned up. Miss Mayton dressed as a man and went to the duke's house about some sort of duel. A kidnapping. And now Lady Rosalind was engaged to the duke.

And then, he was to believe that Shrimps, that young rogue, was a baron? Was he to begin bowing and calling Shrimps "My lord?"

Shrimps?

What next? Would he be informed that Charlie was actually a long-lost marquess? Perhaps he was, himself, the long-lost rightful King of England. Who knew anymore!

How was any of it to make sense?

After all these years, he was beginning to think he did not understand this family at all. Or the world.

It was as if there was a missing piece of information that might tie all these events together, but it could not be found.

Mrs. Huffson hurried into the room. "Goodness, Mr. Tattleton, that pup is going to shred your trousers if you let him carry on like that."

"Who cares," Tattleton muttered.

Mrs. Huffson picked up the dog and deposited him back behind the barricade. She tightened up the defenses, but Tattleton knew it was hopeless. Every day they'd just get stronger and more determined.

"There now," the housekeeper said. "They're all asleep except for that little mite and he'll be going that direction soon."

"You are a very positive thinking person, Mrs. Huffson."

The lady sat at the table with him. "I can see you are shaken up by recent events. I don't plan to say I understand them any better. Still, I suppose it's all gone right in the end. Our Lady Rosalind is to be a duchess."

A duchess. It was true, Lady Rosalind would soon be a duchess.

Tattleton considered that. In truth, he wondered why, in all the things he had considered this morning, that had not been one of them.

It really was something to consider.

When he had occasion to speak to another butler or perhaps

a high-placed valet or steward even, was there not mention of the respective families? Of course there was. A senior servant was very much judged by the rank of the family he served.

Might it not be pleasant to have a duchess to speak of?

Tattleton imagined the sort of conversation he might have. "Yes, you see, Mr. Roberts, we are often entertaining the Duke and Duchess of Conbatten. The duchess is the earl's daughter and I have known her since she was a babe."

Indeed. That would be very pleasant.

"You do look cheered by the idea, Mr. Tattleton. I'll find Charlie and we'll set you up with a cup of tea."

Tattleton nodded. Yes, he would have tea and he would forget about anything he'd seen this season that might have disturbed his mind. He would fill his thoughts with Her Grace, the Duchess of Conbatten, and how he'd known her since she was a babe.

What else could he do, really?

BALTHAZAR HAD CONCLUDED all the business that must be done with alacrity.

There had been Shrimps to interview, as Van Doren had brought him to the house first thing. After seeing the documents, Balthazar had no doubt that he was just now in receipt of Henry Conroy, Baron Dedmont.

As he would personally escort the young baron to Kent before the wedding, and as he intended the wedding to come off at the earliest possible moment, he had directed Henri to contact Ribaldi and have suitable clothes made in all haste.

He had since installed the boy in a bedchamber and instructed the staff that he was to be addressed as a lord, no matter how uncomfortable the boy was with the idea.

Henri had not been all that opposed to the arrival of a boy, especially as he would not be staying. But, as was to be expected, he'd been irate about the dog that had come with him. Surprisingly, since this young baron seemed in all other ways shy, he'd defended his dog with determination. Oyster was to stay and that was that.

Balthazar then set off to White's and met with his future father-in-law. It had been a most pleasant meeting, as the earl was an easy-going sort of fellow and Balthazar himself was inclined to be generous.

Lady Rosalind's dowry income was to be for her sole use and the whole of it passed on equally to her daughters. Her pin money was not to be regulated at all—she might spend what she liked. A property in Hertfordshire that he'd bought the year before was to be given over to her, with all the rents and income for her sole use. That estate would take the place of the dower house, should he predecease her and should she wish it. Generous dowries were arranged for any daughter, and the settlements on younger sons would ensure that they would live most comfortably as gentlemen.

The earl, after hearing all these terms, had said, "Well, I had always thought I'd have to haggle on behalf of my daughters, but so far that has not been the case! I am glad of it, as I do not think I am a very great haggler."

They'd then had a comfortable cup of coffee. The solicitors could work out the rest of what was to be done.

Balthazar had mentioned the idea of taking Lady Rosalind out in his phaeton. After all, they were engaged and nothing untoward could possibly occur in an open vehicle in view of so many other people in the park.

The earl saw no cause against it, as he knew his daughter to be such a sensible young lady.

Balthazar had found himself using all his self-control to stop from laughing. Sensible, indeed.

Now, he'd made his way to Portland Place, having sent a note ahead requesting Lady Rosalind's presence in his chaise.

He hopped down and handed the reins to a footman hurrying toward him. Before he could approach the door, Lady Rosalind flew out of it ahead of the butler.

"Conbatten!" she said.

He smiled at her. Then he smiled more to see her sisters and the deranged Miss Mayton waving from windows.

"Come, my little minx, let's get you into my carriage."

He picked her up and settled her, under the rather disapproving stare of the butler and rather approving stares of her sisters and Miss Mayton.

He urged the horses forward and they were off. As they trotted down the road and headed toward the park, he said, "I've settled with your father. It was all speedily agreed on."

Rosalind held on to his arm and said, "He is such a dear of a man, is he not?"

"He is, rather," Balthazar said. "Though I do not suppose he would have been anything else. I was exceedingly generous—you shall want for nothing."

"Of course I want for nothing," Rosalind exclaimed. "I wanted you, I have you, that is all that ever needed doing."

Balthazar laughed. "Though, I suppose a duchess will wish for new clothes each year, and some sparkling baubles to go with them."

"Of course, that *would* be pleasant," Rosalind said, as if she'd not considered the idea.

"I will inquire of my tailor who is the best dressmaker in all of Europe. You shall have whoever it is."

"Oh, your tailor," Rosalind said. "Did you know that there are so many young men who wish to know who he is? Dear Darden would die to know it."

Balthazar laughed. "I do know that and it is a very great secret. His name is Ribaldi and he is Italian. It will not help your brother to know it, as Ribaldi only tailors for me."

"You have very particular tastes, do you not?" Rosalind asked. "For instance, I immediately perceived at Lady Rawley's theatrical evening that you do not at all care for iced cake."

Balthazar only nodded, but did not think it worth explaining that he was only against iced cake when it was in Miss Mayton's hands.

"And then, everybody talks about your ninety-eight degree bath and that you have iced champagne at the end of it."

"At precisely twenty-six minutes in," Balthazar said. "I have hope that you will join me in it."

"It sounds divine. And I will come to the bath wearing only my sparkly baubles you have bought me. I think that would give it a nice touch."

Balthazar dared not dwell on *that* picture for more than a moment. It would be a bit more than a "nice touch." It would positively fell him.

My god. They'd best get married soon.

CHAPTER TWENTY-THREE

S HRIMPS, THOUGH NOBODY called him that anymore, looked at his luggage piled high in his bedchamber in the duke's house. Oyster stared at it too. Even his dog knew something momentous was going to happen. On the morrow, the duke would take him to Kent and he was to meet his grandparents.

There were times over the past week that he'd pinched himself to make sure he was awake. Why wouldn't he? How many dreams had he had when he'd been hungry and cold where he had plenty of food, a warm bed, and no work to do?

The duke had been very kind in explaining everything to him. First there had been the clothes to be made. A man named Ribaldi had come and spoke in a foreign language. Then the duke's valet had spoke in a foreign language. It seemed not the same languages as they never understood each other very well. Henri had finally told him that he was French and Ribaldi was Italian. However it was between them, it seemed they both agreed that the clothes he'd arrived in were terrible.

Now he had enough clothes to last the rest of his life. And luggage to carry them in too.

The duke sat with him while he ate dinner most nights, before His Grace went out to see Lady Rosalind somewhere. During those times, he talked a lot about being a lord. He'd have to learn to read and acquire manners and know how to direct servants.

Shrimps thought he could memorize manners well enough, though he would never understand why a table had to have so many forks when one would do. He supposed he could learn to read. But directing servants would be the hard part.

He *was* a servant! He'd never directed anybody in his life.

Still, the duke had made him practice it. He'd had to ask the butler, Mr. Alden, for no end of things.

It had been terrifying. Now, there was more terror to come. He was to go to strangers. What would they say? Would they take one look at him and tell the duke to turn his carriage around and go away?

He was not very impressive to look at, after all.

Shrimps glanced at Oyster, his dog lying on a rug and his teeth occasionally chattering. Not even his dog was very impressive to look at.

"Well, Oyster, I suppose we just see what happens. For all we know, we might be back with Cook in two days' time."

ROSALIND SURVEYED THE drawing room with a very satisfied eye. It was the night before Conbatten would take Shrimps to Kent and he'd come to dinner. Beatrice and Van Doren had walked over too and they'd been a very merry party.

Everyone had made a very concerted effort to avoid the subject of any recent kidnapping. Over the dinner, the earl had once more said he could not imagine what London was coming to.

Miss Mayton had leapt to the rescue, lest the earl have questions about the circumstances that nobody was prepared to answer.

She said, "My dear Rosalind, it has been much on my mind that you will take your wedding trip to Sweden. I wonder if you might not make some offering at the sight of Count Tulerstein's tragic demise?"

Van Doren, always simmering with outrage over Miss Mayton's tragic past, though nobody understood why, said, "And how would they go about finding this Alpine meadow where he tragically threw himself over the side since it only lives in your mind?"

Miss Mayton had looked at him sympathetically, as if the viscount had little understanding of such matters.

"Count Tulerstein's spirit lives on in the mountains," Miss Mayton said. "Any mountain meadow will do."

"I'm sure we can arrange something," Rosalind said. "We'll take flowers and throw them over the side somewhere."

"And send him my deepest regrets," Miss Mayton murmured.

"For the love of—"

Van Doren was cut off by Juliet. "I've written a new ode," she said. "It's called *When the Love is True*. I will read it at the wedding breakfast."

"Well, my dear," the earl said kindly, "I am not sure that would be the right venue for your…stylings. The queen will be there, after all."

"Do you say our queen does not care for poetry?" Juliet asked.

"Oh, do not say so, Papa," Viola said.

"If it is true," Cordelia said, "then I expect it is only because she has not heard Juliet's poems. She's probably been bored to tears with Wordsworth and his ilk."

"True," Juliet said, nodding. "Those fellows just go on and on."

Rosalind glanced at Darden, who was looking rather panicked. Conbatten just smiled. Really, her brother should learn to be more like Conbatten. Nothing shook his confidence, not even a kidnapping. He would hardly fear a poem at a wedding breakfast.

"I'll paint a portrait of both of you for your wedding present," Viola said.

"Is the one of Bess and her pups done already, Viola?" Beatrice asked.

"Well, no. You see I kept adding dark colors for the fur, and somehow it ended all dark colors. I think I shall do better painting people."

"Oh I'm sure that's true," Rosalind said. "Goodness, Conbatten, our first portrait together."

Conbatten nodded. "I anxiously await the effort."

They had since moved to the drawing room and Miss Mayton was, as she had promised, reading the conclusion of *The Awful Happenstances of Grimwood Hall*.

The earl had been on the edge of his seat as the story unfolded. The magistrate had attempted to retrieve the dead duchess from the well, as the gentle governess and the duke looked on.

She was not there!

The magistrate was outraged that there was no body to haul up after all that trouble and ordered a search of the entire estate. The duchess was eventually found in an old crone's cottage, deep in the woods. It seemed the crone had found the lady unconscious in a cave and nursed her back to health.

When the duchess was brought to her duke, she informed him that it had been the housekeeper all along. The housekeeper was in love with the duke and had tried to finish her off.

Said housekeeper, when she was looked for, had slipped away.

As the duchess recounted her trials, not the least of which was the old crone's substandard menus and uncomfortable bed, she began to notice that her duke was in love with her governess. As the duchess had always been a very bad-tempered woman, she attacked the governess.

The poor gentle governess ran outside, but the duchess was enraged and would not let her go.

They reached the well. There was a struggle.

And then, a long scream as the duchess fell down the well.

The earl had nearly jumped from his chair at this turn of events. "The irony!" he cried. "She ends up in the well after all, and from her own doing!"

Miss Mayton nodded. "Had she been kinder, I expect that never would have happened. For one thing, the duke would have looked a bit harder for her in the first place."

"Conbatten," Juliet said, "if our Rosalind is ever suspected of going down a well, you will find her, will you not?"

"I will search every well in England until she is recovered."

Everyone was most satisfied with that idea, not the least of which was Rosalind herself.

After that delightful interlude, Rosalind rose and said, "Conbatten, remember that book I was telling you about in my father's library?"

The duke nodded and rose. "Yes, it sounded very interesting. Will you show it to me?"

"Of course," Rosalind said graciously.

And so they left the party in the drawing room and Rosalind knew that they'd all quite given up trying to stop them slipping away together.

They would spend the next hours in each other's arms and Tattleton would frown at all the hairpins left on the floor.

There was nothing for it. They'd really better get married soon.

BALTHAZAR EXAMINED THE young boy sleeping in the seat across from him in the carriage. He had rather fine features when he was not looking panicked over something. The dog that lay at his feet did not have fine features, but at least its teeth had stopped chattering.

They were on their way to Kent, after Balthazar had spent a rather fine evening with Rosalind and her assorted family members.

What a delightful collection of eccentrics they were. Unlike most eccentrics, who seemed to take pride in their oddities, the Benningtons remained entirely unaware of their peculiarities. It was charming, in its fashion.

How earnest Miss Mayton had been in paying her respects to the tragic Count Tulerstein. And then, he did not know where that lady bought her books but it had tickled him no end how enthusiastic the earl had been to understand the mean-spirited duchess had thrown *herself* down a well.

Lady Cordelia was even now sketching out some monstrosity of a portrait as a wedding gift. He could not be certain how bad she was at the activity, but as in her own words her first effort had culminated in smears of black and brown that could not be rescued, he had high hopes it would be entirely ludicrous.

If there had been any little eccentricity that had given him the least pause, it might have been Lady Juliet's determination to read a poem at the wedding breakfast. If *Ode to Hay* was any yardstick to measure with, the queen, and everybody else, was set to be assaulted by the worst poetry in England.

Nevertheless, he would marry into this family and he would be entertained by them. He did not see that Van Doren's outrage always simmering on a low boil did anybody any good. Least of all, Van Doren.

Out the window, he saw the seven oaks landmark.

Balthazar tapped the young baron's shoulder and woke him. "We're nearly there."

"Oh no," the boy whispered.

"It will be all right. They've seen the proof. They are, quite naturally, devastated that your parents did not survive what was, in the end, your grandparents' own obstinance. They will be grateful beyond measure that you *have* survived and are returned to them."

Lord Dedmont looked very dubious over the idea that anybody would be grateful to see him.

"Now, you must gather up all your father's courage, and all your mother's courage. They were very bold people, to have run off like they did and try to make a life on their own."

"Yes, I suppose they were," the boy said. "I'd never have tried it. It's terrible to be on your own."

Balthazar nodded, just as the carriage pulled up to the doors of the house. A crowd of people led by a very old woman in widow's weeds came pushing past the butler and footmen.

"You will not be on your own for long," he said.

The carriage door flew open and the old lady peered in. "Ah yes, it is you, Henry. The spitting image of your father. Welcome home, my boy."

The young lord was pulled from the carriage and passed from one embrace to the next, with many exclamations.

The old woman said to Balthazar, "I'm the dowager baroness. That collection of raving lunatics are my daughter-in-law and Lady Edna's parents. Do come in, Your Grace, and excuse the unorthodox greeting. We are all topsy-turvy here."

Balthazar glanced down at Oyster, who had backed himself into a corner, eyes wide, teeth chattering together.

The dowager followed his gaze. "I'll hazard a guess that interesting looking specimen is not your own."

Balthazar nodded.

"Well, now, if that is my great-grandson's dog, he's welcome here."

The party eventually managed to get back into the house, all surrounding the young Henry Conroy, otherwise known as Shrimps. Balthazar carried the shivering Oyster, lest he run off in a panic.

Everyone settled round a tea tray and after Balthazar gently hinted that their newly returned grandson had been through some difficulties and might require calm and quiet, they did subdue themselves.

Balthazar thought things were well in hand, as the dowager had taken the baron aside and had what seemed to be a confidential and rather cheerful conversation in a corner. He even heard the dowager say, "Shrimps? I like it, we'll keep that between you and me." Oyster had laid down between them and snored, exhausted from all the teeth chattering he'd managed to do all day.

While the dowager occupied the boy, Balthazar spoke at length to the family about what he knew of the young baron's experiences, including the final adventure at Mondrian's hands. They had been shocked to discover Mondrian still lived, suspected it had been he who had stolen a box of papers from the house, and were relieved that he'd been taken in by the authorities.

Having assured himself that all was as it should be, Balthazar took his leave. The newly-installed baron walked him out to his carriage.

"I think you'll be all right here," Balthazar said.

"I think so too," the boy said. "The old lady, she is my Great Grandmama. She says she has the most sense of anybody in the house and she says she will teach me to read and that will be our excuse to closet ourselves away and eat cakes. She also says the dower house has a bedchamber all set up for me. I can go there whenever I want, mostly to get away from the talking. She says all my grandparents talk a lot and most of it is nonsense. She likes peace and quiet and I do too. Oh, and she says my tutors will be examined by her and anybody too sour will be sent packing. Also, Oyster likes her terrifically—he is a very good judge of people."

Balthazar laughed. "I believe the dowager may be relied upon. Now, you are to write me about how you get on. You will get your own stationery with your crest on it and a ring to use as a seal too. You will sign these missives with your proper title. Henry Conroy, Baron Dedmont. It will take time to get used to it, but you will."

"I guess you never know what will happen to you in life," the boy said thoughtfully.

"No, you never really do," Balthazar said.

After all, had he ever imagined that he would marry the lady who had just arranged her own kidnapping?

And yet, the day could not come soon enough.

ROSALIND HAD OF course adored all the gowns that had been made for her season. But there had been one she had not worn. She'd held it back, certain it was to be her wedding dress.

It was the palest peach silk and quite unadorned, but for a Greek knot on each shoulder. It need not be any more adorned than it was. Especially as her father had gifted her a lovely diamond tiara and Conbatten's valet, Henri, had consulted on the veil.

Henri had met Rosalind and Miss Mayton at a dress shop in Cavendish Square. There, he'd sniffed at various offerings, stared down the proprietor, and hinted that if the fellow had anything hidden in the back, he'd best go get it. He'd rounded the entire exchange off with noting that the Duke of Conbatten was to view the lace atop his bride's head and the duke was very particular and had exquisite tastes.

At the mention of the duke, it seemed the proprietor did have something hidden away. A few pieces, actually. Rosalind knew instantly which she must have. An intricate pattern of roses.

The ceremony had been both frightening and thrilling. Conbatten had moved heaven and earth to secure the church on the proposed day and to secure it exclusively. There would be no other couples waiting their turn, as was so often the case at St. George's. It had been packed to the rafters, and then of course, among the crowd, the queen and her ladies had taken up all of the front row.

Rosalind had never had so many eyes upon her!

Though she was so known for her courage, she'd trembled as she walked down the aisle.

But then, Conbatten had been waiting for her at the altar. Her nerves fled when she reached him. Her beautiful, marvelous

Conbatten.

The vows were exchanged and Conbatten produced a lovely gold wedding ring, engraved in the same thyme design as her ruby ring.

Rosalind walked out of the church as Her Grace, the Duchess of Conbatten. She was not really cognizant of that, though. Amongst the cheers of well-wishers, she walked out of the church as the wife of Conbatten. That was the point.

They had decided between them that a Venetian breakfast would take place at the duke's residence. His rooms were larger, so they said to the earl. Really, she and Conbatten thought it would be far easier to slip away. As soon as the queen had departed, they would disappear too.

Alden had been instructed to be exceedingly liberal with the guests' champagne, as they supposed that might assist in the matter.

Rosalind had presumed the queen would not stay long, and yet she still remained. Perhaps Conbatten should not have arranged so much food!

The queen seemed particularly enamored of the pineapple slices. The center of each ring was decorated with a delightful miniature marzipan pineapple. The marzipan was divine and there was much talk about where it had come from. Apparently, along with the tremendous wedding cake, the baker was another one of Henri's discoveries and the secret would never be told.

At least all the guests would leave with their own charming quartz boxes decorated with the duke's arms and filled with marzipan shaped in pineapples, roses, and thyme leaves.

Never in Rosalind's life had she imagined that the queen might be at one of her parties, and that she would wish the lady gone.

As she and Conbatten held hands under the table, a sudden dinging on glass caught their attention.

Juliet had stood and she called for the table's attention.

"I'll wager she's going to read her poem," she said to Conbatten.

He bit his lip and whispered, "I wish I could bet against you."

"Esteemed guests," Juliet said loudly, "I have composed a poem as a wedding present for Rosalind and Conbatten."

The earl had leapt up. "Ah, Juliet, perhaps let us leave it for just the family."

Juliet seemed confused by the idea, as Rosalind was herself. Certainly, she must hear the poem dedicated to her marriage.

"I would be interested in hearing it," the queen said.

The earl bowed. "Your majesty." He sat down with rather a resigned look.

Juliet curtsied in the queen's direction. "It is called *When the Love is True.*"

When the love is true, one cannot be blue
One girds one's loins and races ahead on cue
Though frightening danger circles all around
It is the truest love that's always found.

The silence that followed was indicative of the inspiration Juliet's poetry always did produce. Conbatten stood and led the applause, the rest of the party soon following.

Rosalind even heard the queen say, "Extraordinary."

That royal lady was good enough to leave very soon after.

BALTHAZAR HAD STOLEN his bride away as soon as the queen departed, leaving the revelers to enjoy his ever-flowing champagne and ever-arriving food. It was perhaps not the most proper way to do things, but then there were some advantages to being a duke. The only person who could really challenge him on it was the queen and he had dutifully stayed while she was present.

He did not escape the party without a few comments though.

The queen had been as gracious as she could be, considering

a queen is never accustomed to keeping her thoughts to herself.

As Rosalind curtsied, Queen Charlotte said, "Very charming wedding, Conbatten. Now, Duchess, do inform Lady Juliet that poetry is not her forte. We do not wish to hear of her frightening off suitors with it when it is her turn."

His dear wife seemed entirely confused by it. Balthazar only wished to roar with laughter.

Lady Hightower snorted as she took her leave. She leaned toward him and said quietly, "I will remember this day for the rest of my life. The poetry alone has burned it into my memory. You are in for an exciting sort of life, I think."

She'd laughed all the way out to her carriage.

Of course, Lady Hightower was no doubt correct, and he went into it with eyes wide open.

Finally, the door to his bedchamber was shut behind them.

"Conbatten," Rosalind said, flinging herself into his arms. "I suppose you might throw me on the bed. We're married now so I am certain it is all right."

As he found himself always so agreeable to Rosalind's requests, he did throw her on the bed and then threw himself after her.

Rosalind's divine wedding dress became a shambles, a mere shadow of its former self. Balthazar's perfect coat was rumpled and creased and his neckcloth would likely never be resurrected. Clothes were near-ruined, and then missing altogether. It would perhaps be expected that at least one of the couple might find themselves suddenly shy or hesitant at such a moment.

Shyness or hesitancy was never to be between them, though, as the setting sun streaming in through the windows could attest to had it the means to speak.

Some hours later, they sat in a ninety-eight-degree bath, he wearing nothing and Rosalind wearing only her tiara. It was charmingly askew, and her hair was in entire disarray.

Naturally, now that his bride planned to join him often in the bath, Henri had been sent away and Balthazar would manage the thermometer and the jug of hot water himself. An ice bucket stood nearby, with champagne ready for precisely twenty-six minutes in.

As he gazed at her, this adorable lady he'd married, he thought he really ought to buy her a very elaborate diamond necklace. It would look smashing round her neck in the bath.

"I suppose your family will have been shocked when they realized we ran off from the party," Balthazar said.

"Not at all," Rosalind said, using her toes to march up his chest. "I informed them we would do so at the earliest possible moment. I told my father that we had a lot to talk about."

"And he believed that?" he asked, kissing her soapy toes.

"No, he went to my aunt and told her she'd better explain to me the facts of a marriage. She was very amused by it and informed him that all personal ladies' matters had been thoroughly discussed."

"Your poor father."

"Now tell me of this wedding trip, Conbatten. You've kept me very much in the dark about it. What shall we do in Sweden?"

"Ah yes, we will sail on my own ship, the *Carolina*, making landfall near Stockholm. Then we will make our way to a very charming place called Ekolsund Bay. I have a house there that I inherited from an uncle. We will walk along the water and take horses out to the countryside, we'll have late dinners by the fire and as many baths as you like. I expect the crossing to be smooth. Have you sailed before?"

"I have not set foot on a ship myself, but I did see a regatta once," Rosalind said. "I did feel, as I watched the boats rounding the buoys, that I should have very sturdy sea legs. I am convinced I will take to it exceedingly well."

As it happened, Rosalind did not take to sailing exceedingly well. Or at all well. She spent the majority of their days at sea with either her head over a basin or running up to the deck shouting, "I need air!"

Balthazar held her hair out of her way for her moments over the basin, and walked with her on deck, supporting her arm as she sucked in air and claimed she would never eat again.

Lynette, who had come along as Rosalind's lady's maid, was not much better. Though, she had the further problem of imagining the boat was sinking at every creak and groan.

Henri spent the trip drinking wine and muttering about the Benningtons' peculiar brand of madness.

His dear wife subsisted on dry toast and was decidedly pale by the time they'd landed at port. Conbatten carried her off the boat and she sank to the ground and hugged it.

The change from rolling deck to firm land took nearly a day to readjust to, and Rosalind weaved and staggered through their hotel until she began to regain her balance.

After that, her recovery was swift. When she became dismayed that their wedding trip had begun under such unfortunate circumstances, Conbatten had assured her that she'd looked very charming in her seasick pallor.

After her recovery, the trip was spent gloriously strolling along the bay and having long dinners in front of a cozy fire at night. Rosalind began to inquire of her husband what else he did not prefer, aside from the iced cake she already knew about. He did not like duck, which she seemed surprised to hear.

She went on to tell him that she could not abide fried kidneys and he declared she should never see them. Then, one night very late as they were just drifting off to sleep, she told him she did not read music, despite her originality at the pianoforte.

He did his best to seem suitably surprised.

When it was time to return to England, Conbatten delayed the crossing until the weather would be at its calmest possible.

It really was calm, though that had not prevented a repeat of the trip over.

His duchess was courageous in all respects, but Balthazar would never put her on a sea-going vessel again.

What he would do, though, is provide those little rescues that might be perceived as highly romantic. He might pull her back from the street as he was certain a carriage was poised to swerve and she would have been trampled. Perhaps he would throw his coat over her head to protect her from some unseen wasp. He might even speak of a duel being in the offing if a passing fellow glanced at his wife, that poor fellow never hearing anything about it.

After they'd been married a month, he very cautiously told her of the Queen's Knights and his various activities in service to that lady. Rather than be alarmed, Rosalind viewed it as precisely what a duke ought to be doing.

In the coming years, she would delight in waving to him from the front doors as he set off dressed in black for an appointment in the Rats' Castle. She would wait up for him and have a glass of brandy ready, no matter the hour he returned.

Balthazar lived by the words he had once spoken to Lady Beatrice, upon first encountering a Bennington—the worth of a man was measured by how he took care of all those in his sphere. He did take care, and Rosalind felt it.

Balthazar even went so far as to set aside a particular room in the house as the private family room. It was to be the recipient of the various gifts of creativity launching themselves out of the Bennington household and into his own. Conveniently, that room had been the music room. The pianoforte disappeared, never to be seen again. The travels through the world of music had reached its final destination and would journey no more.

The first installation going into the family room was a framed copy of Juliet's wedding gift poem. The second was the portrait Viola had done of the couple.

Though Rosalind was in general so approving of all her sisters' talents, even she was perplexed over the portrait. Was it them? Was it other people? Was it even people?

They could not decide, but it mattered little. These things were in the family's private room and no outsider would ever view them.

Rosalind herself found she was changed by marriage and the events that had led to it. The kidnapping had taken her into the Rats' Castle and had given her a view of how others lived.

She became a confidante of Queen Charlotte and helped fund the schools the queen was intent on, using the income that was generated from the estate in Hertfordshire that had become her own to use when she married.

Shrimps found himself changed too and over time gave up the name Shrimps altogether. He was Henry Conroy, Lord Dedmont.

As the years went by, he grew quite a bit taller. Rosalind thought it was a testament to good food and a comfortable environment and wished the circumstance for every Englishman.

Though he found stability and no longer feared for his life, the young baron was never to become a boisterous gentleman. He remained rather quiet and retiring.

Balthazar was forever amused by the young baron's letters. Especially the early ones, which centered on who the dowager thought was an idiot, what had recently scared Oyster, and which cakes he favored the most.

Mondrian was eventually hanged for his crimes. Barney and the other boys fared much better. They were taken on as stable hands, and years later, Balthazar had been taken aback to see that Barney was somehow coachman to the Earl of Weister.

Every life saved from the degradations of the Castle had the potential to produce surprising results.

Bess' pups all found themselves situated comfortably. Of course Bess herself did too, as she was to be forever a Bennington. Her smallest pup was kept with her, as the sisters did not believe they could bear to be parted. Beatrice took another of them and of course Rosalind took one, and the other five were enthusiastically gifted to any reliable person even hinting that they might not mind a dog.

The earl concluded that particular season a very satisfied gentleman. His second eldest daughter had married a man he could admire, and he gave all the credit for this smooth sailing to Miss Mayton. Van Doren might be critical of the lady from time to time, but not even Van Doren could argue over how well things were turning out!

As for the next in line, Viola, she dreamed her way through that summer, thinking of the copper-haired lord who had already expressed a genial fondness for ham. All that was required was that he display the quality she found most important—loyalty.

What that copper-haired earl might have been dreaming about that same summer remained unknown. It would not be too big a leap, though, to presume he had not dreamed of precisely how far a gentleman might have to travel to prove one's loyalty to Viola Bennington.

The End

About the Author

By the time I was eleven, my Irish Nana and I had formed a book club of sorts. On a timetable only known to herself, Nana would grab her blackthorn walking stick and steam down to the local Woolworth's. There, she would buy the latest Barbara Cartland romance, hurry home to read it accompanied by viciously strong wine, (Wild Irish Rose, if you're wondering) and then pass the book on to me. Though I was not particularly interested in real boys yet, I was *very* interested in the gentlemen in those stories—daring, bold, and often enraging and unaccountable. After my Barbara Cartland phase, I went on to Georgette Heyer, Jane Austen and so many other gifted authors blessed with the ability to bring the Georgian and Regency eras to life.

I would like nothing more than to time travel back to the Regency (and time travel back to my twenties as long as we're going somewhere) to take my chances at a ball. Who would take the first? Who would escort me into supper? What sort of meaningful looks would be exchanged? I would hope, having made the trip, to encounter a gentleman who would give me a very hard time. He ought to be vexatious in the extreme, and *worth* every vexation, to make the journey worthwhile.

I most likely won't be able to work out the time travel gambit, so I will content myself with writing stories of adventure and romance in my beloved time period. There are lives to be created, marvelous gowns to wear, jewels to don, instant attractions that inevitably come with a difficulty, and hearts to break before putting them back together again. In traditional Regency fashion, my stories are clean—the action happens in a drawing room, rather than a bedroom.

As I muse over what will happen next to my H and h, and

wish I were there with them, I will occasionally remind myself that it's also nice to have a microwave, Netflix, cheese popcorn, and steaming hot showers.

Come see me on Facebook! @KateArcherAuthor

9 781961 275126